INVISIBLE FRIEND

a true story of
spiritual initiation

Laryssa Nechay
and Nick Nechay

LOST
COAST
PRESS

Invisible Friend:
A True Story of Spiritual Initiation
Copyright © 2005 by Nick Nechay

Lost Coast Press
155 Cypress Street
Fort Bragg, CA 95437
(800) 773-7782
www.cypresshouse.com

Book and Cover Production: Cypress House
Design and Cover Illustration: Nick Nechay

Library of Congress Cataloging-in-Publication Data

Nechay, Laryssa, 1928-
   Invisible friend : a true story of spiritual initiation / Laryssa
Nechay and Nick Nechay.
     p. cm.
   ISBN 1-882897-82-X (pbk. : alk. paper)
   1. Spiritual life I. Nechay, Nick, 1955- II. Title.
   PS3614.E28I58 2004
   813'.54--dc22   2003020190

Printed in the USA
2 4 6 8 9 7 5 3 1

Identity? Well, in our sphere, it is vastly different; however, we recognize the shell of the human form which housed us when we were in your stratum of operation.

— *Invisible Friend*

Contents

Preface

✳

To best prepare you for this story, let's cover a few points of perspective.

Although we all share some common ground, an incomprehensible variety of orientations exist in our ways of thinking. Nature expresses itself in many ways, and so do psychic faculties. Not all who hear voices have psychic abilities, nor do all psychics hear voices. Calling this book "channeled material" gets you in the ballpark, but the couple featured in this story never experienced a trance state, nor any lapse of their personalities or consciousness when encountering the Invisible Friend.

In this presentaion, we cover this couple's first year of having a direct line of communication that, once established, remained open for the rest of their lives. Instead of abstruse admonitions and proclamations, the couple received gracious suggestions pertaining to the flow of their lives and interests at the time. They learned, as I also did at their suggestion, that asking questions creates the best circumstances for realizations or revelation to occur. Genuine inquiry of course implies a degree of openness on the seeker's part.

This story encapsulates many of the principles we have come to live by in the decades of our exposure to extrasensory phenomena. Laryssa had many gifted people in her periphery who have given me astonishing information from higher sources. The Invisible Friend's responses, through the couple, to my personal questions gave me sometimes direct, sometimes subtle guidelines with just enough mystery to keep my mind reaching for my own insights. Between the lines, the Invisible

Friend's evolved attitude seems to rub off. Small changes in one's mental orientation incrementally add up to big advances—a personal paradigm shift.

It has taken me a long time to even begin to apply some of the principles touched upon here: to accept unpleasant circumstances as ideal for learning, to develop trust in the justice of karma, and to now know what my rational mind could not acknowledge in the past.

We all have a legacy of ideas about how the world works, and of our own unique set of strengths and weaknesses. We see movies with paranormal themes that generally invoke fear to generate excitement, which cause unrealistic mental associations. We also become entrenched in the things someone told us a long time ago that may interfere with our spiritual progress. In my estimation, those who have a hard time giving credibility to matters of spirit may stand to gain the most from reading this book. A cynical attitude may preclude absorption of anything new, while true skeptics suspend their judgment until their uncertainty dissolves in the light of additional study.

Taking time to question the various components of one's belief system and integrating them into a coordinated whole pays handsome dividends. This continuing effort to correlate disparate bits of knowledge implies keeping an open mind, abandoning some ways of thinking, and verifying or adding others. Peace of mind results from resolution of internal irritations created by conflicting assumptions.

We hope you can resonate with the Friend's ideas as we believe they carry great wisdom.

Nick Nechay

Acknowledgments

✴

In preparation of *Invisible Friend,* our many visible friends made valuable contributions by offering suggestions and editing the manuscript at various stages of its completion.

Our many thanks for the early critique of the manuscript to Toby Jessup, Evelyn Shephard, Pat Nugent, and Kathleen Holmes. Thanks to Shelley G. West, MFCC for her outstanding contribution. We received encouragement from many of our friends, including Toby Bush, Inez Hooper, and Dr. Donald Thronburg. Tim McGarry found in the manuscript "a blueprint for living." Dr. Katherine Powell expressed her feeling that "this book may transform a few lives." We hope so.

The entire staff of Cypress House and Lost Coast Press proved very helpful in the final preparation and publication of this book.

We feel deep gratitude to our friends, whom we shall call Henry and Emma in this story, for making their personal experiences available to a larger audience. They wholeheartedly supported the writing of this book.

The Invisible Friend acknowledged the Holy Spirit as the Source behind the spiritual guidance given to Henry and Emma.

We thank the Invisible Forces from the bottom of our hearts for their generous assistance and wish to share their loving presence with everyone who comes in contact with this unusual material.

Invisible
Friend

Introduction

✳

For over forty years, I have practiced psychotherapy in its various forms and in various settings: University of Florida, Stanford University, Mental Research Institute of Palo Alto, and private practice in the Bay Area and Mt. Shasta, California. Using a variety of techniques as they became available over the years, I have helped many individuals attain self-respect and inner peace.

In 1972, the whole course of my life changed. I experienced a mild stimulation of kundalini, which changed the nature of my perceptions as well as my professional practice. I became keenly aware of the deeper dimensions of personality and the value of including in the therapeutic endeavor the person's needs for spiritual advancement. Soon my reputation as someone who honors spirituality brought me referrals of many individuals who "heard voices." At times, these people seriously questioned their sanity when their budding psychic talents tended to disrupt their accustomed functioning. The majority of psychotherapists would try to indiscriminately medicate away such conditions. In my role as a therapist, I have helped these clients accept and develop their spiritual gifts, thus helping them on their way to their higher potential.

Having contact through my clients with a variety of spiritual teachers stretched my mind with psychological principles far beyond the scope of my previous professional knowledge. While modern psychology sets as its goal adjustment of an individual to the vicissitudes of societal living, the aim of spiritual work, I have found, centers on the removal of obstacles to the realization of one's own unique, authentic, divine self.

After their course of treatment, some of these clients and I have developed close friendships. One such client, prior to our meeting in 1982, began receiving messages through automatic writing and needed an explanation of her experience. A colleague referred her to me for professional consultation, which led to our enduring friendship and an introduction to her family. Her parents, whom we haved named Henry and Emma, had not discussed with her their own ongoing contact with the spiritual realm until she showed her readiness to hear about it and revealed to them her own psychic gift. Henry and Emma take the spotlight as we use their story to convey an example of spiritual life.

As I came to know Henry and Emma, I learned that their encounter with the spiritual realm had resulted in an amazing impact on their lives and had influenced the lives of many of those around them. For decades, they received personal guidance and delivered helpful messages to individuals in search of advice from a source that identified itself simply as *Invisible Friend*. Because of my extensive experience with psychically gifted persons and my practice of transpersonal psychology, Emma and Henry lovingly turned over to me the complete transcripts of their early conversations with their teacher of wisdom. This documentation included both questions and answers, revealing the inner work they underwent with their unseen mentor in the process of their spiritual development. My son, Nick, helped me realize that I held in my hands a treatise of great potential worth.

The relationship Henry and Emma had with their discarnate guide offers an example of the opportunity we all have to attune, in our everyday lives, to the highly intelligent spiritual forces that constantly surround us. These higher intelligences reach out to us in many ways, which we often overlook. Most of us do not yet realize how much help we receive from higher powers. Advanced souls who have completed their education in "schoolhouse Earth" take it upon themselves to attempt, in their non-physical state, to raise our consciousness beyond the concerns of physical existence.

Because Nick and I have benefited immeasurably from the wisdom transmitted by Henry and Emma, we asked and received permission to tell their fascinating story. Describing their experience works well in explaining spiritual principles with which the reader can become familiar and comfortable in a short time.

In preparing the material for this book, we meticulously adhered to the original records of the Invisible Friend's interactions with Henry and Emma. We preserved the unconventional and at times playful expressions and hyphenations, which convey the Friend's flair in using the English language.

During the last seven of our twenty years of friendship, we interviewed the couple extensively to recapture their initial reactions to their conversations with the Friend. We then added our commentary to further illustrate the process of their spiritual education.

Our story begins as Emma unexpectedly receives her first communication from the Invisible Friend in the presence of Henry's business partner. Familiar with paranormal phenomena, he helps the couple understand the value of the unexpected transmission. To Henry and Emma's credit, they defied the convention of the 1950s, when matters of spirit did not yet enjoy their present popularity. They wholeheartedly embraced the proffered invitation to learn from the invisible source.

The guidance Henry and Emma received parallels the teachings of the Bible and reveals the deep meaning of some of the words of Christ. It also parallels what the alchemists meant by *turning lead into gold*—the symbolic gold of personal spiritual attainment.

Henry struggled for many years with his quick temper. He wished to improve his disposition, yet remained strongly reluctant to seek psychotherapy. As if responding to his wish, the Invisible Friend proceeded to steer both Henry and Emma through the conflicts in their relationship, and Henry's emotional difficulties and business predicaments, by teaching the couple the timeless principles of wisdom.

The Invisible Friend also demonstrated a variety of ways in which benevolent entities from the spirit world try to help us: through dreams, inspirations, and events arranged to provide exactly the lessons we need. Why do we suffer? How do we evolve? What awaits us after death? The chapters that follow answer these important questions and demonstrate how everyday events mirror our conditioning, our assumptions, and our karma.

We learn best from personal experiences; however, as our ability to empathize increases, we can take to heart some of the lessons gained by others. Nick and I wish you the benefit of such learning as you read about the true adventures of Henry and Emma with the Invisible Friend.

Laryssa Nechay, LCSW, BCD

1

Invisible Friend

✳

Ever since she could remember, Emma had a sensitive awareness of people and events. As a young girl, she took it for granted that others saw delicately shimmering lights around people the way she did. She also sensed in advance events of importance to her, in school and at home. Emma knew innately when her father would leave for yet another job away from home and when he would return, regardless of what her family had told her.

She got along well with her psychic abilities, unaware of her special gift, until one fateful day in church. During the sermon, Emma saw a particularly vivid play of colors surrounding their minister and whispered her admiration of the beautiful lights into her girlfriend's ear. The grapevine of gossip quickly spread the juicy morsel about Emma seeing nonexistent things. To her surprise, her community of playmates and their families reacted to this story by shunning her. It shocked Emma to see how easily friendliness could turn into alienation. How could they so quickly turn their backs on her? Feeling sad and disappointed, Emma had to recognize that others did not see the world the way she did.

Gradually, Emma lost her ability to see auras. In her adult life, she had hazy premonitions about future events, yet she would have denied receiving psychic impressions had anyone suggested it to her. Her husband, Henry, marveled at her unerring observations of people and her ability to anticipate at times how certain events would turn out. She shrugged off Henry's admiring comments with a pat phrase, "I guess I guessed it right that time." This facile explanation usually quelled any further discussion of her gift. Then one evening, when their friend Donald came for a visit, something strange happened.

Donald wanted to talk about his idea of an instrument that Henry might manufacture in his machine shop. Emma took an active part in the discussion, bringing the two men back to reality when they seemed to get carried away with their plans. She kept track of important points, jotting them down on her notepad, while enjoying their lively conversation.

It happened unexpectedly. Three words kept repeating in Emma's head.

Have polite discourse.

Emma felt compelled to write them down on her pad. As she gazed in bewilderment at the statement, an odd but strangely familiar sensation enveloped her. She felt reluctant to interrupt the flow of conversation between the two men, but finally broke in.

"Something interesting is happening ... I think someone or something is trying to talk to us."

At first, the two men responded with silence, but Donald's curiosity prompted him to ask what made Emma think that.

Stuttering her explanation, Emma looked apologetically at Henry, hoping he would not become upset. Her glance at Donald carried an unspoken plea to relieve her discomfort and help her understand what she had experienced.

"The words keep repeating in my head, *Have polite discourse.* What in the world is going on?" Emma asked with a slight quaver in her voice. "I know the words did not come from me. I would never use the word *discourse* to describe a conversation."

Until that evening, psychic phenomena held no special

significance for Henry and Emma. On the contrary, they avoided any encounters with the occult as something beneath their level of interest. In the 1950s, any mention of otherworldly contact typically elicited the ridicule reserved for little green men from Mars. Donald, on the other hand, had cultivated his involvement with the paranormal. He had visited psychics, and sometimes shared interesting tidbits of metaphysical information with the couple.

"You may have heard from someone on the other side," Donald announced, a hopeful smile lighting his face. Having encountered many similar stories, he did not consider people hearing voices an unusual occurrence.

"Maybe you are turning psychic," he added. "Have you ever had anything like that happen before?"

"I'm not sure," Emma said, fixing her eyes on the pad, uncomfortable with having drawn attention to herself.

Henry's mind raced back to the various times when Emma mentioned her unusual insights. His thoughts jumped from one memory to another, but he remained silent. Obviously agitated, he did not quite know what to say.

"What do you call *psychic*? All of us have strong hunches sometimes," Emma continued, casting a glance at Henry, whose face now betrayed his conflicted feelings. His personable features faithfully reflected his inner states, even when he had no intention of revealing them to the outside world.

"Henry, I wouldn't be too concerned. Some of us are more sensitive than others," Donald opined, trying to allay a mounting tension.

"If these words are coming from somewhere else, they'd better be polite," Henry said, instinctively ready to protect Emma from intruders, but not quite sure how.

"Who are you?" Donald suddenly asked, sending his question into the unknown.

Henry snapped his head in Donald's direction, not wanting to believe that he actually heard Donald trying to converse with the room's ceiling.

The response came without delay through Emma's rapidly moving pencil.

A Force called Friends.

Emma laughed nervously as she read the answer aloud.

"*A force called friends*? What's going on? This is uncanny!" Her voice rose to a high pitch.

Donald raised his voice to give it more credibility.

"It sounds like you are getting messages from the spiritual dimension. This is great! You don't know how many times I've wished I could do that!"

Henry jerked up from his chair and gave Donald a look of disdain. Determined not to put up with any nonsense, although scarcely believing he had allowed himself to enter into this inane conversation, Henry stretched to his full height of six feet and uttered a question.

"Okay. So, what is your purpose in coming here?"

He paused, watching his wife write on her notepad.

To help Henry see the light rays of wisdom.

Stunned, Henry sat down with a thud and let his words tumble out.

"*That'll* be the trick if you can do it!"

A burst of hearty laughter rang through the room. It seemed to momentarily relieve the tension, making the situation appear less strange than it had moments earlier.

Donald hurried to explain the plausibility of the new experience, insisting that such communications took place with increasing frequency now that the intelligence of humanity reached a higher level of sophistication. Emma gladly listened to Donald's explanations, but they seemed to have little impact on Henry, who remained preoccupied with the comment about the *light rays of wisdom,* which lingered in his mind.

Driven by an unexplainable urge that overshadowed his qualms about talking to an invisible someone, Henry relaxed his guard, venturing another question.

"Do you know my need for knowledge?"

More than you like to let on.

"That does it!" Henry muttered. He jumped up from his chair and hastily made his way to the kitchen to conceal his overwhelming confusion. He felt toyed with. The thought crossed his mind that Emma and Donald had fabricated the whole thing as a practical joke, but then, nobody laughed at his reaction. Giving it another thought, he felt certain that Emma wouldn't perpetrate this kind of deception on him or anyone else. He also trusted Donald not to mislead them by his reassurances. Hearing the sound of voices in the living room helped him regain his composure. He filled a glass with water, took a big gulp, and returned to his chair. He found two faces turning to him with sympathetic understanding.

"I think you are being challenged," Donald said with a wide smile, aware of Henry and Emma's penchant for new discoveries. The couple read and traveled extensively, for both enjoyment and enlightenment. Living near a metropolitan center, they had ample opportunity to attend various gatherings, lectures, and seminars. Books covering a broad spectrum of subjects filled their growing number of shelves. Searching, but not always knowing for what, Henry and Emma kept themselves open to new knowledge and good advice.

As if to underscore to Henry her willingness to accept what transpired, Emma continued to sit with her pencil poised on the pad. She well knew she could not have regained her self-confidence in such a short time without Donald's calm and steady explanations. Her trust in Donald and her wish to quiet Henry's excitement gave her the strength to appear less affected by the event than she felt.

"I think they are still here, whoever *they* are," she said.

Fighting his trepidation, Henry decided to go along with the strange happening.

"What would you like to have us call you?" he asked.

Invisible friend who leads you to high wisdom.

"What's in a name?" Henry pondered quietly to himself. "Maybe this is an answer to a longing I've had all my life." His inner sense told him that this invisible source might indeed have the ability to offer answers in his search for guidance on how to lead a peaceful and harmonious life.

Henry had a painful awareness of his quick temper and its aftermath. He had to fight his instant show of dissatisfaction when something appeared not to his liking. He could barely control his actions, let alone his feelings, when his critical attitude rose up, threatening to dwarf his rationality. In those unhappy moments, he desperately wished to find a way out of his difficulty. This invisible someone seemed to know his predicament and did not hesitate to say so. Putting aside his skepticism, Henry wondered if he could allow himself to trust this strange phenomenon.

"Will Henry know when you are helping him?" Donald asked to break the long silence.

Rarely.

Emma continued to write as if taking dictation. A long sentence emerged, apparently meant for Donald.

We sense your attitude in your work and commend your high sense of truthfulness.

Happy to have the focus shift away from him, Henry said that he wholeheartedly agreed with the observation about Donald. Donald acknowledged the compliment and in turn admitted his respect for Henry's conscientious attitude toward *his* work. This mutual exchange of appreciation strengthened the foundation of their friendship, which proved timely in retrospect. Their new joint venture would come to place considerable strain on Henry to maintain a friendship he valued highly.

Emma wanted to understand the process of communication and gave vent to her curiosity.

"Do you know Henry's thoughts?"

Slightly.

"My thoughts?"

More easily.

She laughed. The answer did not surprise her. She valued the complexity of Henry's thoughts. She would have continued, but Donald wanted to know the identity of those who inhabited these invisible realms.

Worthy ones rise to higher realms.

"Do we understand worthiness?" Donald continued.

Not entirely.

"Are you in a state of bliss or is there sometimes turmoil?"

Rest and peace to spare.

"Are you bound by time?"

We take it easy.

The laconic answer brought forth smiles and another question.

"Is there music?"

Great harmony wells up.

Although they enjoyed the cryptic replies of the Friend, Henry and Emma felt they would have asked different questions, but remained silent in deference to their guest. All three felt they could have asked questions late into the night, but Donald rose to leave. He congratulated Emma on "lifting the veil" between the visible and invisible realms. Uncertain of the meaning of these words, Emma protested.

"I had nothing to do with it."

"Nothing and everything," Donald laughed. "Without you this conversation would not have been possible."

Emma and Henry exchanged happy smiles. Something about the evening's unexpected encounter felt exceptionally good. They sensed an unfolding of wondrous possibilities, as this friendly force offered them not only understanding, but also invaluable wisdom seldom encountered in this physically oriented reality.

"Donald, I think you had something to do with it, too," countered Henry, "not to take any credit away from my wonderful wife." He looked fondly at Emma and put his arm around her. "I always knew there was something special about her."

"You speak like a man in love," said Donald, admiring the good feelings that flowed between the couple.

"I am, and I wish you the same," Henry responded, voicing an attitude that would later blossom into a major spiritual attribute. Henry's wishing another well would, over time, transform into a full-blown ability to telepathically transfer serenity to individuals mired in adversity. Before that could happen, however, Henry had to undergo a period of emotional readjustment, which required getting to know himself as he never suspected he could.

Thus began an adventure in personal growth that led Henry and Emma to the unexpected rewards of spiritual attainment.

2

Accepting the Invitation

The following evening, Emma and Henry anxiously waited for their two daughters to fall asleep to assure the privacy they wanted while conversing with the Invisible Friend. They wondered if they would succeed in contacting the Friend without Donald's presence. What risks should they beware of? Deception by dark forces? Irretrievable danger to their souls? They worried about stepping over the line into an unknown realm, but they could not ignore their fascination. Behind the Friend's messages, they sensed high moral principles, a great intelligence, and a genuinely caring attitude. Their hesitation could not match their drive to explore the unknown.

Henry seated himself on the sofa next to Emma, so that he could see the writing as he hoped it would emerge on her notepad. Emma gave him a girlish look, barely containing her excitement. Braving the uncertainty, Henry ventured a greeting.

"Good evening, Invisible Friend."

The response came instantly.

Good evening to you.

They laughed nervously, still feeling uneasy about their contact, but felt encouraged to verbalize their curiosity.

"Are you aware of us all the time or only when we are conversing?"

In more ways than that.

"Is it proper to ask in what ways?" Henry wondered.

Not now. Understanding will reveal. Wait for wisdom. Wisdom rushes not.

Henry and Emma chuckled at the mention of wisdom, remembering the stated purpose of the unexpected contact: *to help Henry see the light rays of wisdom.*

Not wanting to feel left out, Emma chimed in, "Will I get anything out of this?"

Wisdom is catching if tested.

Emma laughed at the answer. Another challenge? She perceived the comment as an invitation to participate in the discussion that seemed to center on Henry. A fear of possibly going against religious dogma lingered in her mind. As if reading her thoughts, the Invisible Friend responded with a strong message.

Humans erect barriers that stop communication. Their stubbornness is like a thick brick wall erected thoughtlessly, blindly. Obstacles make vibrations bounce off, breaking contact.

Henry sensed the truth in the Friend's words and nodded agreement. Emma also recognized the truth in the Friend's words, but cringed at the mention of stubbornness. Accused from time to time of a headstrong attitude, she feared it might interfere with their communication.

"I'm afraid I have more than my share of that," she whispered. Henry smiled at Emma's charming honesty as the Friend responded.

So what! Just don't turn to us with a set chin. Be open to receive. We won't harm, but help you.

The reassurance comforted them.

They noticed the use of the pronouns *us* and *we*. Since *they* offered help, Henry put forward the family's present concern about their house. They had bought it after Henry's discharge from the army, and it had served them well for many years, but they felt they needed more living space for their growing children.

"Is it proper to ask what we should do with the home we live in now?"

Lay low. What's the rush? Take time. Your future is assured. Develop mentally. Round out your spiritual stamina first.

"Sounds like apt advice," Henry agreed, feeling strangely comfortable with the Friend's assurance and familiarity with their future.

Henry momentarily flashed back on the memory of the pain he had felt in the pit of his stomach when he lost his first job after his release from the army. That last paycheck covered the family's expenses, but it had frightened him to think what would happen if he couldn't find employment. Fortunately, things worked out, as he found they usually did. He took a temporary job and quickly organized a small wood and metal shop in the basement of their house. As if by miracle, clients appeared. Henry's income began to grow. Soon after that he quit his outside employment and occasionally even hired others to help him in his shop.

The movement of Emma's pencil caught his attention.

You receive vibrations. Thrill. More can come when the blotter receives harmony.

The puzzling comment made sense, if the word "blotter" implied their ability to absorb what the Friend said. The words definitely conveyed goodwill. Suddenly, Emma wrote in big, swirling letters:

Whee, it feels good!

Emma and Henry laughed. Perhaps the Friend also rejoiced at having established the contact. With great enthusiasm, Henry and Emma expressed their own delight, but Henry soon returned to his usual serious manner.

"Generally speaking, is it better to hire younger or older men for my work?"

Why ask? Do what common sense points out as to which man is apt to show the right kind of interest.

Henry said he did not object to using common sense, but he needed help to resolve a predicament.

"My reason for asking is this: I seem to have an overly possessive attitude toward my shop and my customers' welfare, which causes me to pay a lot of attention to small details. When my employees fall short of my standards, I have to make up for them. I get disturbed about it."

So do I. Don't trail high standards in the dust of mediocrity.

"Well put, Friend!" Henry exclaimed with much satisfaction.

The response pleased Henry immensely. It felt good to have high standards in common with the Friend. A feeling of friendship seemed to emerge between the two inhabitants of the visible and the invisible realms. The Friend apparently held a similar sentiment and expressed it rather poetically.

Waves of vibration sing on wings of appreciation.

Emma's artistic sense perked up at the statement. However,

it seemed to imply that one could only receive *waves of vibration* from the other side if one valued them. The couple came to learn later that *appreciation* sustained their continuing contact with the invisible world.

Eager to continue the conversation, they gave free reign to their curiosity. Emma wanted to know where the communication came from.

"How would you describe your realm?"

Each in his own marked sphere, using tools with which to work.

Henry loved tools and what they helped him to accomplish. He of course inquired about them.

The answer took a long time coming.

Wisdom delegates tools.

"Why the hesitation or difficulty?"

Hard to find words that convey my present sphere.

Henry and Emma could somewhat understand the difficulty, having recently read a book by Stewart Edward White, which illustrated the complex problems involved in describing the other side that the author's deceased wife, Betty, so diligently tried to explain to him after her death. They read the book at Donald's insistence, without giving it much credence.

"Should we read *The Unobstructed Universe* again?"

No.

"Why not?"

All things will be made clear to you directly.

Good. They had something to look forward to. The statement also implied continued contact, and Emma beamed a smile at Henry. She found herself relaxing and enjoying their conversation with the Friend.

Next, they wondered if they could benefit from seeing a psychologist known for his spiritual leanings.

Why? You won't need him to wake up your wisdom.

"Then how do we acquire this wisdom?" Henry inquired.

Think on your own.

Henry and Emma raised their eyebrows and looked at each other. They spotted a contradiction: On one side loomed a source of wisdom seemingly outside of themselves, but on the other, the admonition implied that they should not rely on outside sources. They recalled reading statements to the effect that human beings naturally contain all knowledge within themselves and need only recollect what they already possess as a divine gift. Socrates, Plato, and Pythagoras had referred to this dormant inner knowledge. But how to awaken that hidden treasure? Henry thought of another Master.

"Are we correct about Christ coming from higher realms to teach?"

Make use of the information and read what He said.

"So you think it's good to read the Bible?" Emma ventured.

Go ahead, read, for it will guide you to Wisdom.

Henry remarked about the appearance of the capital letter *W* in the word *Wisdom*, the significance of which would only later become apparent.

A smile of relief radiated from Emma's face. The encouraging comment about the Bible eased Emma's concern about the Invisible Friend's allegiance, though she still suspected that her church would have condemned any communication from the other side.

Emma had grown up with strict prohibitions against dancing, movies, and other so-called frivolities. Observing this religious practice led her to question the severe guidelines for saintly behavior that resulted in torment for many a soul gripped by the fear of spending eternity in hell. Did living a continually churning cycle of guilt, repentance, and forgiveness promise godliness? Hardly. After reading books by Krishnamurti and hearing him speak, Emma had chosen to simply place emphasis on gracious living. Krishnamurti taught reliance on one's own integrity to lead one to God, without religious and societal conditioning. Emma found that her decision to rely on herself liberated her intuitive sense of spirituality and gave her a new and deeper appreciation of the Scriptures. Thus she rejoiced at the Friend's approval of reading the Bible.

Henry shifted to more mundane concerns.

"What about the instrument that Donald and I have conjured up?"

It will be good for both you and Donald. Go ahead, build it.

Henry's question referred to his attempt to design an instrument that Donald envisioned for his department's laboratory. The project would soon stir up many feelings in Henry and would become a frequent subject of conversation with the Friend.

The Friend's last comment offered encouragement, which felt as good as the earlier one about their assured future.

After the conversation in which they agreed on the matter of high standards, Henry began to feel a growing trust toward the Invisible Friend. Henry did not know that his erroneous understanding of high standards had a debilitating effect on him as he tried to live up to an unrealistic ideal of perfection. The Friend would later teach him about perfection and show how it interfered with Henry's emotional well-being.

Noticing the late hour, the couple reluctantly said good night to the Friend, hoping to resume their contact the following evening.

3

Beginning Enlightenment

✦

Although Henry and Emma could readily admit they did not know what kind of wisdom to expect—moral indoctrination or philosophical discourses—they felt that the Invisible Friend's teachings had so far revealed an astonishing and definitely practical psychological foundation. The Friend seemed to focus on emotions, attitudes, and interactions with others. This emphasis made sense, they thought, if one kept in mind that the entire process of human evolution, when stripped of the physical world's various distractions, converged toward the refinement of noble human qualities. They would learn from the Friend that these qualities carried with them respect for individuality, awareness of the value of all life, and the realization of one's potential to love.

With these premises not clearly formulated in their minds, Henry and Emma did not yet recognize that the Friend's interventions in their everyday life aimed at the goal of their spiritual development. They began to see the direction more clearly after an incident in which Emma impatiently scolded the girls for scattering their toys in the living room.

The Friend began after the couple settled down for another session.

We do not welcome rough stuff.

"Are you referring to my blowing up at the girls because they don't put their things away?"

You are too tough and tired to love little girls.

Emma voiced her astonishment to Henry. She felt justified in correcting their twin daughter's behavior when they threw their clothes on the sofa or left their shoes and toys on the floor. "Well," she stammered, "shouldn't they put their things away?"

They will, when my wisdom reaches you.

Emma steadied herself, fighting off a wave of resentment. She and Henry had painful disagreements about matters of discipline, with Henry usually deferring to her in such decisions.

"What shall I do when I feel impatient with them?"

Tread slowly.

"And how can I do this?"

Nine years young.

Emma fell into a reflective silence. She began to realize that her well-meaning attempts to teach the girls orderliness from an early age merely reflected her personal pride in them and the house.

"Oh, I see."

From then on, Emma used the three words, "nine years young," to remind herself to loosen her control over their usually sweet and well-behaved children.

Henry watched Emma's reaction, his strained features gradually relaxing as he sensed her acceptance of the explanation. He remained silent, making sure that he did not remind her of the times when he disagreed with her about their children's discipline. He knew that his occasional outbursts of criticism hurt her feelings. After an explosion of anger, Henry would inwardly punish himself with sharp self-reprimands for not controlling the outpouring of his fury. He never failed to apologize to Emma afterwards, but his disturbance of the peaceful atmosphere in their home would hang like an oppressive cloud for days at a time. They both thoroughly disliked those times and frequently turned to books for help.

Psychology had just begun to gain popularity when Henry and Emma launched their exploration of the various theories available to them. Since the Friend demonstrated an interest in emotions, Henry asked the Friend's opinion on a fundamental premise he found in the field of psychology.

"Is it true that commands and admonitions made when we were young affect us in our adult life?"

YES.

"How do we get rid of the effects of these commands?" Henry asked in a tone of voice that betrayed a mixture of doubt and hope.

Wait in the hills for whatever hides.

"What do you mean by 'hills'?"

Mountains of imagination. Words burn their message into lives.

The answer seemed evasive. Emma tried to change the subject, but Henry persisted.

"How do we get rid of the effects of words spoken to us?"

With my system of recalling the memory of them.

The idea of recalling memories did not sound new to the couple, whose reading of Freud, Jung, and others advocating a psychoanalytic system of therapy had already acquainted them with techniques of this sort. Yet, Henry sensed that the Friend's system might contain something that the others did not.

"Can you enlarge on this?"

When you remember the source of them, my system works well. You imagine what words were said, put them in summary form, and rise above them.

Henry appreciated the Friend's effort to make it sound simple.

"How do we go into the hills of imagination?"

At weak spell.

Henry reflected on the meaning of the enigmatic answer. He took it to indicate that undesirable traits emerge unbidden into full view during weak spells of emotional distress. It made sense to him that such times revealed the weak areas of personality that need attention and improvement. One could then trace the origin of such problems to their source, usually somewhere in childhood, when the words uttered by adults carried great weight and strongly imprinted themselves on the young psyche.

Still feeling the impact of the Friend's comment about her treatment of their children, Emma ventured a question.

"What should I have done in the evening when I got impatient with the girls? Should I have stopped in my tracks and waited to calm down before saying anything?"

Most certainly.

Henry again entered the conversation, trying to divert Emma from her tendency toward self-condemnation.

"Traveling in the hills of imagination, how will we know when we find the command that is affecting us?"

You will suddenly breathe more easily when you hit the harm-doer. Try it.

Although still puzzled about the details of the technique, Henry began to feel a bit more hopeful about the future.

Feeling reassured by these matter-of-fact comments free of blame or shame, Emma decided to ask about communication between spouses.

"Should I have talked to Henry about my problem with the girls last Sunday night?"

May, if desired. Henry understands.

Henry smiled a benevolent smile, making certain that it did not signal "I told you so." He well remembered Emma's occasional grumble, "You just don't understand."

"Should Henry discuss his problems with me?" Emma continued.

Surely, if he wishes to talk about them.

Emma's next question made Henry realize that what he sometimes perceived as Emma's intrusiveness came from her genuine desire to help him in any way she could.

"Shall I offer him my interpretation of what needs to be done?"

Best let him see his own problems.

Sensing that Emma could take the comment as a rebuff, Henry jumped in with a question to ease the situation.

"You mean, allow the one with the problem a chance to search for a solution first?"

Better that way.

Both of them accepted this sensible approach and allowed

themselves some time to digest the preceding conversation.

Still keeping in mind the possibility of freeing himself from negative influences during his childhood, Henry followed this theme further.

"Can we, by doing what you suggest, clear our minds of the hurtful past?"

Wisdom comes with experience, not with learning thoughts of others. Yes.

This answer seemed to set the Friend's system apart from the others they had explored. The strong emphasis on experience appealed to Henry. He did not subscribe to the medical ideas of psychopathology, despite having read authoritative books about neuroses and psychoses. Having observed many instances of parental ignorance, he felt that wrong or bad behavior in children resulted from faulty habits carelessly instilled or ignored by adults. This belief included his own parents, who, he thought, simply did not know any better.

"Do you have a comment on the subject of bad habits?" Henry asked.

Habits result from bad training. Clue resides in the source that trained. Find it. Triumph comes when the source is found. Digging can be slow and tedious at times, but results are certain if sidetracking is avoided. Recognize the source, then laugh away the habits.

Henry took delight in hearing an answer that coincided with his own thinking. The brief presentation of the process sounded familiar, yet the Friend's words intrigued him. Questions crowded in his head. He realized he had to choose his topics carefully and allow time for an orderly progression of the discourse.

Knowing that many parents present their children with a

discrepancy between what they themselves do and what they expect their children to do, Henry pursued the subject a little further.

"Is observational learning more effective than verbal training?"

The Friend responded with a strong statement concerning admonitions.

Blistering words are damaging. Don't stern-word yours. Fertile soil. Words plow deep in youth's field.

Although Emma still felt discomfort from earlier comments directed at her, she instantly recognized the merit of the suggestion to show more understanding toward the girls. Both she and Henry felt the wisdom of the advice and thanked the Friend for it.

Then, Henry recalled a comment from an earlier communication about the need for mental development.

"How does one learn and develop mentally?"

Great knowledge hides in personal experiences and social contact. Ponder your own revelations and get your own results, not hashed theories that produce no effect. Goodness comes and lasts purely from within yourself. Comprehend and enlarge your own decisions. Other views can be of interest, but they do not develop the soul.

Emma and Henry reflected for some time on the Friend's words. The Friend seemed to hammer away at them that intellectual pursuits alone do not develop the soul; that personal experiences, with their gut-level feelings, challenge one's ability to make creative decisions and produce revelations far superior to any theories one may encounter. The couple couldn't help but take such strong statements from the Friend to heart.

"Look at this sentence, Henry." Emma pointed at the middle of the Friend's last paragraph. *Goodness comes ... purely from within.* What does that mean?"

"I think that means that some people put on a friendly act because they think they should, but don't feel that friendly inside."

"That makes sense. It seems right that goodness needs to be felt deep inside to make it real. I never thought of it that way," Emma nodded.

"I really like the way the Friend insists on our making our own decisions. There's nothing like learning from your own mistakes!"

They both began to understand what the Friend meant by *great knowledge hides in personal experiences.* They felt as if they had just come into possession of a small bit of wisdom, and embarked on a discussion of the difference between wisdom and knowledge.

Hashed theories obviously referred to theoretical knowledge. Thus, they concluded, one could possess a great deal of intellectual knowledge about the world, yet remain largely lacking in wisdom. Wisdom, the experiential knowledge the Friend talked about, began to imply to them an inward comprehension, an understanding over and beyond the facts, encompassing a subtle maturity of reasoning where the heart and the mind worked together. Having seen the value of the Friend's advice, Henry wanted to make sure that, in the future, they would have the ability to discern matters on their own.

"Can you give us more information on how we can evaluate the knowledge we find?"

Good question, Henry. Try to understand. Thoughts resolve from facts. You know plenty. The territory now demands rounded-out action of mind, not more information. Don't refrain from absorbing knowledge, however it comes, but do not bind your minds with ropes.

"You seem to talk in abstractions that make us think," commented Henry. "Is it bad for our self-determination to receive specific information from your realm?"

Unused muscles get flabby, so mental processes must receive exercise. To tell all is to feed infants mush. Digest meat, adult mental food. Figuratively, I mean.

The suggestion not to bind their minds appealed to the couple and validated their confidence in their own reasoning. They both observed that solving problems or making personal decisions sometimes presented a great challenge to some individuals. Having made many decisions away from the prevailing trend, they appreciated the rare value of independent thought and welcomed the logic of the Friend's suggestion to exercise their minds.

The Friend's last statement sounded like an invitation to do some mental digesting on their own, so the two felt it appropriate to end the session.

"You have given us much to think about, Friend. Thank you."

Be good.

It seemed that the Friend wanted to cultivate a casual atmosphere with the informal sendoff.

4

Assistance from Beyond

✳

Emma and Henry looked forward to their next conversation with the Friend. They hurried to finish their chores for the day, tuck their girls in bed for the night, and settle down for a session.

"Good evening, Invisible Friend. Can you communicate with us this evening?" Henry asked, expecting the same joviality with which the previous session ended. Emma, pad and pencil in hand, closed her eyes to better concentrate on receiving an acknowledgment of the greeting.

No response.

As the silence persisted, neither of them said anything, but they shared the same dread: the Invisible Friend had left. Mild panic flooded their minds, along with a vague sense of guilt. Could they have done something to disturb the connection?

"Are you with us this evening?" Henry persisted.

Again, no response. Sadness began to creep in. Henry felt that he had to do something to remedy the awkward situation. He thought of asking a question in keeping with the stated purpose of the sessions, one that required more than a yes or no answer. In contrast to his sentiment of only three days ago, Henry did not at all seem to mind talking to the empty air.

"How long have you been observing my progress in obtaining wisdom?"

Emma's pencil began to move. They both let out a sigh of relief. As the new sentence evolved, they had a clear impression that the long silence meant to reveal to them their doubt, so that they would never again question the presence of the Invisible Friend.

Great effort was expended by many through periods that varied in intensity.

The strange answer astounded them. Apparently, these helpers from the invisible world had gone through some kind of trouble on Henry's behalf, without making him feel obligated or even aware of the help they extended.

"I don't know what you did, but I appreciate that you tried to help us." Henry uttered his words with a sense of humility.

This has gone on for long past.

Henry felt his heart beat faster as he puzzled over the unfolding mystery. Wanting to make connections to some actual events, Emma wondered about Henry's remarkable experiences while in the army. Could the Invisible Friend have protected Henry during the war?

Henry seldom spoke of his life in the military. During his wartime service, he had several close brushes with death. On one occasion, he had just moved his gear to another place when an enemy shell hit the spot he had vacated moments earlier. In a similar incident, just as he had leaned his head to one side for no apparent reason, a bullet whizzed by his ear.

On yet another occasion, Henry received an unexpected one-day leave out of the area right before the mayhem of a bombing raid devastated the armored division to which he belonged. That attack killed several soldiers he had befriended, while many others suffered severe injuries. Numerous lesser attacks in the area brought even more casualties, but Henry remained safe.

The more Emma and Henry discussed these remarkable experiences, the more they could sense a connection between them and the unsolicited protection by the invisible forces.

"If this is true, this is perhaps the most astounding realization I've ever had," Henry said.

Why should it be? Why deny what you can't explain? Keep open. You will like it. You will be healthier and mightier. Don't worry, we do not lead astray.

"It must be truly a labor of love." Henry felt a heavy emotion welling up inside, but he braced himself. His long-held prohibition against crying worked well. Emma sympathized with Henry's struggle to contain his emotions as the Friend continued.

Our work is beyond your comprehension. Our part consists of efforts to clarify perplexities. Happiness comes from results we observe in children wandering in the world's hills and valleys of hardship. By degrees, we acquire satisfaction and proceed upward to Wisdom's dictates, as do you.

Henry and Emma tried to grasp the higher meaning of the statement, but it implied a familiarity with some principles of which they had little recognition. They did understand, however, that the Friend cared about them, and that many besides Henry received unrecognized help.

"Your effort is to teach us wisdom," Henry mused. "I wonder if we have enough wisdom to even ask proper questions." He felt awed by the Friend's dedicated service to mankind.

Crowning achievement of your future powers makes your present strength appear as weakness. Remember, wisdom proceeds slowly but firmly through experiences.

The conversation seemed to have reached its natural stopping point. Henry and Emma sat in silence for a while, reviewing the messages, trying to better understand them. They felt immersed, beyond any doubt, in an overwhelming amount of love, more than they ever thought possible. As if waking from a heavy sleep, they reached out toward each other, recognizing the deepening love they felt for one another.

✶

A busy week went by before Henry and Emma attempted to contact the Invisible Friend again. Reflecting on previous sessions, the two realized that everything the Friend had said up to this point felt exceptionally good and right and helpful. A brighter attitude had in fact spread into their daily routines. Emma found it easier to deal with the children, at times feeling waves of love flowing toward them. Henry, while working in his shop, realized that his thinking sometimes felt different from his usual inner dialogue. He now began to carry on mental conversations with the Friend, receiving some hints in his work as helpful thoughts appeared in his mind. At one point, Henry asked the Friend to help him find a missing tool and almost immediately found it.

Henry began to sense that several different voices spoke to him while he worked in his shop, although he could not always hear or discern them clearly. He chuckled, imagining what people might say if he told them that he heard voices. They would, no doubt, try to convince him that he had hallucinated them and probably recommend that he seek psychiatric care.

Starting their next session, Henry and Emma immediately felt the close presence of the Friend. The session felt light and cheery.

"I appreciate your pointing out the location of that wrench after my extensive search," Henry began, as if resuming an ongoing conversation.

Did you like that? Remember the old saying, 'Use your head and save your legs'? Yes, the direct approach has a number of benefits that are useful and step-saving.

"But if I were to ask you where things were every time I lost them, wouldn't that be dependency?"

We certainly would not tell you things if it came to that. But don't demand, merely accept; there is a difference. Many work well with these practices. For example, Donald and his ability to find parking places. Why not try this once in a while and see if it works?

Donald had told Henry of a game he played: When he drove somewhere and found a parking space nearby, it signified a welcome for him and a blessing on his activity. If not, he would reconsider his timing or his plans. He claimed he frequently found a convenient spot in crowded situations and thanked his "parking angel" for it. Hearing Donald's experiences encouraged Henry and Emma to look for the Friend's assistance even in such mundane matters as finding a place to park their car.

"Today I asked myself questions and thought of answers almost immediately. Were you or anyone else responsible for that?"

We watched that mind of yours working on answers to questions. Fine way to face perplexities and conquer problems. We delight in your progress.

"I was concerned as to whether those answers came from my mind or from yours."

Why divide so exactly? We work with you, you work with us.

"If I consider these thoughts as coming from your realm, I may have a tendency to depend on you. I don't think that would be good," Henry said, feeling that he presented a well-reasoned argument. Again the Invisible Friend surprised him.

Such confusion in not necessary. Our realm is all about you.

Apparently, the Friend did not see a sharp division between Henry's world and the invisible realm. The explanation also seemed to hint at the idea of omnipresence. This stirred up questions about the Friend's place in the big picture and in relationship to God, but these curiosities floated vaguely in his mind, not yet clearly defined.

Consider yourself always adequate to comprehend. Our help reaches you in an indefinable way. You can't grasp its method now. Only know that we work harmoniously, dislike turmoil, and seek to guide you away from disharmony. Haven't you been aware of that often?

The Friend's statement identified yet another area of help, that of directing Henry into a harmonious way of living. Although he didn't think the Friend really expected him to have such an understanding, Henry felt uncomfortable admitting his ignorance of the benevolent, behind-the-scenes influence.

"I've always tried to avoid disharmony, but I never thought of the possibility of receiving help from your realm."

Now you know. Peace is pleasant, isn't it?

"Yes, and disharmony is very unpleasant to me," Henry said. "It must be a tremendously tedious job to guide someone properly, as you do. From what I can see, your teaching is precisely tailored to fit and enlarge an individual's current understanding."

Henry and Emma began to admire the high quality and appropriateness of the Invisible Friend's presentations. Even though they had kept their senses alert for indications of impropriety, they failed to detect any. They also felt reassured, rather than threatened, by the Friend's claim to have influenced events in their lives in the past. In their delight, both now found themselves wanting to share their experiences with others.

"Friend, have you any thoughts as to whether reading these messages can be beneficial to others of our acquaintance?"

Ponder well. Debates ensue if the recipient is not ready.

Oh, yes. They could see how debates might ensue, and neither of them felt strong enough yet to offer explanations of the phenomenon. These wonderful communications would have to remain a private matter, at least temporarily. Still taken aback by the Friend's surprising revelation of assistance, Henry indulged his curiosity.

"Is it proper to ask you why we were selected to receive this particular type of communication?"

A rare combination. Development has gone on for long past. Concern yourself not about the future. At present, the foremost task is to receive as given. Regard privately the amazing truths, so further wisdom can be recognized. Continue to gratefully receive.

Sensing closure, they reluctantly ended yet another informative session.

"Good night. Thank you very much for giving us your amazing help."

You are welcome.

"Just like that," Henry said to Emma after the session. "They say 'You are welcome' as if I had thanked them for a simple favor like 'Please pass the salt.' They saved my life several times; who knows what else they've done for both of us and for humanity, and I say a simple 'Thank you' to them."

True to her down-to-earth nature, Emma reassured him.

"What else can you say? I think they know how limited we are in what we can see of their activities. They understand our position. And they are trying to teach us wisdom, for which we, indeed, can be very thankful."

"You're right," Henry responded. "All of this is so mysterious but, as they say, God works in mysterious ways."

5

A Fine Team

✳

In the days that followed, Henry encountered seemingly insurmountable difficulties in his effort to design the instrument he and Donald had set out to develop. When mental conversations with the Friend did not bring the clear answers he needed, Henry relied on Emma's help in getting his questions answered in the evenings.

Having finished their chores, the couple took their usual places on the sofa and began a session.

"Good evening, Friend. What should I do in my perplexity?" Henry asked.

Movements make good turns, if they are followed to conclusion.

Once again, the Friend spoke in riddles.

"What do you mean by movements?"

You made them with your pencil.

"Do you mean the sketch I made? Is that the way the instrument should be built?"

With some changes. Draw the instrument as it will finally look.

Just as Henry readied himself for a more detailed discussion, Emma lifted her head and stared into space. After a mysterious pause, she announced she had received instructions from the Friend to use a typewriter. On her pad, she quickly scribbled the Friend's words.

We make a fine team.

"It sure looks that way!" Henry's hope for securing guidance from the Friend reached new heights. He rose to retrieve Emma's old Royal from the hall closet.

Using the typewriter meant leaving their comfortable sofa and heading for the more austere chairs at the kitchen table. Emma hadn't typed for years, but her training as a legal secretary allowed her to feel comfortable at the keyboard. Henry pulled up a chair beside her, ready to fire questions. Emma, however, seemed to need some time to adjust to the new method of communication.

"It feels to me like the Friend is trying to connect my fingers to my brain. What a strange sensation! Wait a minute. Here it comes."

She began to type.

Here is what you do whenever in perplexity: stop, look, and listen.

"I understand, but that's hard to do under pressure," Henry remarked.

When confusion enters your thoughts, look out that you make no decisions. Be calm always when important events come to you, Henry. Look ahead. Your work is growing up with foundation of good sound principles. My help will always find you when in perplexity and not quite sure, whatever problem has you licked.

Henry and Emma chuckled at the Friend's use of slang in an obvious effort to express familiarity with their earthly vernacular and to help them feel at ease in their relationship with their otherworldly instructor.

Emma reflected on the fact that once again the Friend had addressed only Henry, rather than both of them. With a start, she remembered the original statement as to the purpose of the encounter with the Friend — *to help Henry see the light rays of Wisdom* — with the option for her to join in the conversation. She silently chose to remain a part of the proceedings, while sensing the special quality of the relationship forming between Henry and the Invisible Friend. Meanwhile, the Friend's assurance of help eased some of the weariness Henry felt after seemingly endless discussions with Donald about their joint project. Henry now continued to probe for advice.

"Friend, do you have any thoughts on the instrument?"

Your perplexing problem requires detailed drawings. Downright honesty of purpose can be revealed by tangible evidence that clutters not with voluminous words.

Accustomed to working with his hands, Henry knew how to put together materials to match the ideas in his head. He seldom made blueprints for parts he made in his shop. The Friend's suggestion to make detailed drawings did not appeal to him.

"From my limited viewpoint, detailed drawings may not be convincing. I suspect some deeper mystery. Can you enlighten me?"

Henry sensed that something other than his reluctance to spend time on drawings stood in the way. He did not yet fully recognize that his frustration had more to do with his relationship with Donald than with the details of the project. The Friend seemed to refrain from pointing this out to Henry, waiting for him to come to his own realization.

Tension mounts. Wordology is senseless because only debate ensues. Limit your talk to an object that is seeable, *tangible, useable, transferable into action. **Proceed boldly and count on definite progress. Crowning achievement will be delightful.***

Henry could see the value of the Friend's advice to make practical suggestions more tangible for Donald, but he did not feel bold enough yet to act on his own ideas.

Over time, Henry would come to acknowledge that, due to his childhood experiences, he had a big emotional barrier to hurdle whenever confronted with people in authority, even his friend Donald. Henry felt apprehensive about the situation and asked the Friend about it.

"Fear is a tremendous subject, and one perhaps close to us all. I wonder if I am ready to receive some wisdom regarding fear."

Considerable fear is unwarranted. New circumstances frighten unnecessarily. Crowning quality is peace of mind. Mind admits fear in small degrees to remind one of the weakness of flesh.

"Interesting point, Friend. In this case there's no physical threat, but somehow the situation feels dangerous to me."

Undue caution is regrettable. Milestones remain unnoticed in the quest for an elusive, fanciful condition altogether devoid of fear.

"How true!" Emma exclaimed. "Just think how much time we waste worrying about making mistakes. You know, I assumed that if I did everything just right, I could reach a blissful state of no fear or worries whatsoever. But I suppose such expectations are unrealistic."

Henry nodded, acknowledging Emma's words, but to him the Friend's statements did not deliver the relief he had hoped to get. He presented another problem to the Friend.

"In view of the great amount of work in my shop, I don't see how I can find enough energy to do it all. I can see but one alternative—farming out some of the work."

Considerable effort already expended would be lost if not concluded. Plan carefully. Delegate details outside. Sure, you can accomplish lots more, and bigger tasks.

"Thank you, Friend. I appreciate your efforts."

So be it.

Emma wondered if the Friend might find Henry's persistent questions about the instrument annoying. She asked a mental question about it and received an answer through her fingers.

Quickly matured fruit lacks what slowly ripened fruit contains.

To Emma, the answer implied a reassurance, while Henry took it to mean that he needed to fully comprehend what he already received before asking for more. As a confirmation of Henry's thoughts, the Friend answered before Henry could speak.

Quite so. Rarely does an experience validate revelations given without action-testing the honesty of finds.

Henry tried to understand the statement. One could interpret instructions in a variety of ways, he thought, but only by testing the Friend's suggestions could he prove their worth. The word "finds" reminded him of a treasure hunt and brought a smile to his face. Searching for answers and finding gems of good advice promised a thrill of discovery, if only he could find enough determination to build the instrument the way he saw it in his mind.

"Thank you for your suggestions. I'll try to absorb more of the material already given. Good night, Friend."

Ditto to you.

Feeling encouragement from the Friend, Henry read between the lines a hint to devote more time to the instrument, but he also knew that to action-test his own ideas would challenge Donald's specifications and thereby his authority.

6

Matters of Authority

✴

A bright engineer, Donald had several inventions to his credit. His colleagues and employees held him in high esteem and some hailed him as an indisputable authority, making it that much more difficult for Henry to question Donald's opinions. Successfully built, the instrument would fill a need in Donald's laboratory and provide a sizable income for Henry.

In the process of discussing the project, however, Henry observed that the great man didn't have all the necessary information on how to choose the best materials for the instrument and how to best configure its components. Seeing Donald as an absent-minded professor—brilliant, yet lacking in practicality—bothered Henry. Although they hadn't planned on a session that evening, Henry interrupted Emma's activities to ask for help in talking to the Friend.

"My relationship with Donald confounds me. I value Donald as a friend and I am flattered that he seems to be interested in my friendship. On the other hand, you probably know my anguish about having to reject many of his ideas for the instrument. Can we have some enlightenment on these matters? Am I being taught wisdom by his seemingly unnatural insistence, or is he being taught wisdom through my having to reject his ideas?"

Great men seldom choose friends without adequate response. Sound principles underlying your ideas are paramount. Greatness overlooks minor differences and enlarges

on cooperation. Trying conditions require tact. Good inten-
tions surmount obstacles. Learn kindness, Henry. Reveal
answers without condemning. Donald prefers honesty.

The next day, Henry again found his range of options limited by Donald's instructions and by his own desire to honor
Donald's expertise. His efforts to build according to Donald's
specifications repeatedly frustrated him. Once again, Henry
found himself unable to continue and asked for more help.

"Good evening, Friend. Again, I seem to be stymied by the
instrument problem. I'm still not sure which way to go—show
the spirit of cooperation by plodding away at Donald's instrument, or make my own? My design can lead to a much better
machine, but at the risk of antagonizing Donald. He could easily interpret my action as stubbornness, lack of cooperation, or
selfishness. Can you perhaps offer an additional thought? I am
confused about this and would appreciate any assistance."

Clamoring noises are creating confusion, Henry. The noise
of authority sounds so loud that clarity of understanding
is getting dimmed. Pause to consider how much is at stake
if you yield. You would despise yourself, regard your friend
less, if forced to do contrary to enlightened judgment. Fear
frightens. Do not let momentary gratification sacrifice an
enduring result. Proceed in kindness and with caution. Your
desire not to hurt is commendable. See what happens. It
won't be as disastrous as you think.

Henry weighed the Friend's words carefully. Emma added
her observation that Henry's lack of success in building according to Donald's design might contain a hidden message.

"True, I've had great difficulty making Donald's version of
the instrument. With a different attitude toward his ideas I
could have finished it by now. My attitude of resistance seems

unusually strong. I never thought it would be so hard to get it done when I started out. Is there an explanation for this?"

Careful scrutiny of the finished product will tell you why your decision to follow the dictates of another is not conducive to the best originality in you. Now your teacher of wisdom will not need to repeat the lesson again. Enlarge your force of imagination lest stagnation creeps in unknowingly. Christ spoke of an abundant, fully lived, dynamic existence when He said, 'Let not your heart be troubled.'

"Your words make me feel better. I much appreciate them."

Concrete help is gladly given. We try to construct lasting energy. Use the available source of power directed youward.

Knowing the statement had more depth than he could fully comprehend, Henry ventured a comment.

"I feel I am missing some key concepts that may be hindering the progress of wisdom."

Brilliant revelations congeal into mind matter slowly. You are lacking details that are responsible for your troublesome attitude. Remind yourself how far you have come. Delight in your accomplishments. Recognize that much foundational work is already done.

"Thank you for the encouragement, Friend."

By the next evening, Henry grasped the core of the problem and faced it squarely. Had the Friend indicated the nature of his difficulty to him earlier, Henry would have dismissed or minimized it, but now he arrived at his own understanding. The Friend had patiently waited for Henry's inward search to yield an awareness that gradually brought his problem into perspective.

"Perhaps you are teaching me by showing me my vulnerability to powerful people. Donald seems to insist on doing things his way, but he is also very kind. I seem to be immobilized by my confusion over his behavior. Is it proper for me to ask you for more help on this?"

Avoidance might not necessarily be a kindly act on your part. A friendly assurance of authority is not necessarily ultra.

"Well! I take it that Donald's assurance of his authority to me is not the best attitude on his part." A deep frown indicated Henry's mounting anxiety.

Your concern is proper, as tender kindness should be developed. However, trust not the thought that you mean well when confusion results. Your objections are noteworthy, but words alone do not build adequate structures. Present your ideas in tangible form. It will help verification of do-ability. A good machine is, after all, what is needed. Convincing with words is foolhardy. Be not afraid, exact details are left up to you.

With this big dose of encouragement, Henry resolved to build the instrument his way. Emma noticed an immediate change in Henry's demeanor. He seemed to regain his self-confidence. He finally understood the Friend's comments about constructing *lasting energy* and *slowly ripened fruit*. He had to chuckle about the irony that Donald, who had helped Henry contact the Friend, should now cause him the problems he encountered.

A new Henry presented Donald three days later with a practical and beautifully designed instrument. Donald found himself confronted with an elegant creation. The novel design and the meticulous execution of detail astounded him and far surpassed his original idea. Donald spared no words in praise of Henry's accomplishment. Henry felt great relief from his concern about hurting Donald's feelings and losing a valuable friendship. On the contrary, Donald expressed his confidence in Henry's abilities. Impressed with Henry's innovations, Donald also decided to relinquish all rights to his idea, making Henry the sole proprietor of the product.

But receiving the approval of his highly influential friend, however wonderful it felt, did not end Henry's problems in dealing with authoritative people. Donald immediately wanted to show off the instrument at his lab and proposed to invite several VIPs to view Henry's achievement. He assured Henry that introducing him to his business contacts would open the possibility of many purchase orders, which would generate considerable profits. Henry's financial future brightened instantly, but the thought of having to interact with more authority robbed him of a full appreciation of his good fortune.

With the exceptionally trying days behind him, Henry realized that the time arrived for him to confront the origins of his emotional quandary. He now set out to explore his childhood memories for traumatic incidents relating to authority. His first efforts at examining his childhood quickly overwhelmed him, as issues of authority confronted him wherever he happened to look. Henry resolved to pursue the theme.

In the middle of Henry's reflections, a commotion broke out.

One of his daughters came home from school in tears, complaining that her teacher had reprimanded her for talking in class. Henry took the pain he heard in her sobs right into his heart. His indignation condensed into a heavy cloud of wrath. In his view, the teacher had punished his daughter unjustly.

The more Henry centered his thoughts on the mental image of that teacher, the stronger the injustice burned in his imagination, and the stronger waxed his heroic determination to right the perceived wrong done to his child. He thundered a bit in Emma's presence, but she gently reminded him that their daughter did not seem particularly concerned anymore. Could his feelings have flared up because of the tension in his work? Henry shrugged his shoulders and went downstairs to his shop to cool off.

As the evening arrived, Emma said a silent prayer of thanks for the presence of the Friend in their lives and looked forward to their next session. Henry's anticipation of talking to the Friend markedly tamed his unruly feelings, although he still felt inner turmoil when the session began.

"Friend, you are aware of my emotions, so you must have noticed my negative reaction to the incident with my daughter's teacher today. I sense trouble in this situation. The effects of authority from the past obviously tainted my reaction. It indicates to me that I must fix my problem or bury it deeply for all our sakes."

Too bad that so many tried to force their thoughts of conduct, speech, habits, procedure, plans, and purposes on you when it was not needed. You have already grasped the significance of the terror, lest you submit to unlikely authority. Authorities can dull a person's individuality to such an extent that camouflage looks easier than traveling the ultra path.

Yes, hiding his feelings, rather than revealing a genuine response, did make life easier for Henry in some situations. With a welcome blend of analysis and sympathy, the Friend masterfully bolstered Henry's self-respect.

Retaining the understanding that submission is better than fisticuff attitude will smooth out the uncomfortable situation. Furthermore, starting healthy, un-revengeful thought influence is a most effective tool. It dulls the edge of sharpened blades of the authority's thrusts. Needless to detail too thoroughly each past incident, as in your case, Henry. Your countenance could even become bitter, such a conglomeration of them exists. This is a massive problem with you, very deep-seated. Take eradication in easier strides.

The highly descriptive language—_the edge of sharpened blades of the authority's thrusts_—illustrated the Friend's ability to infuse just a few words with a great deal of meaning and to do it in a way that made Henry feel completely understood. But what about the statement that _submission is better than fisticuff attitude,_ he wondered. Shouldn't I fight for myself, defend my rights and protect my honor? If I couldn't do it as a child, shouldn't I at least do it as a man? Only wimps let people walk all over them.

Emma's eyes skimmed over the line of type about the _un-revengeful thought influence._ Unaware of Henry's self-assertive thinking, she offered a comment.

"I wonder if the Friend is telling you to turn the other cheek."

"Turn the other cheek?!" Henry shrieked. "I could have clobbered that teacher for intimidating my daughter!"

His tone of voice worried Emma.

"Let's read again what the Friend said," she suggested.

Together, they nestled on the sofa and began to reread the Friend's most recent message: *Too bad that so many tried to force their thoughts of conduct... on you when it was not needed. You have already grasped the significance of the terror, lest you submit to unlikely authority.* Bingo! Henry saw that he responded with a feeling approaching terror at the thought of the teacher browbeating his offspring, an obvious extension of him, into submission.

"That's what the teacher tried to do! She tried to force *her* thoughts of conduct on *my* daughter," Henry interjected. Emma fell silent.

Suddenly an image of the Golden Rule as a balance scale of sorts came vividly to Henry's mind along with the familiar saying "Do unto others as you would have them do unto you," as if suggesting a closer look at his own attitude. It occurred to him that he had tried to force *his* thoughts of conduct on the *teacher's* thoughts of conduct, who had tried to force *hers* on his daughter. The whole thing seemed insane.

After admonishing himself to simmer down, he returned to the typed message. Yet the Friend's words, *submission is better than fisticuff attitude,* kept ringing in his head. He then recalled the image of his daughter chirping with an impish laugh, "Oh, the teacher was just in a bad mood, and I did talk too much." After a glass of milk and a cookie, she had easily dismissed the incident and scurried off to play.

Henry felt a rush of tender emotion toward his little daughter, who had handled the situation much better than he did! She had probably forgotten the incident by now, while he continued to stew. From his new perspective, he beheld the absurdity of the scenario.

"You know, Emma, I think our daughter is ahead of me. She already has forgiveness in her heart, and I am still trying to get hold of it. I don't quite understand this bit about turning the other cheek, but maybe I'm getting closer. If only I could keep my past from interfering! Let's ask a question about living in the *now*. Maybe that will help me understand."

Let us consider the problem at another time. It is not 'timed to interest' now. The paramount problem is of another kind. See how undependable your feelings are? They are wafted about with even a slight breeze, aren't they? That's why it is so essential to become grounded in basic fact-principles. The surface of the ocean may be churned with storms, but deeper waters remain unruffled. This is a good picture of fact that surface emotions will not disturb Wisdom's principles.

This comment meant to Henry that if he could better align himself with the "deeper waters," then the emotional upsets wouldn't matter so much. Knowing this seemed to help. Instead of floating helplessly on the waves of his turbulent emotions, he could rely on basic principles of wisdom to keep his peace of mind. The sound of the typewriter broke his reverie.

Conforming for the sake of conforming, as opposed to rebelling, with the full knowledge that one is conforming, is liberty.

"Well, what a statement!" Emma immediately sensed the value of the premise that choosing to conform could fit the category of freedom.

Despite seeing the wisdom in these words, Henry still felt the throb of unsettling emotions, and not only those in reaction to the school teacher. During the day, he struggled to control his annoyance when the telephone rang or a customer appeared at the door. He resented these interruptions in his work and tried his best to calm himself. Rational thinking had to prevail, he told himself, but it faltered in its arrival.

"Along with this turmoil about the teacher," Henry continued to reflect, "many frustrations today seemed to have greater than usual power over me. I could barely restrain myself. There may be a time and place for righteous indignation, but I honestly can't see any justification for getting angry and snapping sharp answers at my customers who did nothing wrong."

You are not 'yourself' when in the midst of turmoil. That is why I would teach you early to abate its force.

Through the process we have traveled together, you have loosened up a good deal. It is for that reason that you see yourself, when in the midst of turmoil, more free to express your feelings rather than to adhere to your parents' instructions to be a little man and hold in those sobs and cries.

Do not be alarmed about this, Henry. Recognize, when you see these contrary traits, that they would not be there, except for your twirling in the whirlpools, and it isn't smooth sailing. I would encourage you ever to retain an open attitude, so you need not be twisted and torn.

The explanation seemed clear. He had a greater awareness of his feelings now, simply because he paid more attention to them. In the past, his denial blocked a clear awareness of what he did or did not feel. He could not quite grasp what went on inside of him, let alone in the lives of others. Experiencing his feelings and understanding the changes in him offered some relief, but this understanding did not take away the passionate force of his emotions. Henry now wondered how he could abate the force of his anger, and received a very helpful answer.

These sudden flashes of anger are merely like a sudden temperature rise in the physical body — a type of evidence that indicates the presence of something causing the temperature, or the fit of anger. Now, can you apply the same complete lack of blame in having a temperature to feeling anger?

"I feel I have no excuse for losing my temper," Henry replied.

You see, in reality, the flash of temper in the emotional body is no more to be condemned or shamed than a fever in the physical body. When that matter is fully settled and completely understood, then real progress can be made. Both anger and fever should be controlled, but there is a great need to be altogether aware that one is only controlling the anger or symptom, and not by such controlling solving the underlying cause of the anger or fever.

An aspirin, properly and timely administered, aids in the subduing of fever. So, too, the use of willpower subdues the anger, for the continuation of either one is a draining and weakening experience. So, we might say that the controlling of anger is like taking an aspirin. The progress itself is not in the aspirin, but in a complete understanding of anger.

If, when the anger flash is present, at once, immediately—before some prior conclusion clouds the immediate vision—the consciousness can be opened and the 'why' question immediately injected, then light can come, and lo, there is no anger left. Alertness reveals the source of trouble and causes the condition to be remedied or accepted, as appropriate.

Henry and Emma had to read the lengthy statements several times to grasp what the Friend intended to convey. Negotiating the difficult passages, they understood, at least intellectually, that one *can* handle anger without passion. Henry could see that becoming conscious of the rising emotion, and immediately asking *why,* would serve to detach him from the situation. Trying to find a reason for the anger would introduce an emotional distance between him and the event that provoked his anger.

Henry could see that the Friend's discourse on anger contained much wisdom, but he knew that implementing it in daily life would require more effort than he could immediately muster.

7

Understanding Unfolds

✳

Having gone through too many emotional upheavals in connection with the instrument project, Henry determined to clean up his emotional life. Although he couldn't change his life history, his angry, hurt feelings about authority had to go. Emma decided to join him in his mission of self-healing, remembering that *wisdom is catching if tested.* This quote occasionally punctuated their family conversations. Their girls even played "catch the wisdom" games, making up the rules as they went along. The whole family became involved in a search for wisdom, each in his or her own way.

Some time ago, among the many books they had perused, the couple came across *Dianetics* by L. Ron Hubbard. Much of the book made sense, but the overly self-assured manner in which the author presented his information annoyed them. The odd new terms coined by Hubbard, such as "engrams" and "aberrations," made Emma cringe, but Henry used them as commonsense descriptions of the emotional scars and unhealthy behavior patterns adopted as a result. The Friend would gradually modify Henry's borrowed terminology as the couple progressed in understanding the wide range of consequences that followed their formative experiences.

"I wonder if you can give us more details to help us remove our aberrations. It seems we need to learn how to examine our thoughts and feelings. If we can get a feeling that we can remove at least one of these engrams by ourselves, it would give us a little more confidence to proceed."

Good you seek further enlightenment. Yes, the process is detailed, for many regrettable instances, as you know, stem from one general root. The very fact that certain incidents are remembered, while more momentous events slip from memory, forces into view the fact that these important clues must be followed backward to effect elimination. Your attitude is correct. Now on to details for working out the perplexities.

First, to identify the existence of an aberration, as you term it, remember to recognize, in your concern, that your present response to an event is not as it should be.

Ask 'why, why, why,' over and over, with imagination of what happened. Continue to painstakingly search all possible angles, avenues, personalities involved, and as many details as seem important to you.

When basic root is tapped, understanding will tell you and relief will come—sometimes immediately, sometimes later. Again, a warning must be voiced that no two people may react exactly alike. Did roots get planted in the same way? They certainly didn't, so elimination will necessarily be different.

It is important to tap the root and eject all poison of the weed. How will you know when the root is gone? Once again, results are what counts. Dare face the truth. If an evidence of bad reaction to a current event pops up, the root is still there. Sometimes it takes longer than at other times to trace back to the source, but as long as an improper reaction remains, there remains digging to do.

Through it all, relax, relax, relax. Don't strive too hard, or a barrier can be created. Try gently venturing onward in specific problems. Our aid is there to guide you, backward as well as forward. Generously ask, and you will generously receive.

This lengthy presentation gave them precise instructions and assured them of sustained help. When Henry and Emma finished reading, the Friend continued.

Careful scrutiny leads onward. Unrest and strife are needless if full understanding rules. As enlightenment brightens, perplexities vanish as fog before the sun. You will witness relief after uncertainty is clarified by rigorous searching for the basis of conflict.

Face the facts fearlessly, uncompromisingly, unafraid. Days' tasks and responsibilities exceed not the strength present. Relaxed attitude is desirable, but somewhat difficult to acquire. You will be helped, as understanding unfolds. Feel its effects even now.

True, Henry and Emma felt their understanding increasing, but they also needed to remind themselves of the virtue of patience—to not expect instant results. The knowledge that full understanding would eliminate strife, even if only sometime in their future, served to encourage them in their efforts to follow the Friend's guidance.

✦

As they prepared for another session, Emma noticed an unusual thought that came without her having asked a question. She wondered if it came from the Friend.

"Where did I get that thought: 'Church attendees may be in touch with wisdom even though they go through various forms of worship that seem superficial.' Did it come from you?"

Crowning idea is that Wisdom is reachable to all who honestly seek. Place and position are not important. The attitude is important. Wisdom hides in unexpected places.

Ready, fertile soil is a requisite, not formal or informal setting.

This time, the capitalized spelling of *Wisdom* alerted Emma that the Friend did not seem to differentiate between the concepts of God and wisdom. Emma also felt that the Friend addressed her desire for more people to know God by saying that everyone who wanted to could seek and find God on their own, without formal worship. Henry, however, wanted to make sure they understood the Friend's terms correctly.

"How should we regard your use of the word 'Wisdom'?"

Wisdom's dictates rule both our realms. Entire limits are unknown. Only be sure it surpasses any definition. Fullness of brightness is blinding to un-advanced beings. Limited viewpoint demands a shaded vision.

A wave of humility swept over them as they realized their limited capacity to fully appreciate the grandeur of what the Friend referred to as Wisdom. They gleaned to their satisfaction that Wisdom indeed implied God, encompassing realms beyond their ability to fathom. Wisdom alluded to much more than a wise conduct of everyday affairs.

"Can one consider evil as lack of Wisdom?" Henry continued.

It's a partial definition only. Much more enlightenment is on the way.

The Friend didn't seem to show much interest in talking about evil, but Henry had asked his question because he associated evil with war. Thoughts of war had surfaced in Henry's mind again. His horrendous World War II experiences left him harboring deep resentment about the insanity of legal murder. He had expressed his feelings to Emma in the past, but now wanted to discuss his viewpoint with the Friend.

"Friend, I see little wisdom, even evil, in conflicts between nations. It seems that if only mankind would communicate, much trouble would cease. Do you have any thoughts on this?"

An ideal situation is sadly un-attainable, Henry. Selfish motives rule many hearts that seek to guide nations. Barriers they build block entry and refuse access of true wisdom. Penetrable only occasionally. We would so gladly help, if given an opportunity. Self-made savers of lands are so sure in their foolishness and pride, that honest hearts, so burdened by seeing the conditions, leave to seek purer climes of thought. It takes a strong man to stand alone in the face of un-responding and overly confident leaders. Support with pity, but support nonetheless those in command.

Henry saw some of his fellow soldiers make the ultimate sacrifice for their country and felt a thorough disgust for politics; however, he could also accept the need to support the efforts of the government officials to govern. Somebody had to do it. The Friend obviously understood the prevailing conditions on Earth, and later explained that those in leadership positions have chosen this particular path of learning, since everyone comes to Earth to advance consciousness.

Henry continued his questions regarding humanity's shortcomings.

"Can you tell us a little more about selfishness?"

Selfishness manifests itself openly, but also behind a cover that looks like thoughtfulness. It may be un-recognized by the person. It dreadfully hinders pure Wisdom's brightness and is classified as vice to be overcome. Strenuous effort is necessary to conquer the foe called selfishness. The attribute is almost universal. Few rise completely above its entangling, subtle manifestations. Bear in mind to eradicate its every appearance and suggestion of presence. More about it later.

"It seems to me that an overly selfish person is an unenlightened person, hence to be pitied." The words fell effortlessly from Henry's lips. He spotted a new sensation and quickly added:

"These sound like your words, not mine. Is that true?"

From where do you think has come to you all that uplifts, Henry? We guide in various ways. You observe and desire more. The un-enlightened know not true wisdom, hence respond abjectly. Wisdom's seed can spring even in unsuspected hovels, high and low. It is limited only by refusal to allow entrance.

"It seems to me that people hardly ever think about wisdom, let alone search for it."

They satisfy their inherent hunger by lesser means. They dull the sensitive mechanism by their refusal to care for, culture, respond, seek, ponder, wish, long for, yearn for wisdom. If attended, wisdom's seed takes hold and thrives, if slowly, carefully, cautiously, unhurriedly nurtured. Quench not the flame of desire to know. One who seeks wisdom learns from Wisdom's storehouse.

Receiving these weighty words, Emma and Henry once again remarked to each other about their good fortune in having the opportunity to catch glimpses of eternal truths. They noticed that they began to treat each other and their children with greater respect, which they attributed to the contagious influence of the Friend's altruistic nature. Henry noticed something else.

"Some wondrous things are happening here, as I think of it. The informal way I conduct my business seems almost opposite to what is generally considered good practice, yet I seem to draw more and more work to my shop, and it seems strange to me. It's true that I am conscientious, but so are other people; my work is fairly good, but other people's work is also good, at times even better. It almost seems like I am using a principle of wisdom that I don't comprehend. Can you enlighten me a bit?"

Do you recall words that were meant for you, 'Blessed are the meek for they shall inherit the Earth'? Modesty is a more crowning virtue than is often supposed. Relaxing in the shadow of others' compliments won't strain like bragging would. Vibrations emanating from your work, the results you get, are conducive to stirring proper vibrations in users. As your hands toil with painstaking effort, tender handling commences good vibrations in motion. Calmly proceed shedding onward and forward your good influence on metal. Inward peace follows outward thrust of superior product.

Besides validating Henry's inherent modesty and its merits, the Friend opened up another mysterious subject with the mention of vibrations emanating from Henry's handiwork. It immediately stirred Henry's curiosity, but the Friend suggested they retire for the night. Henry knew he had a tough day ahead of him, but he had no idea how thoroughly it would tax his emotional stamina.

8

Perfection Standard

✳

Henry awoke to the patter of raindrops on the roof. Reluctantly, he swung one foot out of bed and sensed that his whole body felt heavy. He had to force himself to start moving. He could hear lively voices coming from the kitchen, which, in contrast to his cheerless mood, seemed to worsen his unhappy disposition. He slowly pushed himself through his morning routine. Emma had suggested that he wear his new shirt and slacks for the special occasion, which he had reluctantly agreed to do. The day had arrived when he would demonstrate his newly built instrument in Donald's laboratory.

In preparation for the big event, Henry had done quite a bit of digging into his past to examine the sources of his dread of authority, starting with his earliest memories. He had not expected to discover so much tight-fisted control and manipulation when he started his exploration. He recalled his mom and dad pushing and pulling him in different directions and vividly felt the confusion that had overwhelmed him as a youngster. Demanding and critical at times, they would also indulge their only child with unrealistic praise and costly presents, causing him to feel uncertain about his real worth to them.

His mother dressed him in outfits of her own creation, which his father criticized for their fancy appearance. His father tried to counteract his mother's attempts at refinement by gruff games that often brought little Henry to tears. His mother would then step in to protect him, and the usual tangle of words and accusations would fill their small cabin, leaving Henry quietly shivering under his covers.

His father worked in the oil fields and frequently moved the family from one place to another in search of work. Their living quarters usually consisted of one room, with Henry feeling either constantly observed and victimized by his parents' faultfinding or pampered with promises and apologies. No matter what he did or did not do, he saw himself as falling short of one or another of his parent's expectations. His parents lacked empathy for his feelings, thus causing him to initially hide his feelings from them and, eventually, even from himself. As he grew older, he gradually forgot about his feelings altogether.

Looking at the overall conditions of his childhood, Henry wondered why someone with his sensitivity would find himself born into a family of such limited understanding. Maybe the ways of evolution intended just that, he reasoned, each generation arriving at a higher level of sensitivity and intelligence.

In the process of looking at his early years in relation to his dread of authority, Henry opened his eyes to other negative attitudes he harbored as well. He thought of his dislike of having visitors dropping by unannounced. It now occurred to Henry that his avoidance of company affected his wife's world in a significant way. Emma had grown up in a large, intimate family with a tradition of casually stopping by each other's houses. Henry told himself that he should spend more time with Emma's relatives.

The reconstruction of early events that shaped his attitudes proved difficult and painful. Nevertheless, each incident remembered and evaluated through his increasing understanding gave him a measure of relief. He even found that he could view with humor what he usually remembered with frustration and resentment. The Friend provided invaluable help, nudging some of Henry's memories into sharper focus and encouraging him to continue his endeavors.

Henry's well-intentioned efforts to prepare himself emotionally for his big day hadn't completely resolved his intense reluctance to subject his work to the anticipated critical judgment of powerful strangers. He thought of them as capable of thoughtlessly crushing his feelings and his sense of accomplishment.

Once the meeting started, Henry valiantly endured an onslaught of know-it-all commentary and critique. He suspected that even some of the praise given him contained subtle digs and hidden barbs.

Henry had previously tested the instrument many times in his shop and knew it performed well. The demonstration and tests in Donald's laboratory, however, proved more rigorous, necessitating minor adjustments. Having to stop and perform these adjustments midstream did not unsettle him, but he simply could not shake his resentment of what he perceived as pompous, judgmental attitudes on the part of the experts.

As a result of his inner tension, Henry gradually receded into the background, glad to have Donald fill the need for conversation. As the meeting came to a close, Henry realized that he had remained overly quiet during the proceedings and berated himself for not getting more involved in discussion to actively promote his product.

By evening, the emotional strain had severely drained his energy. The excitement, the uncertainty, and the self-criticism had concocted a toxic mix of internal frictions. As he teetered at his crisis point, Henry knew he had only two options: he could continue with his resentments, which would eventually consume him, or he would have to conquer his problems by finding the cause of his ill feelings. He knew that these negative engrams, patterns, aberrations — call them what you will — undermined his peace of mind and feelings of goodwill toward others.

Emma wondered if Henry wanted to talk to the Friend. Henry responded by setting up the typewriter on the kitchen table, as usual. Dejected, he let out a big sigh before beginning the session with his usual greeting and a request for help.

Good that you ask, Henry. No stars in your crown when you flounder in the midst of turmoil. Much better when we, together, can shake it off. The basic tendency in this turmoil arises from the old bugaboo perfection standard.

What? Hadn't the Friend approved of high standards earlier?

Henry had fully expected a suggestion to search the dungeon of his personal history for more dragons of authority. He knew that vexing emotional snarls do not unravel of their own accord. Instead, he found himself directed to ponder the theme of the *perfection standard.*

The Friend's comment brought to Henry's awareness his subconscious tendency to insist on supreme quality in work and ethics. Having a family to support, he took for granted the need of pushing himself to the extreme while remaining silent about the ensuing pain.

"Did I impose this standard of perfection on myself just to make myself look better? I thought I was just using my skills to the best of my ability."

The Friend seemed to know Henry's innermost feelings, even those he had kept hidden from himself.

There are, however, a few other aspects, too. You find it difficult to give voice or put into words the sentiments of your inward knowledge.

The Friend's astute observation struck home with Henry. Indeed, he did have difficulty accessing his feelings and expressing them, especially about matters that concerned him personally. What appeared as reserve, politeness, or even humility, frequently veiled his clamped-down anger.

His frustrations had many facets and layers, with tendrils crossing back over each other, confusing his attempts to sort them out. After struggling with them for some time, Henry isolated some of the factors of his predicament:

First, part of the frustration stemmed from the fact that he did not feel right about having any angry feelings at all.

Second, trying to find proper words for these awkward things called feelings took time and generated more frustration.

Third, his frustration mounted even further when he did find the words that portrayed his feelings, only to discover that those words brought on either confrontation or embarrassment, or created misunderstandings when people took him the wrong way.

Fourth, the combination of frustration, embarrassment, and lack of verbal skills had a self-compounding effect, which quickly took a big toll on his patience and reserve. At those moments when he most needed to rightfully assert himself, he found himself least equipped to do so with any grace.

The Friend approved of Henry's efforts at self-analysis.

Recognize this, acknowledge it to yourself, and note immediate improvement, when you grasp this much of the problem.

You also tend to overplay to yourself each minor defect, gladly taking responsibility whether justified or not. Remember, Henry, you are a vessel containing a piece of Wisdom Himself, and you have the privilege of demanding the courtesy and respect due you. This does not, of course, imply a demand to be babied. Indeed not. Wisdom does not welcome pampering.

No doubt the Friend had Henry's well-being in mind by bringing up these problems. Indeed, Henry found it easy to personally absorb any differences to avoid confrontations. He would go along with other people's views and assumptions to spare himself the trouble of having to face his tangled emotions. Guilt and shame found a ready home on his shoulders, heaped there by even the most casual of remarks. With sympathetic encouragement, the Friend gently but firmly guided Henry toward his rightful sense of self-respect.

The Friend's words *a vessel containing a piece of Wisdom Himself* reminded Henry and Emma of the expression "God within," which they had encountered in their reading. To them, this notion felt like a breath of fresh air, compared to the forbidding image of a distant God glaring down upon their sinful nature. The idea of personally containing a bit of God gave them an uplifting sense of divine origin, elevating their outlook on themselves and others. This light yet energetic feeling brought them closer to understanding the remarkable way the Friend spoke of God — the word "Wisdom" meant God, while simultaneously alluding to the *means* of getting closer to God.

It is correct that you demand from others the honest treatment that you render them. Your instrument contains a bit of you, Henry. You exerted your influence on that device. It speaks for itself as an outstanding accomplishment.

The recognition felt good, but the Friend offered a startling suggestion, indirectly serving to unmask yet another of Henry's debilitating attitudes.

Cancel out, however, for your peace of mind, any right

to ownership. The troubles, such as you are made aware of now, feel too personal, as if they were thrust at you, instead of at your instrument. You are advancing fast into heights of Wisdom's experiences, so these troubles, by contrast, seem greater than they are. Can I help you more? Feel free to ask.

What could he ask at this point? With all due respect to the Friend, the suggestion that he relinquish ownership of his invention sounded like an absurd and totally unreasonable request. The instrument felt to him almost like his own flesh and blood.

"That's how a parent must feel letting go of a cherished offspring," Henry muttered, softening to the Friend's suggestion.

The more he thought about letting the instrument stand on its own merit, the more reasonable the advice appeared. He did not take the comment to mean that he should not benefit from his labors financially, but rather that any forthcoming criticism of his brainchild would not feel like an attack on him personally. Despite the difficulty of breaking old habits, making such a distinction would certainly serve to protect his feelings.

Still, the amount of emotional investment and physical effort he put into his unique creation loomed large in his awareness.

"I can see a problem here. I feel that people judge me by my work, so I try very hard. On the surface, I can say I always do my best, yet doubt creeps in and says I could have done better. That somehow translates into I *should* have done better, which makes me wonder if I've ever done my best. I should be able to walk away from my work with confidence that it speaks well for itself."

We are now bumping smack into the perfection standard. The best is not perfection: Openness is perfection. Forget not the word 'doing.' If you obeyed that perfection standard of yours, there would simply be no do-ing. Nothing would ever be accomplished, nothing would ever be done. For ever and always there would be that mirage of the perfection standard. Your 'best' is doing, as of the moment, that which appears the most reasonable, the most feasible, the most enlightened manner of conduct and approach. In openness, allow new concepts to enter, as your fingers fashion and your mind outlines procedures and plans.

"I try to do my best to make a product without flaws. I admire perfection in proportion, in clean appearance, and in other ways, but striving for perfection to the point where it becomes something to worship seems totally out of line. I find it difficult to properly balance my attitude toward my work."

First of all, Henry, recognize that your general attitude is an enviable one, much better than fighting the foe from the opposite angle! Your aim to produce a superior product, moderately priced, and pleasing to the eye, is commendable. Tenaciously cling to that high ideal. Let me illustrate from a completely different angle.

Did you pause before a fine work of art or a piece of statuary? There before you is a finished product. Perfect?

To your eyes, possibly. To its originator, flaws appear that in the next rendition will be improved upon or eliminated. Only as the originator remains open, can new, fresh, original ideas continue. The designer must not leave himself in the piece of art at which you look.

You and many 'yous' who see the work receive the vibrations that result from the efforts of the artist, but that is not a part of himself. Perfection is not in a completed object, no matter how complete, but in an ever openness to new, delightful vistas.

It comforted Henry to know that he didn't have to abandon his drive to achieve high quality in his work. The Friend caused Henry to re-examine his understanding of perfection by placing emphasis on the person and the process rather than on the resulting product.

Now, to take us back to the instrument, your beautiful handiwork. Your careful thought and plan, your interest, all these are in the finished product, and their vibrations will continue to be felt by those who use it. But—and this is very, very subtle—you should not be in it. This does not imply that you are incorrect in considering your customer's viewpoint and standing back of the goods; oh, no. But not because of the reason you give yourself.

Practice thinking on this; I feel sure you will grasp the difference between extent of responsibility and your perfection standard that permits no room for kindness to self.

Kindness to self? Emma and Henry looked at each other as if to ask "what's that?", but Henry noted the late hour and reluctantly ended the conversation.

"Thank you very much for a very enlightening session."

You are welcome.

Talking to Henry afterward, Emma said she had never before heard of kindness to self. The idea of extending kindness to oneself sounded strange to Henry, too, yet, as time passed, the subject gained definite importance.

9

Observe Your Turmoil

✳

Henry noticed his level of tension increasing after dealing with several potential customers who presented him with their needs. Their talk seemed to fray his nerves more than usual, if not to the limits of his self-control. He managed to respond as graciously as he could, but, inside, he boiled. He tried to look at the *why, why, why* of his inner agitation, but with negligible success.

"Good evening, Friend. This turmoil is getting rather rough to handle. I don't know how to deal with it. I have noticed that many small things stir my emotions. They fall under the general category of authority, which, to me, means fear, anger, and continual resentment that I can't rise above. I feel like my emotional maturity resembles that of a two-year-old."

Henry's self-condemnation reflected his disappointment with himself, which the Friend attempted to counter.

What a turmoil! You are baking in the oven of adversity, emotionally speaking. Can't blame ol' Sol, either. Let's take it piecemeal, Henry.

The Friend's humorous entry—exempting the Sun from overheating Henry's emotions—had an immediate relaxing effect. The words might as well have said, "Don't worry, we can cut any problem down to size."

First, that authority angle. Your resentment, I might say, is now unfounded. You have been granted your release and

the ropes no longer bind you. I am speaking about out-
ward actions in relation to authority figures. So surely have
you proven your adjustment and stability that you have
reaped a harvest of respect and admiration. However, the
psychological strings—the ropes in your mind—are just
as firm as ever. Now, to get relief is of very much concern
to you. Why?

The Friend paused, allowing time for reflection, but Henry
could not find an immediate answer. He thought of his recent
argument with Emma about music lessons. Henry favored their
daughters' musical education, while Emma felt they could not
afford the expense. Before Henry said anything, the Friend
answered the question by complimenting him.

Because you are progressing so well, Henry, you dare
to face the existing conditions without fear, but in kind-
ness—not to excuse self, but willing to face uncompromising
facts. Carefully pull apart every possible aspect that pres-
ents itself, asking 'why, why, why?' Permit to come to your
memory any events that may present themselves. This is no
easy task, but one you can master with head unbent, emo-
tions ruffled but intact, feelings in turmoil but not scarred,
senses churned but not tangled.

Closely watching you is a group of us, ready to lend our
aid, so think not that you are going through this by yourself,
alone. Converse freely with Emma, your wife, as she enters
another room full of turmoil when you distance yourself.

True, Emma felt quite upset after Henry abruptly walked
away from her after their disagreement. What they thought of
in the past as their private domain seemed to present an open
book to their apparently all-knowing Friend. They felt like mis-
chievous children caught in the middle of their antics.

'Tain't funny. These predicaments are definitely upsetting when you tend to live moments of the past over and over again. This tendency is burdensome, and intense kindness must be exercised, and that means Henry to Emma and Emma to Henry. You gain nothing by erecting barriers. Now proceed to ask more, if you wish.

Henry didn't feel like asking anything at that moment. He suddenly realized that he lost awareness of his effect on Emma's feelings in the midst of his turmoil. It dawned on him that people in emotional distress paid little attention to anything other than their own feelings — precisely the definition of self-centeredness. Henry flinched at the thought that he adversely affected those around him while spinning in his world of personal concerns, blind to his surroundings. He wondered how he appeared to his daughters and how they felt during his bad moods. Did he frighten them? He hoped that they did not notice his temper that much, yet he knew they did. Seeing himself in such unfavorable light confused him and sent him groping for something rational to say.

"I can't see any benefit from frying in turmoil other than the observation of our wrong attitudes, engrams, selfishness, and so on. Am I right?"

Only if your term 'observation' is inclusive enough. Observe how much can be observed while in turmoil. Think how understanding develops, how kindness is learned, how hypocrisy is detected, how energy is sometimes aroused, how silences are invoked, how talking reaches completion, how involuntary movements come about, how compromises are impelled, how strength and weakness are discovered, how truth is unearthed, how conscious upsets reveal unconscious threats — and that does not exhaust the subject.

Does Wisdom err in permitting these experiences? Oh,

no, Henry, oh, no. When your soul shall echo back, 'Come whatever will, in that I find my contentment'—yes, when you can say that and mean it, peace will descend. Regard with gratitude these approaches by Wisdom, Henry, as they are given with generosity and for your growth in spiritual stature.

Henry fell silent. Each item the Friend mentioned deserved extensive thought. The many things yet to learn and the negative traits still to overcome brought Henry near a state of shock. That night, his feelings manifested in a nightmare about snakes. They wiggled in the water at the bottom of a large tank, raising their heads and hissing at him ominously. On awakening, Henry concluded that the hissing snakes symbolized his unresolved conflicts.

In the evening, Henry mentioned his dream to the Friend.

"Come to think of it, the snakes actually looked more like eels."

We tried to make them look less offensive.

Henry's mind reeled. The seemingly innocuous comment by the Friend amounted to an admission of control over the contents of his dream. Henry did not know whether to feel intruded upon or blessed. Leaning back in his chair, he cast a blank stare at the typewriter. Emma tried to suppress her giggle at the sight of the befuddled look on Henry's face, until laughter overtook them both, enlivening their rather strenuous enterprise of emotional growth.

✳

For several days, the couple made sure, whenever their ideas differed, to listen to each other closely, discuss their viewpoints in detail, and give each other room to express their thoughts without undue emotion. Feeling completely heard for the first time, both Henry and Emma found the process very satisfying.

"We are curious as to whether looking at our turmoils produced any benefit. Can you see any?"

Revelations present themselves in many forms, but the premise remains the same: unless you observe, comprehend, and are present at the scene of revelation, the benefit to you is lost. You can absent yourself from the possible benefits, if you desire. It is entirely up to you. As to ultimate benefit? You are creatures of haste. If no apparent change appears, you think nothing happened.

Try to place yourself in perspective, with eternity in focus, and understand that an entire lifetime is but a flash, so why enlarge each individual incident? But, into that flash can go a great deal of growth and progress, if the life is adequately handled. The matter of choice rests entirely with you.

So ended another brief session. Henry and Emma agreed that their troubles would indeed appear minor in the immense perspective of eternity; however, they knew that their experiences nevertheless served a meaningful purpose of fostering their emotional growth. They could also see that difficult times provided windows of opportunity for rapid spiritual progress, given proper attention and technique.

The Friend's comment that *you can absent yourself from the possible benefits* required some time to ponder. The meaning of the statement became clear when Emma understood that full awareness needs to accompany the experience for the learning to become effective. What the Friend described as remaining *present at the scene of revelation* meant actually experiencing what the event revealed.

After some discussion, they also realized that a person can try to eliminate negative traits by deciding to behave better, but unless the change rests on sound inner convictions and principles, the attempt remains futile. If one simply believes that the banished trait will no longer appear, in an unguarded moment, it may reappear with an even greater force.

Henry soon came to face such an unexpected challenge.

10

Misevaluations

✳

Henry woke up to a blue Monday. At the breakfast table, he tried to pull his thoughts together while mulling over how to schedule his workday plans. His frustration about beginning a day on unsure footing mounted, and when the girls played their radio too loud, Henry's irritation spilled over into a harsh voice demanding quiet in the house. The girls immediately obeyed.

"Daddy is in a funny mood today," Emma whispered to the girls, trying to laugh off Henry's annoyance. Henry felt forced to join in the laughter, which infuriated him even more.

He spent his day struggling with petty aggravations. When the time came for the evening session with the Friend, Henry wanted to understand his reactions, since he knew that he had handled the morning situation in less than admirable fashion.

"Do you know what was behind the turmoil this morning?" he asked. "It was connected with the radio, but it started before that, if I am not mistaken."

You are correct, Henry, in your discovery that the center pole around which you have treadmilled today commenced before the ether waves sent their din into your ears. This illustrates the fact that when a misevaluation chains you, other grievances appear magnified all out of proportion — sort of that downhill trend, that once-set-in-motion-off-we-go type of happening.

Reading the Friend's apt description of what happens when irritations begin to mount, Henry and Emma exchanged knowing glances. The Friend understood. Every new annoyance enlarges the one before, and then things spin out of control if not stopped in time. Maybe it did not have to work that way, if one could remain free of misguided emotions, or "misevaluations," as the Friend termed them. Henry realized that what feels real may or may not truly reflect the circumstances as they exist. These misunderstandings on the emotional level reveal areas where a person needs to unlearn faulty preconceptions by replacing them with more accurate perceptions.

"What was my problem in the morning, if I may ask?" Henry tried to open himself to a fresh view of his behavior.

The unresolved weekend floated into an unresolved workweek, and the transition was uncomfortable.

The situation seemed to involve a chain of events. Henry's previous workweek ended with an unfinished job, which upset him. The art exhibit he had looked forward to attending over the weekend with his family offered little of interest, despite a good review. Henry's hope for an uplifting distraction had ended in disappointment, and his gloomy mood continued unabated.

"When stress builds up, it's hard to shake it off. I felt the burden of it all day today."

The element of coercion, of being forced to laugh, also had its effect, Henry. It is as if situations were saying, 'This should be done' and yet, the ease of obedience to these commands eludes you as yet. It is coming, however, as you expand into the glorious realm of full understanding, but considerable misunderstandings and misevaluations yet block the full release.

"Yes, I have a really hard time with being told what to do, and having to laugh felt so artificial that it turned my turmoil into exasperation. You are right, I knew better than to act as I did, but I didn't have what it takes to instantly change my mood."

To deal with being forced to laugh was an intense injury to you, Henry. Facing it completely now will drain out some of the poison of the occurrence. Note that, with some individuals, a laugh in identical circumstances would be the masterstroke of accomplishment. Emma is largely that way. For instance, a laugh lifted her out of her emotional toboggan speeding downhill at the art exhibit. So, the tool is a useable one, but not at all times with all persons.

Now that he looked at it again, Henry could see that he wrongly evaluated the forced laughter incident. He found himself admiring Emma's resilience in controlling her attitude. With the help of his loyal wife and the Friend, life didn't seem so bad after all. He affectionately acknowledged Emma's good intentions, and she playfully responded with an invitation:

"Next time, laugh with me, will you?"

He sheepishly nodded his assent and received a big hug from Emma.

Later in the week two state officials arrived at Henry's shop unannounced, presenting a new challenge to his ability to keep his emotions under control. They talked to him at length about regulations and new requirements concerning safety measures in his business. As a result, Henry's opportunity to catch up with his schedule suddenly vanished and so did his precious equilibrium.

Once again, Henry turned to the Friend for help.

"I had a rough day today. I guess you know about those two gentlemen showing up to boss me around. It's just too bad I couldn't make my delivery today. Would you care to comment about it?"

Say rather, 'The product was not delivered today.' Just a statement, not a designation into good or bad. And of course, no experience comes to you, except as attracted by that big magnet.

"What magnet?" Henry asked, wondering what the Friend would present to them now.

We call it the 'magnetic attraction principle.' It means that no experiences come, except those that are attracted to you by your need for the experience.

The concept startled both of them. Emma flashed on the statement in the Bible to the effect that not a sparrow falls without God's knowledge. However, the idea that experiences come based on the need for them sounded like an extravagant notion.

"So, by what means did I attract this last experience?"

Shall we look carefully, kindly, but firmly into this one?

Most of the important conclusions, or I should say lessons, which you learned from your pop arrived as an opposite in the mirror of understanding. In other words, you discovered by negative example what was best not to do. But not all. Some became positive. One of them said something like this: 'Son, don't you let anybody push you around.' Remember that? Somebody pushed you around today.

Something shifted in Henry's mind as the clarity of understanding began to dispel his confusion. According to the

Friend, the experience of his interrupted work schedule came to him because a misevaluation distorted his view of reality and he needed an opportunity to correct his father's well-intended but erroneous teaching. Henry would have never guessed. The Friend continued.

So, of course, there could be no acceptance, no agreement with circumstances, no relaxation in assurance that all things work together for good.

The two officials had indeed offered some good suggestions, but Henry found his irritation too great to see their helpfulness.

It was to be that way, Henry, for your over-concentration said this morning, 'I will finish this job,' instead of 'I would like to finish this job.' There is a world of difference, for one is rigid, the other flexible; one is unyielding, the other passively active; one is stern, the other kindly.

Once again, the Friend alluded to the need for kindness to self. The habit of excluding all else but the job at hand eliminated any regard for self as superfluous to a firmly set course of action. Henry could feel the Friend's gentle tenacity in showing him that a flexible approach worked much better. He could now easily imagine how a kind, accepting attitude could have smoothed away some unpleasant edges.

In addition, Henry saw that an awareness of the *magnetic attraction principle*—if indeed it operated as the Friend described—could certainly cast a more benevolent light on even some of the least desirable events in life. One would know that the events appeared in one's path for a reason, even if one did not always comprehend the purpose at the time. It amazed both Henry and Emma as they considered how a necessary experience could weave itself into the fabric of everyday life.

Now, there is a karmic reason fir this, certainly.

"Karmic reason?"

Henry and Emma remembered Donald's attempt to tell them about karma. They had argued with him, obviously not ready to accept a concept that did not fit into their worldview at the time. The Friend's comment now piqued Henry's curiosity, especially since he recalled Donald using the Biblical words, "Judge not lest ye be judged," as an example of a statement about karma. To Henry's surprise, the Friend used similar words in explaining the reasons behind the events of the day.

Your judgment of your pop was something like this: 'You don't have to do it that way,' without the recognition that behind the action lie driving forces like runaway horses, most difficult to curb. To him, you would say 'stop that.' But now, can the karmic incidents you meet be equally met with a 'stop that'?

Henry had to laugh. Someone on the sidelines could have easily judged him today the way he had judged his father.

"So that's what karma looks like! You attract to yourself the same experience for which you have condemned another!"

Henry remembered his embarrassment when his father self-righteously attacked people verbally when something did not go right for him. Henry had wanted him to stop, but it would have taken more than a simple request for his father to change such ingrained behavior. As Henry recalled the hard time he had containing his own "runaway horses" in the presence of the two unexpected visitors to his shop, he felt a wave of warmth toward his father. New comprehension dawned on him that he had severely judged his father without any compassion for the strong emotions that drove him into so many calamitous predicaments.

You are finding, Henry, that the intense drives that forced your pop into action spelled a hurt to him in his losing jobs, in telling people off, etc. Understand this clearly, and your problem dissolves into nothingness.

Is this too direct, Henry? Is this too bluntly revealing? Sooner or later we will face this; can we do so now?

"This is not too bluntly put. In fact, I have often wondered if I would ever have a chance to speak as candidly with anyone as you have spoken with me."

The straightforward way in which you yearn to approach matters is well known to us. But in the great work of progress, all steps must be in accord with Wisdom's dictates. As a definite example, you would find yourself in the strong bonds of unkindness to self, if these matters were placed before you in a rapid, haphazard fashion. It is better this way.

Just then, Henry realized that he did not even think of condemning himself for having so harshly judged his father. The Friend had delivered to him a bitter truth about himself, but in a manner that avoided the pitfall of self-condemnation. Instead, his eyes opened to a compassionate understanding of the pain people bring upon themselves by not accepting the events that Wisdom places in their path for a specific learning experience. To validate Henry's thoughts, the Friend continued.

Your progress has been tremendous and most satisfactory, Henry, for the content of consciousness, seen by us, contains reams of progressive material gathered during your present lifetime. As to the karmic aspect, yes, Henry, much has been understood before now, but this one premise was yet unresolved, for if it were, you would not have faced that turmoil today. You still do not wish to be pushed around, according to the edicts of your teaching of early days. You see, it is not the work that the visitors presented, or the act of an interruption, for these identical factors have occurred in the past, and you have welcomed them at times. It was that it all caught on to that unresolved premise, and suddenly, you were being pushed around.

The explanation made sense. The premise that he should resist anyone telling him what to do had etched itself on Henry's memory as fatherly advice to his son. Henry felt good about resolving his long-standing misevaluation, which distorted his perception of even well-intended actions toward him.

Now, added to this was the further consciousness-acquired premise learned from your pop, in the what-not-to-do aspect of speaking your mind. For let it be known that had your pop felt as you did today, he would have dismissed the visitors for good, for he did not have the brake to stop the runaway horse. Furthermore, he would not allow himself to admit that a better way was available. He would have insisted that it was 'manly' to tell them off.

Understanding all of this will give you strength—no, I don't like the word—will give you acceptance. It doesn't take strength to accept; it takes relaxation, peace, poise, just that letting it happen, and swing along with the event in rhythm and ease. Think you this a big hurdle? Not so, Henry. We have risen above many others in our sojourn together, in past lives, as well as this one, and the ease of another day will spell the acceptance you have achieved.

"I sense a great deal of material connected with this premise. The 'not being pushed around' was made quite a point of honor, as well as 'manliness,' as I remember."

Your pop learned much in the years after the textbook was exhausted on you, Henry. As a matter of fact, during his tender years of older age, he took many things which, had they occurred in his younger days, would certainly have entirely upset his equilibrium. He learned much, and could have told you many things, had he revealed his innermost feelings. But he learned the hard way, and it is in his consciousness now as an asset of great worth. So, the lessons he taught you, he later admitted to himself were weakness, but he could not transfer this learning to you. Even to know this thoroughly, Henry, assists in pointing out the instability of the structure of these many, many of your father's teachings.

In the quietness of your being rests the gold of accomplishment; in the depths of the soul are the diamonds of worth revealed. That is all, and now good night.

Reflecting on the session, as they frequently did before retiring, Henry and Emma shared their admiration for the wisdom of the Friend. Henry felt more at peace than ever, and yes, even if the Friend did not choose the word, he felt strengthened. Emma also felt fortified in her attempts to ease situations with humor. Both agreed that not having any misevaluations to work around in the first place made the most sense of all.

11

Direct Communication

While in his shop, Henry again received direct communication from the invisible realm without the mediation of Emma and the typewriter. This time, he clearly understood the answer to his question. He mentioned the incident to Emma and the Friend as they sat down for their session that evening.

"I had a curious experience. I was prying off a board with a crowbar when it slipped and I hit my thumb. Pain aside, I had a funny feeling that something wasn't right, so I asked directly about the trouble, and got these words: 'Openness implies alertness, not a trance state.'"

In hindsight, Henry laughed at how he had roused himself from his daze and saw the value of keeping a clear focus on the task at hand. The Friend complimented him.

Your success in receiving communication comes from your openness to the presence of Wisdom's messengers. I enjoyed it, too.

Next time, don't hit so hard. I'll teach you my short-cut definitions with just a little tap on the finger!

Emma winced at the sight of Henry's swollen thumb. No, he did not want any help with it; he had a bigger problem that he wanted to discuss with the Friend. News had reached him from Donald's laboratory that one of his instruments had broken down. This would have upset him greatly in the past, but now, since his conversations with the Friend, he lost neither his composure nor his self-confidence. He realized that even without knowing the nature of the failure, he could at least temporarily remedy the situation by providing a new unit to replace the broken one. Despite feeling somewhat shaken, he managed to joke about the problem.

"Could you enlighten me about the replacement of the instrument, or is it rather a matter of replacing an unbalanced attitude of mine?"

Could I? Well, now let us see. You are still feeling too heavy about this matter. Lighten up! Your basic tendency to view with perfection standard the finished product is hampering a proper viewpoint on the subject. Feel not as though mama slapped you for not producing a hundred percent product. That is where the sting lies. Are you aware of that?

No, Henry had not thought in that direction, but he got a chuckle out of the Friend's comment. The perfection standard had stepped on his toes again, but now he knew where it had originated.

It is far more important, actually, that you comprehend this most important aspect than whether or not you replace or repair the instrument.

Henry made a mental note to follow up on the steps by which he learned to overreact to ordinary occurrences in life. He thanked the Friend for shifting his priorities and decided to assemble a parts kit so he could repair the instrument in the morning. The following day, he paid Donald a visit and corrected the problem.

When he returned to the shop, he heard an entity speaking to him in a casual, friendly manner. A definite Scottish inflection lent a pleasant coloration to the visiting personality. Without ado, the Scot proceeded to explain the characteristics of the particular metal at hand, and assisted Henry in the process of polishing it. Henry had some difficulty explaining exactly how it happened, but the result of the assistance pleased him immensely.

"The entity with the Scottish accent gave me some information about the manner in which he coordinated my hands with my mind. His influence seemed to mingle with my consciousness and a sort of synchronization took place. Does this sound as if I received it correctly?"

Correctly deciphered, Henry. It pleases me to see you using other avenues by which Wisdom reaches you. Regard it highly, but do not worship it any more than any other method. It is a pitfall into which many a sincere one stumbles. Never 'halo' a manifestation, no matter how sacred it appears to you. Try hard to regard all these manifestations, including the part I play in this great scheme of things, as methods, as means, as avenues, by which Wisdom reaches you. So long as you permit us to retain our rightful place, we can exert our influence. That was the basis of my caution not to lean too heavily. The feeling of enthusiasm matures with experience — it does not get overly or underly emphatic: you retain an even balance, and more and greater manifestations can come. Proceed now, good people.

"Friend, thank you for the stabilizer. These new experiences are very strange. It helps to have them evaluated in a sensible manner."

I sensed that you needed this. Try hard to remind yourself of this attitude often. Wisdom's many manifestations seem strange because of their uniqueness. Do not be surprised, as you have others in store for you. Wisdom, Who made the mountains, has many unlimited avenues. Retain your open attitude. You will witness many mighty things if you do not hinder their appearance by slamming shut the door. The choice is entirely yours.

Not even once did it occur to Henry and Emma to slam the door on something so fascinating, enlightening, and helpful. In the past, they would have deemed such happenings impossible, even frightening. The Friend's sensible explanations made all the difference between accepting the strange manifestations or rejecting them as wild imagination, if not insanity.

Separating the influences that reach you is paramount. The unfailing clue is the results you reap: happiness or depression, understanding or perplexity, peace of mind or turmoil, sense or nonsense, clarity of mind and thought or mere agitation of mind-matter.

"Is there any way we can tell the difference between receiving wisdom and an active imagination? I am talking about receiving directly."

Good question, Henry. Here is a clue: Wisdom continuously uplifts, benefits, and inspires; mere imaginations dull and perplex. Wisdom results in peace and contentment; imagination can lead to unrest and dissatisfaction. It is easier to determine, actually, afterwards. Look at results. That is your final, absolute, and concrete assurance.

If a new thought or idea enters your focus of mind and results in backbone-builder type of instruction, consider it as sent from Wisdom; if not, imagination has taken over. However, do not regard imagination as kin to selfishness, for example. It is not a foe to be overcome. The only caution to be expressed here is not to make the mistake of letting the fruits of imagination become basic fact-principles in your thinking. Imagination is a useful tool to be used occasionally, but it is more desirable to receive directly from Wisdom.

"I am always pleased to use the direct method, but a while back, I asked a question and the sentence came up to the point where the next word would have given me the information, and it stopped! From that I judged that you considered that I had best not ask too much, or that you saw it as dependency."

Yes, I remember your experience. That was twofold in implication. For one thing, a measure of fear and a twinkling bit of pride you allowed yourself permitted a 'meddler' to intercept the fullness of the message. In other words, the words were there, but the ground was not quite clear for receiving.

A valuable lesson emerged for Henry from this experience. Henry learned that pride, as well as fear, could interfere with communication. Something to keep in mind, Henry thought, since his struggle with negative emotions seemed far from over.

Recall another basic clue, Henry: we don't demand or command. Should questionable material present itself, you will be aware of it. How? By its lack of coordination with the previously carefully learned truths.

That made good sense. Having the basic points of reference, such as kindness and awareness of the Golden Rule, one could pretty much figure out what Wisdom's realm embraced and what simply wouldn't fit.

Then another aspect, Henry, is the tendency to evaluate such statements as 'absolutely so,' or 'positively this way.' For even our words, Henry, you must qualify with a 'So it seems now … According to present indications … As it looks from this angle … ' rather than take them as a flat 'This is it.'

"Yes, I can see how I might oversimplify matters to have them fit neatly into a box."

This time the Friend pointed out that deep understanding of a situation includes the consideration that conditions change with time and circumstances. The necessity to abstract thought into word-symbols, and the natural tendency to generalize, can introduce distortions and degrade the accuracy of the thought process. Reasoning in black versus white absolutes may have sufficed in the earlier stages of human development, Henry mused, but expanding consciousness required more discernment and flexibility in thinking.

"Proper understanding is tricky business. Am I on the right track?"

Regular communication with you is becoming increasingly available, as Wisdom's avenues are becoming more and more unobstructed. You are learning well and solidly. Your concepts remind you that thinking with powers you possess is vital and delightful. Continue daily to broaden your vista of understanding, contacting new ideas and more ideas.

The next day, Henry had another experience to share with Emma. While working in his shop, he noticed a recurring thought he could not shake off: wanting to tell other people about their communications with the Friend. The thought persisted to the extent that it occurred to him to question his motivation.

A mental conversation with the Friend led him to an entirely new concept—"undesirable desires." Henry's desire to spread the word apparently took on the form of missionary zeal. The Friend then showed him the unwelcome nature of his apparent temptation. Henry could not remember every detail of his impressions, but wanted to share with Emma whatever he retained of the experience.

Missionary zeal, the Friend had explained, consisted of grasping one piece of enlightenment and assuming that one has the whole of it, which happens more often than not. Each new morsel of comprehension becomes the end of the road. In general, today's knowledge seems to make yesterday's mode of thinking obsolete, and encourages a now-I-absolutely-know attitude. The body of knowledge in many fields, including religion, psychology, and even science, becomes permeated with fragments of truth passing for complete theories, without an awareness of the limited horizons of such truths. This fervor then leads to condemnation of previously held beliefs, and strenuous attempts to teach the new, without appreciating the rights and the necessity of individuals to have their own personal experiences and draw their own conclusions. The Friend explained that this attitude played an important part in such events as the medieval crusades, the fascism of recent history, and wars in general. The sum of the various aspects of zeal, as it pertained to Henry's desire to share his experiences, the Friend described as good intentions without wisdom.

It shocked Henry to think of himself as a zealot. The intimation stirred up many questions about himself. He felt he wanted to share with others that which felt so right to him, but then, wouldn't a zealot think that way, too? Henry began to suspect having misevaluations in this area. He thought that possibly because of his feelings of inferiority, he wanted to impress others with his possession of great truth.

Another reason to think himself capable of zealotry he attributed to the stern admonitions in his youth to not talk unless addressed. The words "keep your big mouth shut" rose up in him like an echo from the past. A rebellion against his childhood prohibitions could possibly explain some of his eagerness to communicate. With these thoughts clearly articulated to Emma, Henry opened the session with his usual greeting, to which the Friend immediately responded.

Good evening to you! Your training is progressing constructively. The seeming strangeness should not be taken to indicate that the process is complicated. Soon a familiar feeling will replace the oddity of this type of communication. Your alert, questioning, and aware attitude makes for workable soil for Wisdom's seed to sprout. Let the sunshine of His smile, the raindrops of His caress continue to cherish, protect and burst forth into brightest bloom the glorious workings of Wisdom.

The moisture in Henry's eyes made the air shimmer, and caused him to blink a few times.

Lead others, as opportunity presents itself, but go not out of your way to create opportunities. Your firmness, assurance, and calmness will attract the bewildered ones. That's the time to encourage open minds. The clinging vine types who would try to glom on to you are not what you want to attract. Your aim is to lead them to drink from Wisdom's fountains for individual benefit.

The brief session ended with uplifted feelings.

"Well, are you going out to change the world now?" Emma could not resist teasing Henry after the session.

"Not so fast, dear. I need to put it in committee." Henry liked to spoof the bureaucratic procedure used to dismiss important issues, but Emma knew in her heart the great importance Henry placed on helping others.

12

The Expression of Self

✳

Henry had many talents. He expressed some of them through painting, making jewelry, and especially through woodcarving. He experimented with various techniques of gluing pieces of chiseled wood to burlap, or connecting carved pieces with strings, to make representations of different themes in the Bible. Using this technique, he fashioned a set of two abstract carvings depicting the Old and the New Testaments in a unique interpretation of their meaning. Following his whimsy, he almost felt the hands of some invisible power guiding his movements. Henry felt an indescribable joy while working on these projects.

"Friend, I wonder if you could tell us what is in back of the urge or desire for self-expression?"

There are several aspects of this so-called self-expression. You may regard it differently from your neighbor, Martin, for example. His self-expression emphasizes the self part, not the expression part. There must be a clear understanding of this particular term, or confusion is sure to result.

For the time being, let us corral that term to mean expressions of the finer, the energizing, the beautiful, such as the lofty expressions in prose or poetry, in fine art or uplifting music. That, Henry, is the essence of consciousness breathing in those things necessary for the ability, shall I say, of grasping the greatness of the next step in progress Wisdomward, the next realm.

Very often, it is difficult to ascertain, even for yourself, wherein lies the distinction between self-display and inspired self-expression. But if your awareness can catch the beauty of the profile of a tree against the setting sun, the blue of the wing of a flying bird, the lilt of the song from the throbbing throat of a songbird, the grace of a sparrow in flight, the delicate coloring of a wild rose—yes, if these awaken within you a responsive thrill, then you can invite yourself to enjoy self-expression, for then surely the consciousness within is reaching, reaching, reaching for the beauty, the comprehension presented by one of the many self-expressions of the Creator. Is this helpful?

"That was a splendid comment, Friend. Can you tell us if inspiration is given according to how diligently one works for it, or according to how closely one has attuned oneself to Wisdom?"

Inspiration comes in many forms, sometimes recognized as such, but not always. Conscientious effort is amply rewarded, as you suggest. Duty inspires at times; also complicated circumstances. Wisdom trains in diverse ways. Many attempts are made to stir action Wisdomward.

The information needed a little pondering. They already knew that Wisdom tried to inspire humanity and worked through many avenues even when not recognized. People may proudly or mistakenly lay claim to inspiration as all their own, when in reality the credit belongs to Wisdom working through them.

Comprehend and learn to use more fully this generous gift. If inspiration is not self-stirred, it won't be hindering any other activities inspired by Wisdom.

Henry became curious about "self-stirred inspiration." Apparently not all inspiration came from Wisdom.

"Is that when I push myself to create something and it doesn't seem to work?"

Self-stirred inspiration versus Wisdom's inspiration? Results clearly indicate whether the source is proper. Indiscriminate, heartless, brutal crushing of others to gain supremacy indicates self-stirred inspiration at work. Amassing terrific evidences of security at the expense of enslaving fellow creatures indicates self-stirred inspiration at work. Craving the advantages of another, called jealousy, is indicative of this wrong attitude.

Evidence of Wisdom's inspiration is ever and always kindness and peace; not envy, but goodwill. A helpful attitude toward others will result in good for receiver and giver, too. Reduce desire, if gluttony is evidenced. Needs can be refined to include that well-rounded society you desire. Sincerity is pretty basic, too, with kindness.

"I wonder if you could give us some more clues as to how kindness works. Can it reach the self-engrossed souls? The influence of kindness must somehow transmit itself to another, and that other person then shows kindness in return, at least so it seems. It also appears that if you are kind to others, you actually end up being kind to yourself in some mysterious manner."

You are correctly headed toward marvelous basic truth, Henry. Kindness, as has been revealed, is Wisdom's attribute. The transferable quality appears in somewhat different aspect than you now recognize. Think of it more exactly as tuning in to a matching vibration already existing in another. Total absence of kindness in another is rare, but complete absence of this quality would find no answering vibration, no matter how hard you might try to impart kindness. Remember, too, that the Creator's handiwork contains some of His attributes. You just keep on absorbing more and more of the attributes of the Creator.

The idea that one can increase divine presence in oneself by absorbing more and more of the divine attributes sounded simple enough, yet unfathomable in its depth. Henry began to see that growing in kindness contributes to the general process of increasing enlightenment.

"Can you tell us about the mutual benefits we receive when we show kindness to each other?"

Nurturing seeds of Wisdom encourages growth and expansion, as when seeds receive rain, sun, and nourishment. A dwarfed plant indicates a lack of vital needs being met for growth. Nothing may be wrong with the seed, but it is not properly fed and nourished. When you impart kindness, you figuratively water and nourish the spark of kindness within you, as well as prompt the receiver to do likewise.

Thus the Friend explained how by showing kindness we nurture it within ourselves. An outward display of kindness may prompt the other person to express it in kind, but one cannot transfer kindness to another. A certain degree of kindness already resides within individuals as part of the package of attributes they bring with them to Earth, but each person has a choice to cultivate it or not during their lifetime. Once again, the Friend's respect for individuality and free will became clearly evident. We cannot control the responses of others, but we can offer them an opportunity to show their kindness in return.

This type of interaction respects the individual's freedom of choice, in contrast to the prevailing practices, Henry thought.

More often than not, people try to influence, manipulate, sway, persuade, control, cajole, convince, insist, or otherwise pressure others in order to impose their own will, while overriding the other person's preferences. No wonder the Friend saw Wisdom's gift of free choice to humanity as a sacred, yet largely disregarded, right. The Friend also emphasized the need to understand the importance of kindness.

True unselfish kindness that seeks no reward implies presence of Wisdom's attribute. Kindness reveals itself in many ways. Sometimes acts may appear otherwise, but be basically kind. Generosity, for example, could be a most unkind act. However, in another situation, generosity could be kindness personified.

Examine the difference between a self-centered act meant to appear as kindness and one that reveals true kindness. The driving urge behind the act determines whether a kindly act is done. To give kindness—true kindness—implies much, Henry. The outflow to others is completed as you tap the true fountain, which is Wisdom.

The observation of how generosity could clash with kindness made sense to Henry and Emma. One can indulge someone with generosity and yet rob that person of an opportunity to exercise his or her own capacity for growth. Yet in a different context, generosity can become an appropriate, necessary, even life-saving act.

"A person under considerable stress may find it tremendously difficult to be kind. It seems to me that kindness can come easily only when backed by confidence and a substantial reservoir of spiritual strength."

Strains and tensions tend to separate you from Source, and the confusion that results often breeds unkindness.

Yes, that is what happens, and frequently. This is, however, not the only cause of unkindness. It's a delightful thrill for us that you so constructively enlarged on the thought of kindness.

"Are we sufficiently advanced to cope with the question of evil?"

Absence of color is black. Absence of light rays of Wisdom implies the darkness of confusion, unrest, self-seeking, lack of understanding—the downward spiral. Do clarify your thoughts much more before too definitely remarking to yourself that such and such is evil. You will comprehend in due time.

Knowing himself as vulnerable to kindness, Henry at times felt wary when someone acted kindly toward him.

"Some people use kindness to manipulate or induce guilt. It's a shame that something so nice can be turned into a subtle weapon in their hands. Or maybe what I'm talking about is not kindness at all."

Kindness is a shining example of Wisdom's effectiveness in reaching mankind. Shallow thinking overlooks the force and power that kindness wields. It is truly a weapon, as you suggest. It plows under mistakes and errors of others, hides defects, proves eternally trustworthy and loyal. Its breath is the essence of love and goodwill, ever and always. It gently nurtures the weakest ones and crowns the strongest with meekness. It is the most desirable of attributes, if one understands kindness as a breath of love itself. The crowning delight is basking in kindness completely."

"Breath of love itself," Emma repeated. "What a lovely expression!"

✳

The following day, Henry found himself composing a poem while sweeping his shop. He stopped to jot it down.

> The world's a cathedral,
> The altar's within,
> The mind is a lens
> To be focused by Him.
>
> For we know not our nature,
> But stand manifest
> As a structure of time
> That's eternally blessed.
>
> Who walks in the light
> Sees a bird on the wing,
> Whose soul is cast down
> Sees a terrible thing.
>
> Now, life is a lesson
> From which we can learn
> That to the altar within
> Is the place we should turn.

This verse would win no acclaim in a competition, but it marked great progress for Henry, who had long held a conviction that "poetry is sissy stuff." Emma loved poetry and greeted Henry's first attempt at rhyming with genuine delight. She also noticed Henry becoming more gentle in his demeanor. Looking at Henry with admiration, she knew she had married the right man.

13

Be Kind to Yourself

✳

Having read many books on theology and psychology, the couple could not fail to notice discrepancies between diverse theories and ideas. Every author seemed to have his or her own slant on numerous issues, and some who claimed authority sometimes sounded strange, baffling, or simply preposterous. Henry and Emma asked the Friend about several ideas they found in these books. While occasionally clarifying the points of view in question, the Friend left room for the couple to form their own opinions.

"We have just been reading a book by a man who interprets the teachings of Christ in an unusual and highly unorthodox way. I doubt that any of the churches would approve of his thoughts, but they still sound like they may have some validity. I wonder if this man has the deep insight into Christ's teachings that he appears to have. Would you care to comment?"

Consider every avenue of learning, whether new and untried or old and familiar, as means of approaching Wisdom and not as ends in themselves. You have correctly opened your mind to receive the intentions of the author. It will benefit you. However, don't consider it absolutely necessary to approve of the whole book. Take from it what proves beneficial, but recall that it may not benefit all who read it. Some may not have progressed as far in search of truth and wisdom.

With kindness and consideration, the Friend encouraged Henry and Emma to maintain an attitude of flexibility and acceptance of differences in thinking.

"In one particular instance, an author presented well-founded arguments for receiving emotional influences in the womb before birth. I am inclined to doubt that such a possibility exists."

The response to Henry's comment came in keeping with the Friend's attitude.

Carefully investigate. This point sounds to many ridiculous and impossible, since the concept is new and startling. Cast it not away for that reason. But neither is it healthy to entertain as a positive fact each new concept introduced as being factual. The best approach is an attitude that there is the possibility that it might be so.

As to this specific problem, Henry, it is better that you wait and find out for yourself. It is not nearly as important as you have been led to think by the authors, but do not deny the possibility of the existence of such. Reported to you are largely imaginary incidents, in an effort to prove something of which they themselves are not sure.

It is well to bear in mind that often individuals will expound the loudest, speak the most eloquently, when in greatest doubt. Again, do not apply this observation too literally or confusion will result.

Despite their introduction to the idea of reincarnation, Henry and Emma had their reservations about claims that one could remember past lives.

"What about those who write about influences from their previous incarnations?"

The Friend again handled the matter in a typically gentle manner.

After all, Henry, interpretation enters the picture very largely. Imagination can play tricks on careless people. Don't conclude from this that those who are so certain are necessarily entirely in delusion. The most important lessons for you to hold is that the possibility exists, as far as you are concerned, but remind yourself that it is not good to be too certain, or too positive. In questions of this nature, a neutral, I-don't-know approach is admirable. This is the type of subject where uncertainty shines as a desirable condition.

Yet another book employed a technique of distilling life's stressful events down to a few words to portray the influences that had the most disruptive effect on one's life, and emphasized relaxation as a means of identifying them.

"Some of what this author has to say sounds a lot like your advice. Am I entertaining any deep-seated 'command phrases' that hinder my relaxation?"

The chief difficulty with you, as of now, Henry, is your insistence on blaming yourself. Are you looking for chances to scold Henry again? To pin him down? To demand instant obedience? Certainly, all of these will hinder relaxation.

You have put on a garment of relaxation, but it is just a garment. You have successfully concealed from even your intimate friends that un-relaxed Henry. Congratulations!

Seriously, though, Henry, it isn't a bit funny; it is a burden you have carried for too long a time. We must work to eradicate it. Use every possible tool you find to enlarge the peace you know is yours by right of heritage. My four-inch type for you is:

BE KIND TO YOURSELF

Don't chide, blame, blaspheme, compare, indulge in self-pity (a subtle form of unkindness to self), or bemoan. Only look and see.

"What right of heritage do you refer to, Friend?"

I'm glad you asked. Consider what makes you the real you. It is the Wisdom's piece of Wisdom allotted to you. What is your destination? Absorption into Wisdom. That's your heritage. Thrilling, isn't it?

Henry and Emma wondered what such transition might feel like. The idea of dissolving the boundaries between the God within and the God beyond gave them insight into the ultimate goal of spiritual evolution. Yet the prospect of absorption into Wisdom seemed such a profound and abstract proposition as to elude comprehension. The possibility of divesting himself of everything connected with life on Earth stirred in Henry a chaotic mix of feelings, including the instinct of self-preservation and one of the very sentiments the Friend suggested to avoid—self-pity.

"I find myself feeling undeserving and incapable of living up to these wonderful teachings you lay at our feet. When I look at myself, I don't like what I see, and that happens quite often. Do you know why I would indulge in this kind of self-pity?"

Certainly, Henry. As a small boy, you observed that you must make all the decisions because others were not dependable. Poor little boy, with such a responsibility! Recall also your 'discovery' that desire attracts the opposite. That's how the misevaluation started. And it has grown through the years with many incidents that reinforced your early conclusions. You will recall these incidents, as you pump your way to the present.

Henry felt he still had a long way to go in finding the sources of his emotional injuries. He tried to hide his discouragement, though he knew he could not hide it from the Friend.

✳

Henry continued to peruse books for ways to access the archives of his memory and probe for the origins of his negative attitudes. He had found several suggestions couched in theories that sometimes played tricks on his sensibilities.

In one book, for example, Henry found a similarity between the statements of the Friend and those of the author emphasizing the importance of thinking for oneself. Disenchanted with psychoanalysis, the writer advanced a seemingly convincing notion that psychology places too much emphasis on the negative aspects of personality instead of on appreciation of one's inherent strengths. This seemed to imply that Henry should ignore his shortcomings.

"I wonder if one way for me to be kind to myself is by not paying too much attention to my misevaluations, like my aberration of self-pity. If I dwell too much on negative thoughts, don't I grant them extra power? But isn't it also true that I must think about them if I intend to remove them? There seem to be opposing views here, if I am not mistaken."

Carefully picking off rotten fruit to be discarded is an apt illustration of plucking out so-called aberrations. It drains strength unnecessarily from the tree, if the rotten fruit remains on it. (Of course, this analogy is rather vague, because rotten fruit usually falls off, but aberrations cling.) Another disadvantage of rotten fruit is the appearance to any who come in contact. They may admire the tree in spite of the rotten fruit, but more sincerely if it's plucked off.

Also, consider the angle of permanence of habits. Unless eliminated, they remain. To pluck off the offenders does not require continual harping on the subject. That gets pretty tiresome. But when the presence of offenders is noted, it is best to eliminate them. Polishing will not do.

"By polishing, I take it, you mean glossing over the offenders; but by being kind to myself, am I not excusing myself from jumping into some hard and ugly work?"

Excusing self is not the same as kindness to self. Attempts at polishing would be apt to give 'power' to aberrations. Remember, though, the process is sometimes slow and tedious, especially when dealing with deep-rooted issues. Care should be exercised that continual attention to this work not be given over long periods of time, or surely depression would overtake. Circumstances will assist, if an open attitude prevails.

As a hint, if you sense anger toward self, that's the time to smother the possibility of a downward spiral with good thought influence. You have choice, you know.

This is a difficult procedure, because each type of circumstance requires specialized handling by you. Create healthy attitude of confidence and the foes will yield.

Henry saw the need to maintain a balance by heeding the warning to neither avoid the difficult work, nor obsess with addressing his deficiencies.

"The fine lines of distinction between excusing self, working on self, and kindness to self seem very important to get right. It seems there's a constant standoff going on inside of me."

It is not unduly paramount in you, Henry, but it pays to pay attention. Careless habits of conduct may interfere with reaching the goal. Excuse not yourself by regarding all instances of plucking the offenders as a long, drawn-out procedure, lest laziness take the place of alert openness.

"Okay, now I have a question about reincarnation. Did I absorb any of my attitude of self-pity from a previous life, or was that solely a bad evaluation I made because I assumed my parents didn't know what 'poor little Henry' needed?"

Your so-called aberrations hooked themselves on to you (for a free ride) because of your misunderstanding of values and lack of experience. Consider in what light such a suggestion would be received now! You would have the understanding, because of your advanced knowledge, and it couldn't hook onto you now. You would be able to properly evaluate the situation, hence no self-pity would result.

The effects of scars from past life don't reach over to you in that forceful a manner. The influence is vastly different. You haven't heard all I have to say about the subject of reimbodiment. Familiarize yourself first with this concept and its existence as part of Wisdom's plan of action.

The next day, they visited a metaphysical bookstore and bought a book on karma. The kindly woman at the counter assured them that reading about karma would help them to understand the interrelated concept of reincarnation, or reimbodiment.

Upon their return home, Emma began to read the book aloud. Before long, she noticed Henry fidgeting in his chair and wondered about the reason, which they then discussed in great detail.

Henry told Emma that he had trouble accepting the concept of karma. The difficulty had to do with the subject of authority once again. The authors interpreted the Biblical expression, "As you sow, so shall you reap," as representing the law of karma. His and Emma's strong indoctrination with the thought of inherent human sinfulness had left them with an intimidating notion that the words meant: "If you do wrong, God will punish you." Henry admitted that the description of karma as a strict, unbending law reminded him of his childhood fears of punishment. He found himself resenting the implied ruthlessness of authority. Emma had to remind him of the Friend's teaching—as she understood it—that the Creator has no malevolence whatsoever. Henry pondered the thought, let out a deep sigh, and asked Emma to continue reading from the book.

The idea of reimbodiment also felt confusing to both of them because the author referred to different kinds of bodies, not just the physical body. They decided to ask the Friend for clarification.

"There are a number of new concepts in the karma book that we have never heard before. Astral body, desire body, spiritual body—were all these bodies described as such to make us think of them as having distinct functions, or do they overlap?"

It is conceivable and understandable that confusion results whenever thoughts are clothed in words. These various 'bodies' exist as attributes, Henry, as definite leanings and tendencies, or divisions of being. But, for instance, you could not separate the so-called desire body from consciousness. It remains an attribute, a commingling into the area of awareness—that is, to you, on your Earth sphere.

Certainly, learning about them by such terminologies as you have read makes you more alert to those aspects of your being. Look at these words with a transparent glance: see through the words to the basic consciousness.

It will assist you to think in terms of rays of light. Colors manifested are many, and decidedly defined, yet are aspects of a single ray of light. Is this understandable to you?

"Yes. That's a nice comment, Friend. Thank you."

Henry would learn more about the ramifications of karma and reimbodiment soon after the Friend bid them good night.

14

Special Dreams

✳

Henry had an unusually vivid dream. It made so strong an impression on him that it stayed with him throughout the day, while he tried to fathom its meaning.

In the dream, Henry found himself, with Emma by his side, in an ethereal realm, standing inside a handsomely furnished cathedral-like building. Framed within an elaborate arbor, sat a Chinese man of great distinction. Dressed in a golden robe, he seemed to signify a manifestation of Wisdom. Henry did not know how he knew the name; he simply *knew:* Wu Li Tsung. A deep wound across the man's face suggested a possible reason for his transition to this other realm. As dreams would have it, the image of the wound began to disappear. The man's face then took on the very kindly sort of features that would characterize one dwelling in the higher realms, Henry thought. Next he became aware of a transparent plate hovering a few inches over his head, and noticed an identical one over Emma's head as well. These plates accompanied them at all times, serving as means of communication. While in his presence, Henry and Emma felt deeply indebted to this man who had bestowed great gifts upon them and benevolently expended efforts on their behalf.

Upon awakening, Henry tried to understand his feelings and realized that his impression of owing the man something of equal value in return came from his social conditioning. In the dream, nothing at all had indicated any sense of obligation. Henry concluded that his dream attempted to illustrate relationships between the two realms, and felt that the Friend might reveal important details.

"Is there more significance to my dream that I should know?"

My willing service youward includes visitations even during sleep. It is good that you recognize the visitation as a picture of fact. You are learning through many channels. Keep this in mind, as it will clarify many mysteries of our relationship with you. Treat the visitation humbly, realizing that it is a generous gift from Wisdom's outstretched hand. You deciphered correctly the meaning, but make it clear to yourself that Wisdom is unlimited and, therefore, could not be contained in Wu Li Tsung. He might be more correctly considered one who is Wisdomward bound, even as you, though graduated to a higher class.

This modest explanation gave little indication of the true significance of the man in the dream. It seemed that the Friend, appearing as Wu Li Tsung, wanted to gradually introduce Henry to the notion of past lives by providing vignettes of a story, one at a time.

As Henry pieced together the fragments, a panorama of their past relationship unfolded in his understanding. According to the Friend's account of events centuries ago, Henry—at that time a monk named Gurda—came upon a man waylaid and severely beaten by roaming bandits. Gurda took care of the man and nursed him back to health. The injured side of the face in the dream image of Wu Li Tsung derived from that incident. A deep friendship developed between the two men. Together they traveled from one remote mountain village to another, teaching the wisdom of the day, and sustaining themselves by helping and working wherever they could. Their ancient bond of friendship provided a foundation for the special attention now given to Henry and Emma in their present communication with the invisible realm.

It amused Henry to think of himself as a traveling monk. In his present life, he had felt a great affinity to the teachings of Lao Tsu, and the occasional visits he and Emma made to antique shops steadily enlarged their Oriental collection. The revelation of the story helped Henry to accept reincarnation as a real possibility.

"This past-life business seems to explain my fascination with Lao Tsu. I wonder if you could tell me more about his philosophy—it holds a strong attraction for me."

Lao Tsu? His wisdom was devoured by you with much the same intensity as you are now receiving our treatise. You dwelled long, and I mean long, in your search for the hidden meaning behind every scrap of instruction you could find. As a matter of fact, in those days you were a walking compilation of Lao Tsu's teachings. You relished his philosophy—it was like bread to your body. You quoted Lao Tsu loudly and frequently in our many discussions. Not that I found no common ground with you, for I, too, admired the experiencer who hesitated to verbalize lest words become traps.

Few realized your inward struggle, Henry, for your display of loyalty to your beliefs in all public appearances was masterful. It's quite natural for you to be loyal to your Emma and your friends in this lifetime, too.

Since his last dream had unfolded so beautifully with interpretation by the Friend, Henry wanted to discuss two more of his recent dreams.

One of them featured a man happily dropping seeds into the holes he dug with his primitive hoe. Sowing the seeds, for some reason, did not seems as important to the man as making the holes, which felt rather odd to Henry. The Friend explained, to Henry's further amusement, that from this simple hoe, the first device he had ever fashioned with his own hands, stemmed his present imbalance—his infatuation with tools. Henry's inordinate attachment to his various implements clearly showed in his present existence. First the shop in the basement, then the garage, quickly filled with specialized gadgets and machinery. Once acquired, the equipment remained in Henry's possession regardless of its lack of usefulness. He simply refused to part with it.

The other dream involved a man playing a lyre-like instrument. The musician cut an impressive figure in his long, heavy robes, with gold chains around his neck. As if burdened with heavy thoughts, he fixed his gaze on the marble floor of a magnificent hall with tall columns. Alone, surrounded by an atmosphere of opulence, he looked sad and forlorn. Henry noticed a striking contrast between the idea of the man playing a musical instrument, which to Henry implied gentleness, and the harsh expression in the man's eyes. Henry called him "the wicked-eyed Peter."

The Friend confirmed that these dreams depicted experiences from Henry's previous incarnations. The Friend also told Emma that she had carried over her great love of poetry from one of her past lives.

Its root belongs to an English family of which you were a part, Emma. Your earthly father, in that day, was a poet of some renown, but his work is lost to the ages. That is why you, in your young days, delighted in verse and rhyme, and found it delightful in school, as part of your familiar past.

Emma thought of her present-day father, Imre, and wondered if she could share with him the wonderful knowledge they had received. An outstanding member of his church community, Imre helped many in times of trouble.

Imre is a tired old man. His sympathies lie already with the prospect of eternal bliss. His comprehension is not complete, but after all, who knows complete truth? As to seeing our treatise, why not allow the circumstances to dictate that? Don't jam it into his hands, but note the response and act accordingly. It will never mean as much to him as you might think, nor as much as it does to you. But, if he tried, he could receive much encouragement and benefit from it. However, let this matter take a natural course, or you will create confusion.

Emma sensed deep warmth and sensitivity in the Friend's suggestion. It helped her to subdue her impulse to burst into her father's calmness with an exuberant "Look what I've got!" Her father's hidden desire to leave this Earth for a more peaceful state revealed to her a deeper meaning of his tiredness, and filled her with respect for him and his imminent transition.

✦

The couple found the continuity of consciousness intriguing, and the history of their own reimbodiments fascinating. Their previous lives revealed details that had definite bearing on their tendencies and inclinations in their present existences.

Henry's dream of Wu Li Tsung impressed him so much that he did not want to ask questions about anything else but his life as Gurda.

"Is there anything else you can tell me about our adventures?"

We traveled together for several years and enjoyed a close relationship. You were my coworker, as we trained and mingled with a group of people seeking enlightenment.

Because of the closeness we felt, even though distance separates us now, my consciousness can reach you. I understand you so well, Henry, and you understand me. Of course, we will meet again and recognize each other. It has been so greatly beneficial to have this intimate contact, Henry. We both have benefited.

"Frankly, Friend, I find it exciting to learn about all of this. Did we actually know Lao Tsu back then—I mean in the flesh?"

Well, well, Henry. Now you know. You are getting keener, sharper in your discernment. Of course, we knew Lao Tsu, for it was his enlightenment that was partially contained in our propaganda spreading. And why else would there have been that inward stir when you met with his teaching recently?

It was a blessed experience to absorb the delightful aspects of his teachings. Recall our exuberant enthusiasm? We knew he had something deep to reveal, and wanted in haste to tell others, although your forceful exhilaration did exceed your understanding at the time, Henry. Good you recognize this, as you will look for other clues in your interests that attract you as a magnetic response, as they did in this case.

"I take it that all of this must have happened in China."

We taught in the hills of the Himalayas. Our course was through China, too. If you went there now, you might even recognize, in a sudden flash, some of the places we inhabited. I spoke the Chinese language and you interpreted for the folks in the hills. We reached many bewildered and puzzled people. This experience followed the wicked-eyed Peter incarnation you visioned. You needed to undo the damage, in a sense, or, rather, to enlarge your conscious-ness to include service to others.

Henry showed insatiable curiosity about their past coexistence, but the Friend hesitated to provide more details, explaining to Henry that his tendency to want to live again his past life would not have a beneficial effect on him in his present life.

Henry, we have all eternity to talk this over. Continue in your present realm, daily adding volume to your conscious-ness. Yes, we'll reminisce, and watch the clouds go by, and the spring change to summer, and enjoy the thrill of con-tinued, expanded friendship. And Emma will join us, too, for she is a kindred spirit.

It delighted Emma to know that she would remain part of their company. Any doubt, which she occasionally entertained about her importance in this remarkable relationship, could now drop away.

The conversation came to an abrupt halt when the Friend demonstrated concern for their worldly affairs.

Well, you plan a trip tomorrow. Best your bodies keep up with your spirits, and the best preparation is a restful sleep.

15

Moment to Moment Living

✳

The family enjoyed occasional weekend getaways. While traveling, Henry and Emma did not have access to a typewriter. At those times, Emma had used her stenographic skills to jot down the Friend's comments as best she could. At times the Friend surprised them with spontaneous remarks. One such remark caught their interest. The Friend had spoken of the realm of spirit as free of the limitations of space and time, adding that living in the moment on Earth approximated conditions on the other side. The couple wanted to learn more about the idea of bringing their attention into a clear focus in the immediate instant—moment-to-moment living—as a way of life. The Friend offered to teach them this rarely understood approach to living.

The teaching implied, in essence, that if you live in the present moment, you leave behind the effects of the past and oppressive concerns for the future. Instead of having preconceived expectations, you attend to your need or interest of a given moment according to an inward feeling of rightness. The Friend also explained that every individual lives according to his or her *master plan,* which may serve as reassurance that one can entrust oneself to the daily flow of experiences as they arrive. Henry and Emma, naturally, became very curious about the suggestion.

"Is the master plan the same thing as destiny?" Henry asked.

What meaneth destiny? The only destiny actually is our final absorption into Wisdom; that's our destiny. The master plan is in a sense the map that points the way to that delightful heritage. Did I say map? Well, partly. An instruction of directions is more applicable.

"I'd hate to think that everything I do comes from a script."

In your realm, you have choice; you can follow in openness into the center of the master plan, or you can take a great big walk in the opposite direction, or onto by-paths that lead over some rough territory. The all-wise provision of Wisdom does not include the explicit laying out of the plan before you (although there are instances when this is done). It appears more to your benefit to discover the fullness of the master plan through moment-to-moment living. Capture the essence of that experience, and you won't miss the fullness of the master plan for you. Learn early, Henry, that your tendency to approach matters slowly and methodically has a beneficial policing effect, in that it keeps you out of hurried, agitated movements that would lead to confusion.

But Henry and Emma found the teaching about existence in the moment difficult to apply. After struggling with the idea for a few days, they posed a question to the Friend.

"What is the main blockage that is preventing us from entering the moment-to-moment existence as you explained it to us?"

You hesitate to comprehend that moment-to-moment existence is a true reality and can be commenced without stage setting—it is a recognition of what is, and is now. It is seeing the now as it is, without viewing it through rose-colored or smoke-filled glasses, tinted or smoked by past experiences.

Moment-to-moment living implies a recognition that the future is unattainable now, and now is now. It is an acceptance of every element that enters the now as directed by Wisdom and, consequently, not to be marred by contaminating influences from the past.

Henry reflected that, if he contaminates Wisdom's benevolent intentions for him in the present with influences from the past, then indeed he would do well to keep trying to eliminate those influences from his life. Perhaps the Friend's method offered just that kind of freedom, Henry thought, as the Friend continued.

Moment-to-moment living implies an acceptance of every picture that enters the horizon of your being, whether colorful or dull and gray, buffeting or applause, disregard or acclaim, energy or inactivity. Can you conceive that it is possible to respond to everything with equal equilibrium?

Christ was the master. He saw true conditions and was unmoved by palms waved in His honor, or thorns pressed into His flesh in ridicule. Moment-to-moment living implies a serenity of being. But I must not attempt to describe it too much, or it will become cloudy with detail.

Henry closed his eyes to reflect on the Friend's explanation. As Emma waited for Henry to ask another question, a different voice began to speak to her. Poised to type, she hesitated when she realized that the voice had a different feel to it. The unfamiliar voice praised her ability to tune in on the world of spirits. It promised to reveal a secret, when the Friend suddenly intervened, and her fingers typed an odd message.

Cancel out.

"What happened just now? Cancel out what?" Henry asked.

Still flustered, Emma continued to type.

These busybodies—trying to confuse you into living tomorrow today! Beware of promises of this nature, Emma.

Emma shook her head, as if to shake off the unwelcome interruption. Apparently, an intruder took advantage of the open line of transmission. The Friend then issued a warning that anyone communicating with invisible forces needs to heed.

This is an example of what often happens with zealous seekers. You need to be very cautious, as there are many who want their voices heard—like the politicians in Chicago!

Henry got a chuckle out of the comment, an obvious reference to the raging political convention at the time. Emma, however, experienced the intrusion as a shock and decided to terminate the session. She felt fortunate that she had noticed the difference in style enough to alert her to the need to question the message. Thus a valuable lesson presented itself to both of them to always maintain a keen sense of discernment.

The Friend had assured them of protection and had provided an evidence of it by canceling the impostor's message.

The following evening, Emma still expressed concern about the intrusion into their session with the Friend. Henry suggested that they redouble their vigilance and ask the Friend to give them more information on how to remain open while guarding themselves against interference from undesirable sources. Emma agreed. Henry put forth his question, readying himself to scrutinize the reply.

"I wonder if we can talk about the subject of openness again. We have some concerns about it."

Openness is a state of being, a mode of action, a sensitive-ness to change if necessary, a tremendous inner relaxation. This and much more is implied in the openness theme. If you remain in an open attitude, open to guidance from within, to the inward something that prompts or holds back, you will know the right action.

Openness is the ability to walk in the now, not in the yes-terday or tomorrow, but in the now. And walk in the now alert, sensitive to the proper urges and leadings.

Emma singled out the words, *open to guidance from within,* as the most important part of the answer they needed. Henry agreed that when they listened intently to their own inner impressions, they could discern the quality of messages that reached them.

"Thank you, Friend. Surely, we know deep inside what is right and proper."

Obedience to the inner guidance leads to confidence, though un-sought, though un-searched for. Confidence is more nearly a result, while openness is, in a sense, the means by which confidence comes creeping in. This is quite a subject!

"Quite so!" Emma agreed, but she still had some concern as to whether she could tell with certainty where the mes-sages originated.

Even the leadings must not be absolutely certain, or one would insist on them and that would not be openness. You may rest assured, however, that if openness reigns, some, yes, some method will be available to let you make the right moves moment by moment. This is a big statement but a true one. Methods may vary, and do vary with each pass-ing incident. Make no shrines, set no bounds, and cling not to methods.

Emma couldn't help but laugh. She hoped for some solid, reliable guidelines that would assure the safety of their transmissions. Instead she received reassurance that if she remained open to her inner sense of rightness she would avoid problems.

Henry also had some uncertainties he wanted to clear up.

"Today I was in a hurry, and did quite a few things awkwardly. Suddenly I became aware of what I thought might be you, or some other friendly entity, suggesting that I be more open, but when I mentally asked if there was something you wanted to say, there was no reply. So I wondered about this aspect of openness—whether I interfered or nothing more was said. When I am working and become aware of you, and you have nothing to say to me, I immediately start working again and, in a sense, forget about communication because of the need to direct my attention to the job at hand. Should I have a listening attitude constantly?"

There are several matters involved in your question. First of all, your entry into the moment-to-moment existence will clear up any pondering you may have about listening, hearkening, attending. Suffice it to say at this time that you are very correct in your procedure.

It is especially imperative that you do not attempt to force something when it is not timely. You may be aware of us as we are just breezing by, as it were, and lightly reminding you of our presence with a 'Hi, there' greeting. Your recognition at such times is an adequate response.

Henry wondered how he could better tune in on the Friend.

Now, the matter of tuning in. Consider this subject from the standpoint of vibrations. You reach us, and we reach you, when our vibrations are in tune, sort of on the same wavelength. That is a picture of fact, of course. We are ever there; it is you who break the connection. However, this does not imply that there shall be continuous conversation, as relationships are often knit closer together by sharing experiences without words. An easy, rhythmic, relaxed, open, assured, confident condition maintains the proper attitude of a tuned-in position within you.

You approached another matter in your question that permits me to enlarge on the thought of continual expansion, that is, preparedness to receive more and more. Think of this as an attraction to spiritual seeds that will be sown in your heart field. Cold, frozen soil is not conducive to the sprouting of seeds; so, too, an indifferent, cold-shoulder response will not awaken the possibilities of growing. An overheated (with anger, for instance) condition is not desirable either.

It is the broken soil, devoid of poisons you call engrams, nurtured with heavenly manna, and watered from heavenly flow—it is that soil, so to speak, which brings forth sturdy growth. So, it is necessary for you to break up and expose your soil so that nourishment can reach you. This is all a picture of fact, of course.

The Friend managed to convey a picture that openness does not require constant effort, but an attitude of preparedness to receive at any moment.

The preparedness to receive, however, presented a definite challenge the next time Henry and Emma sat down to a session. Earlier that day, they had quarreled a little, and ended up feeling tense and uncomfortable before their contact with the Friend.

"I would like to talk about improving my openness. If I am

not mistaken, one should have no desire other than to experience and accept reality as it exists. It's very hard for me to comprehend. If we are given trouble, even though it is meant to develop consciousness, are we supposed to like it? If not, are we supposed to be indifferent about it? It seems to me there are three choices in the matter: liking it, indifference, or getting upset. I nearly always take the last one, but I don't like it. Usually, I try to change myself or change the situation, until it is pleasant or more acceptable. I am confused. Can you help?"

Can you conceive of the moment-to-moment aspect while dwelling in trouble? In turmoil? In confusion? Witness the poetic quality stirring in your cathedral verse. Was it unsettling? It could have been, if you had been living in the past command. You freed yourself up in that instance. Therein you tasted the moment-to-moment pear pie.

Relinquishing, throwing away, abandoning every hindrance (or engram, as you call it), surrendering each misevaluation and every obstacle, getting rid of all of them permits you to see reality. Be thankful for every incident in life that reveals to you that hindrances are blocking complete comprehension, for then they can be made to release their power over you. The crowning achievement possible for you is to accomplish, with many tools, the eradication of hindering obstacles.

You weary yourself patching up the holes; let's get a new garment of true humility, and live in peace.

Then the Friend delivered a soliloquy perhaps suited for a poster on a wall.

Though thunder crashes without, the moment-to-moment one is tranquil within; though breakers snarl and threaten, the peaceful one is unafraid; though clouds hide the sun, the understanding one knows its rays are there; though mad winds howl and foundations shake, the one living reality is alert, responsive to energies that are needed to accomplish the task without furor or haste, but in serenity and poise adapts self to the situation.

All this information sounded good, but far beyond their reach. The attitudes the Friend described felt unattainable.

Henry had a sudden desire to go away and sit quietly by himself. In the next moment, he had a vision of himself as a child, sitting in a corner, pouting. He instantly recognized the situation as a replay of an old pattern and quickly returned his attention to the immediate situation.

"We certainly could not consider our recent turmoil pleasant," he said, thinking of the argument he and Emma had prior to the session. The difficulty had revolved around the question of how to deal with their children's numerous requests.

Would there have been this recent turmoil if there were no engrams?

Even the word "engrams" felt irritating to Henry. Everything irritated him right now.

"On Earth, one is continually being taught lessons until one dies, isn't that true?"

Henry's question contained unmistakable bitterness, but the Friend responded with a steady and comforting explanation, as if to indicate the insignificance of Henry's temporary emotions.

Henry, why limit it to Earth? The entire progress Wisdom-ward is a continual learning process, although we learn differently than you. We do not live in a static condition of no new comprehension. Advancement for us is also included in Wisdom's dictates.

In your realm, lessons are learned best when openness prevails, or shall I say, less painfully, if openness obtains. It is the 'don'ts' you impose on yourself, rather than the 'dos' that make lessons difficult.

True enough, both of them thought. They frequently used the word "don't" with their children, as well as in their heated conversations.

In the moment-to-moment aspect of living, activity is not hampered by prohibitions. Your past misevaluations are continually bearing down on you, trifling incidents enlarge into massive events and block out opportunities for truth to reach you. Engrams, as you choose to call them, prevent your reaping from many instances in life the fruits of learning that would bless you. That's why shedding them is a delightful chore.

Still trying to somehow correct the jagged feelings of the recent turmoil, Henry asked for more explanation, but this time, the response surprised him.

Too much has already been said. Each one involved is looking at it from 'my viewpoint,' and understanding has taken a back seat. So much dust has been thrown into the atmosphere that the true situation can no longer be seen. Why waste any more time and emotion on it? Ruffled feelings don't penetrate into engrams, they only help to hide them farther from view.

Emma nodded emphatically. Henry still felt sad, but not as hopeless as he had earlier. Emma's forgiving smile and something about the Friend's explanation comforted him.

"I've heard that a wise man won't engage in an argument because, if someone defends their point of view, they only succeed in entrenching the opponent's viewpoint more thoroughly. In other words, you unconsciously create a stimulus that calls forth an opposing response."

Yes, Henry, yes. Now is it apparent why propagandizing is so ineffectual? Note the extraordinary exception when there is an openness on the part of the one with whom you are conversing. Imagine, fancy the progress that would be made if two sat together, both open, both unbiased, both searching, both willing to listen, to learn! No wasted time there! And neither one would be propagandizing, only learning. When the visit was over, they would each go their separate ways, much wiser, but note that their conclusions might not be identical. The asset of openness is amply recorded in a life of ease, of energetic poise, of dynamic calm, of crystallized flowing, of loud silence that comes in a walk of moment-to-moment openness, and the possessor of such life is most greatly benefited.

"A splendid comment, an excellent piece of wisdom!" exclaimed Henry. "Certainly an asset to remember. At times I wonder if I knew all this in a past life and must learn it again each time I come to this realm. I'll try to keep my mind as open as I can in this life!"

Life can be so simple, Henry, when uncluttered with lots of details. Certainly, openness is an asset, if you proceed to use the tool.

Did you know about openness in a past life? I tried so hard to convince you, but how you argued back! Shall I tell you something? You are a great deal more open in your present than in the past life. As a matter of fact, you heard much of this before, but it is not entirely familiar to you now because you didn't allow it to be experienced then, so it did

not become an asset, a quantity of your consciousness.

The Friend's point implied that, unless deeper layers of self become activated through actual experience, one can spend a lifetime mouthing words of enlightenment—intellectualizing like Gurda did—but remain untouched on the innermost level. If Henry had truly realized an attitude of openness in his past life, an added measure of consciousness would have come into play and he would have retained the wisdom in his present life.

The Friend went on to explain that the *quantity* of consciousness referred to the learning we accumulate in our lifetime and take with us when we leave the physical plane. We examine the *quality* of the acquired consciousness between lives, when deciding—with the help of guides—what type of life experiences we need to gain in our next appearance on Earth. While contemplating this information, Henry and Emma had the impression that great portions of knowledge pertaining to the divine organization of the universe remained veiled and inaccessible to human awareness.

Henry admitted his embarrassment about his bitter words at the beginning of the session. The question he had asked implied trouble deliberately meted out—but by whom? By an angry God deriving pleasure from punishing us? Maybe instead we run into trouble at the fringe of our ability to make wise decisions. It all started to come together in Henry's thoughts: Wouldn't a loving God, who gave us free will, allow us to experience the unfolding chain of events that stem from our decisions, even from the ones we make beyond our capacity to comprehend their consequences? How else could humanity expand its consciousness and increase its store of wisdom if not by making mistakes and deriving from them learning experiences?

The Friend's gentle reminders to Henry and Emma that they came to Earth to relinquish their foibles and uncover the true beauty of their inner divine essence felt very heartening. They felt as if the Friend, speaking to them from behind the veils of earthly existence, guided, encouraged, and most of all, loved them unconditionally.

16

Our Christ

✳

"We are going for big questions tonight," Henry announced. "Could you say a few words as to the correct use of the word 'God' and what it implies?"

I intentionally and deliberately try to sidestep that word, because the term God has, unfortunately, limited and warped the conception of the Creator, the Great One, the Exalted One—the one we term 'Wisdom.'

As soon as the term 'God' is used, a definite idea, a definite entity, a form appears in the thoughts and comprehension of Earth children. It is not the word that is in any sense objectionable, Henry, if that term can be understood to include all truth, all wisdom, all comprehension, all that begins and ends (as far as time is concerned), all that is, transcending beyond and above and over all. To anyone whose understanding includes that much, and more, in the term 'God,' there is no reason why that term should not be used. Even such names as Wisdom, Truth, All-Wise One—all are just words. Understanding must grasp the vast scope of the intent, regardless of what terms are employed in an attempt to partially clothe that which is greater than any definition, than all words, than all possible concepts. Does that help?

"Yes, it does. I can see how we limit the meaning of a term by our preconceptions. Could you tell us what Christ meant when He said, 'Take up your cross and follow me'?"

The 'follow me' is interpreted also as a picture of fact, a decision of allegiance, not a literal laying down of tools to pursue what appears as the vision of the Christ leading.

Our Christ saw deeply within the hearts and beings of those with whom He conversed. He knew where their greatest problems lay. He understood the extent of self-sacrifice that would be entailed for each individual, and He knew how far their consciousness had developed into the spirit of Wisdom.

Do not fret, Henry, that, to some, alignment on the side of Christ frequently does entail a degree of sacrifice, although when sacrifice is made, it actually does not appear so to the follower. In the exuberance of the new experiences, any relinquishing or parting or any required changes could not be compared with the glorious walk with Christ.

It is as if someone said to you, Henry, 'You give so much of your time to the sessions with the Friend and are missing some terrific fun of sundry pleasures.' Now, this does not make the sundry pleasures undesirable, but, to you, they pale by comparison.

"You are right, our other interests pale by comparison. And it makes sense that the words 'follow me' were symbolic rather than a literal command to join in a procession."

It was His way of saying, 'Come now, make your choice — to stay with your nets, mingle with your townsfolk, entertain local interests, or do what to you right now appears to be the magnificent program, the enlarged life. Press forward into larger landscapes, greater visions, higher heights.'

On the lives of still others, the effect of Christ's invitation may be most far-reaching perhaps in a path of solitude, or quietness, of apparent inactivity, where Christ would surely walk beside them also.

The depth of feelings the Friend implied in this reference to Christ pleased and intrigued Henry. To his sensibilities, the name *Wu Li Tsung* signified a background of Eastern tradition, yet his invisible teacher spoke with high regard about Christ.

"I noticed that you referred to Christ as 'our Christ.' Did we embrace Christian ethics as well in our travels together?"

You and I have missed the time of the appearance of Christ, Henry, because our lives were united in Earth experience before His coming to Earth. We were not acquainted with the Christ, but His revelation was contained in many other, earlier manifestations, some of which the keenly-eyed, the sensitive ones could fathom and understand.

Think of the profound prophecies contained in your Old Testament. Although His feet touched not the hills of Galilee until His physical appearance on Earth, His influence, His energy, His spiritual being preceded and reached many. In that sense, to a slight degree, He already—and I say it reverently—belonged to us. But now you have the witness of His appearance contained in your Holy Bible, and have sketches of what He said, how He worked, and the extent of His influence. I say sketches, for your records are, of course, far from complete.

"Our records say that He has 'risen.' Can you say something about that?"

The visitation in the visible form by Christ was yet another of His manifestations, a wonderful, beautiful one. Does He exist now? Of course, He continues His influence, but through a different type of manifestation.

In our realm, we know not all of Christ, for He belongs to Wisdom. But His greatness, His majesty, and His power are sensed by us in greater measure than by you. He is our Christ, and He is your Christ, so that makes Him our (yours and our) Christ.

His visit to Earth brought a touch of Heaven; His existence prepared the Earth children for an entrance into the deeper, more profound understanding of Wisdom. The Earth sphere is privileged in receiving the attention of one so intimate with Wisdom.

Henry remained silent for a few moments, touched by the Friend's degree of reverence for Christ.

"Somehow, I was under the impression that our experience together was later than Christ's visit to Earth. I'd like to find out why I had this impression."

The hills of the Himalayas existed before the advent of Christ, of course. However, they were not then known by that name. I just peeked at your present map of China and read your mountain names. As to time, Henry, yes we sojourned early in this phase of existence. As a matter of fact, we taught an earlier type of revelation. You found out about Christ in a later life form, and we didn't meet each other then.

Note, too, that impressions sometimes appear as facts. We can't trust our feelings too far! Again, I caution you to keep the large concepts, the basic truths in correct focus, and the details will fall nicely in place.

"I guess I've gotten the chronology of my lives on Earth a bit confused. If you think it's unimportant, we can proceed to other matters."

It is certainly not unimportant, if it concerns you, Henry. There is no reason to dwell in doubt. There is no virtue in confusion.

This emphatic response came with speed and force through the typewriter. The Friend took the opportunity to stress the importance of clarity and understanding, with the following qualification.

I would like to make the point that it is not always feasible to provide all the details in the exact order, but if information is withheld for a season, it is for a definite, specific reason. When you fully understand the reason, you will see the necessity of having done so.

As to your past lives—in your dream you saw the early man sowing seeds because he had a great love of tools. This life was followed at a later time, not necessarily with no other appearances on Earth, by the 'wicked-eyed Peter,' and in the next manifestation, you and I became acquainted.

Later, you appeared as a sheep-herder, far from pursuits that required tools, but even then you found your staff and relished that instrument. Your nearness to nature, your fondness for animals, and your solitary tendency in the present stem from that immediate past life. Now, is that clearer?

"Yes, that does make it clearer. I would not have connected Peter's clothes and his musical instrument with the pre-Christian era, but perhaps there was a more advanced mechanical ability to build an instrument like the one I played at that time than I had thought possible. Perhaps the vision was intended to play up the wickedness of Peter, rather than the fashions of the period. Incidentally, the visual manifestations of you and of Peter were excellent! Is that one of the attributes that consciousness attains as it advances?"

Visions, such as you witnessed, are given because of a need. They are not necessarily the property of only a far-advanced one. Visions are not a measurement of a soul's progress. That is not a temperature taker!

The clarity of the vision given to you was intended to set it apart from your regular pursuits when asleep. The details were correct. It is well to add another 'allowing' to your list, that of visions.

Henry and Emma had by now made many allowances for their unusual experiences, with so many more possibilities opening up for them than they had ever imagined. Their evolving belief structure seemed to provide a framework for the accumulation of ever finer comprehension. They also felt a deepening appreciation of the Friend's teachings.

Even their view of history changed as they continued learning. The development of string instruments, for example, as portrayed in the large picture book they had recently bought, emphasized the evolution of modern forms, while neglecting ancient creations in the overall comparison. Perusing the book, they had the impression that mankind had little musical ability before the time of Christ. The Friend pointed to a possible reason for the inaccurate recognition of mankind's achievements by providing a new perspective on the bias with which humans evaluate their accomplishments.

It is the tendency of Earth people to attribute to themselves, at the time of their lives on Earth, the greatest culture, the greatest advancement, the sweetest morsels, the classiest existence.

"We think we are smart because our knowledge has increased, but we can't memorize and recite lengthy epics the way people did before printing was invented."

Progress has gone on for long past, and many people, as vessels for the housing of consciousness, contributed to

*humanity's knowledge. But recall the necessity of conscious-
ness to add quantity, to expand.*

"Are you saying the expanding consciousness is something
apart from increasing knowledge?"

*People in jungle lands, for example, may know nothing
of weather charts, but can read the language of the skies;
they may know nothing of the finer points of vitamin study,
but gain for themselves a fairly balanced menu; they hear
not the blast of radio from captured wave bands, but are
attuned to hear profound remarks without the use of an
external device. This does not imply they are more advanced,
but that they are advanced differently.*

Henry liked the idea of different ways of advancement. It
reaffirmed his thought that modern civilization's accumulation of formal knowledge and invention of labor saving devices
don't necessarily reflect the qualities that lead humans closer
to God.

"Thank you for fortifying my understanding."

You are welcome, and good night.

One evening, Henry decided to clear away his misgivings
about Christian faith. He felt conflict about what he had
observed in his occasional church attendance.

"If all that you tell us adds up to something greater than
we can conceive, then I suppose the Christian concept of faith
got it right. But to me, the faith of the so-called faithful often
seems shrouded in hypocrisy. I wonder how many times I've
seen the real McCoy."

Faith is another one of those worthy words trampled about so badly it becomes grimy with misuse. Faith, Henry, is a result, not a cause. The tendency of Earth people is to make faith a means to an end, when it is the result of experienced experiences. Until the meaning is swept clear of its unhealthy hue, it might be just as well to presume to not know — or, in other words, be open.

With one short paragraph, the Friend clarified Henry's confusion about faith. One puts the cart before the horse when one doesn't have the strength of inner conviction. Henry could understand that not everyone has yet acquired enough experience to develop strong belief in God. But he could also see that if one's faith rested on the proclamation of authorities, or a fear of burning in hell, no wonder so many people had a problem in this area.

Emma agreed with Henry that the tactics of instilling fear may have positively influenced some people's behavior in the past, but she mentioned the Holy Inquisition as a prime example of gruesome misuse of religious precepts. Both felt that the present state of human development seemed to ask for something more than an inherited repetition of rituals and proclamations of dogma whose original meaning had become obscure with time and misinterpretation.

The couple readily absorbed the spiritual nourishment provided by the Friend, ever hungry for more. They wondered what else they could do to solidify the emerging foundation of their knowing — rather than blind — faith.

"What type of information would be best for us to pursue to work toward the development of higher consciousness?" Henry asked.

That which is timed to interest. It indicates the need and is reflected in your questions, Henry.

"Like the saying 'When the student is ready, the teacher will appear'?"

It is so easy to overlook some matters that introduce themselves to you, for reasons that openness is not yet permitted to function at a high enough level.

Henry and Emma thought themselves sufficiently open while receiving such a wonderful education, but the last comment left Henry wondering how he could increase his openness and stretch his mind to receive even more wisdom. The reply to his silent call came in a very unexpected way.

17

Growing Pains

✦

"Good evening, Friend. I had an odd headache today, and I noticed an interesting thing about it. I felt the pain, but as soon as I fixed my mind on it, it would vanish. Some pains felt more severe, and did not leave immediately, but lasted for a minute or so. They came in different parts of the head. I have never had pains like this before. Perhaps you have a comment."

Tonight you relax in the knowledge that the temporary pains reveal workings of Wisdom directly on cell tissue. Expansion of thought material requires growing room. Great things are happening, Henry, and all beneficial.

So, Henry had experienced a novel form of growing pains! His apparent brain surgery from the other side would serve the purpose of accommodating more of the spiritual advancement he wanted so much.

"Now I've heard it all!" exclaimed Henry, feeling invigorated and encouraged.

But his headaches continued for several days. They reminded him of the biblical story of the sudden conversion of Apostle Paul. Talking it over with Emma, he admitted he could not understand why Paul had so many struggles with himself after that moment of immediate enlightenment.

"I am curious about Paul's battles with himself after his transformation. Did he have difficulties adjusting to his new life? Is that what's in store for me? Is there any similarity between what happened to Paul and what's happening to me?"

Do not hesitate to clear up these points that prevent a clear understanding, Henry. Apostle Paul, for apparent reasons, needed an experience that would completely reverse his direction, as it were. His misplaced zeal was transformed into respect for the objects of his persecution, a complete reversal of his previous attitudes and policies.

To him had to be handed a startling enough experience to stop him in his tracks and, by the very brightness of experience, dispel any doubt of the supremacy of Christ, Whose followers were feeling the lash of zealous energy at Paul's hands. But Paul's consciousness was not at that moment of enlightenment fully and completely integrated, as you would say. Other experiences, other events, other lessons—yes, and karma, too—needed to be included, before that far-advanced one could graduate to an even higher class.

Among those experiences was the sobering clash he felt within himself, but recall that it was of a far advanced nature.

Furthermore, it should ever be remembered that consciousness is continually being quantitied, added to, expanded, so long as you traverse the Earth sphere. These stopping places, these arrival goals, these landmarks of integration often cause confusion, for the tendency to discontinue advancement can lead to lethargy and indifference. It is well to say 'I've arrived,' and in the same breath add, 'but I am on my way again,' so as not to miss even one golden opportunity for comprehension.

Even a great transformation, then, such as the one bestowed on Paul, does not include a final point of arrival, but requires in its wake additional learning and expansion of consciousness. Henry now knew that his mysterious head pains prepared the way for a long series of personal transformations.

"I understand that Paul suffered losing his sight as a result of what happened to him. I wonder—if my transformation came suddenly, could it conceivably strike me blind too?"

Yes, and it would so intensely frighten you that further work would be rendered more difficult, as there would be the additional factor of fear to combat. Also, Saul, before his transformation into Paul, was steeped in zealotry. He believed in all honesty within himself that he had been helping mankind by persecuting these new-doctrined Christ followers. In his case, had the transformation not come in the manner it had, he would have invented excuses to himself for dismissing, ignoring, or combating every new thought and every argument.

You, Henry, have set your feet in the right direction. But there are briars and barbed-wire fences that make going difficult. It is these obstacles, these handicaps that we strive to eliminate from your pathway. Note, too, that Paul still felt the jabs from these types of briars even after his one masterful transformation. But again, his sensitive, far-advanced attitude sensed much that would escape others.

Your fears vanish as the gentleness of progress informs you that it is forward-going, and life is better, more livable.

True, Henry and Emma related to each other and their daughters in a more loving manner, and frequently commented on the privilege of having contact with the higher realm. Their lives continued to feel more peaceful and harmonious as their loving attitudes took greater hold.

"I wonder if we could now discuss the subject of love," Henry ventured.

Much has appeared in print about this massive subject, Henry, but Christ summed it up in His three word (as translated) summary: God is love. In the measure that consciousness contains the development which permits an emanation of that most beautiful of all attributes, to that extent is love freely poured forth from and by any human in his term of wandering on your planet Earth.

I hesitate to dwell on any one aspect of the subject, so as not to shadow other aspects, for it is all so intensely alive. Capturing its significance, even in small measure, portrays the essence of the Wisdom's piece of Wisdom within.

Concern yourself for the time being with the largeness, the extent of the subject, as we will return to it frequently.

Your toils of the day are ended. Your energies will best be restored by peaceful sleep, so good night.

"Good night, Friend, and many thanks."

The expression "God is love" contrasted vividly with the couple's youthful impressions. Their parents had unabashedly used their authority to instill in them an image of an all-knowing Father poised to lash out at His children's misconduct. Recalling events from their childhoods, Henry and Emma shared stories that reflected their fears of punishment by God for even the most trivial transgressions. Their reminiscences left Henry laughing despite the pain in his head.

Now that he knew the purpose of his pain, he could more easily cope with it, feeling grateful for the gift of a granted wish.

18

Karma in Action

✳

Henry had another vivid dream. This time, he saw a moving column of motorized vehicles in a setting of war. The apparent leader had an unearthly quality about him. Although bitterly aware of the futility of war, he nevertheless showed intense alertness and fierce determination in the execution of his duty. Yet kindness also radiated from him, a quality uncommon in military personnel, in Henry's opinion. Henry presented his dream to the Friend, who offered a surprising interpretation.

Regard this visitation as a timely urge for you to forsake the bitterness entailed because of your experience in this slice of life.

An invisible finger pointed at Henry's negative feelings about his war experience.

Truly, that experience offered much more enlightenment than you could permit at the time, because of blindness caused by your bitterness. In other words, the necessary teachings available to you at that time could find no entry, because they were blocked off at the door marked 'bitterness.' Remember and sense the relief that came when a helper from our side, Luigi, was permitted to show you a thing or two.

Sometime after Henry had begun speaking with the Invisible Friend in his shop, an entity by the name of Luigi presented himself unexpectedly. He identified himself as the master craftsman who had assisted Henry from the other side in crafting exceptional smoking pipes during the war. No longer surprised by such visits, Henry had expressed his gratitude to Luigi for all of his assistance. Luigi's timely intervention had helped preserve Henry's sanity in a desperate situation, and the Friend now acknowledged Luigi's valuable help.

At the mention of Luigi, Henry had a sudden awareness that not all of the exposure he had during the war had negative aspects. The good came with the bad, and some events now seemed quite extraordinary when Henry considered the circumstances under which they took place.

The paths we walk while traveling through a period of time are devious and often strange, but all are necessary for the development of our experiences into the ripeness of a finished state. The war experience was a class in the schoolhouse called life. The lessons were 'toughies.'

That the Friend knew of Henry's struggles no longer surprised him, but the Friend's knowledge of every detail of them impressed him greatly. Henry marveled at the degree of empathy coming from the Friend's words, as the Friend continued to reveal unsuspected deeper meaning of Henry's dream.

In the dream, your guide appeared as a spiritual being to show that often even natural leaders contain, beneath an assumed stern exterior, a devotion to a cause that transcends your understanding. But that is one aspect of your vision. Another aspect concerns and directly implies to you that our influence must and does reach into remote corners where danger lurks. Intense effort is exerted to provide a measure of leadership, even though unasked. In dire instances, even actual control is attempted, but all this operates according to Wisdom's dictates.

The comments left Henry speechless at the mention of the caring attention accorded human activities by spirit beings. The Friend once again revealed protective activity on the part of invisible forces that went quite unnoticed by those reaping the benefits of this gift.

There is still another aspect of this vision—your part in a past scene. I am leaving this subject open for definite reasons. It will be mentioned later, if we continue our relationship of openness.

Staggered by the latest messages, Henry squirmed in his chair, feeling reluctant yet eager to get a closer look at his experiences. He had strenuously avoided recalling wartime incidents, but the dream seemed to have reactivated his memory beyond his ability to squelch it. Recollections of various war scenes intruded on his mind, sometimes as clear images, sometimes as avalanches of disjointed impressions.

Henry's four years in the army coincided with World War II. His tour of duty had taken him to Italy. He arrived there with the First Armored Division after the American forces had landed at Anzio, a beach infamous for its fierce battle engagements. The German troops had tried to recapture the beachhead and staged hellish attacks. Henry had suffered sudden enemy fire, bombs and flying debris, and a tremendous amount of fear. These unnerving exposures to peril and to people killing each other had gone beyond the bounds of his rationality. Throughout the extended combat, Henry's mind teemed with morbid thoughts, but he resolved to outlast the inescapable, outraged at his powerlessness to stop the mayhem.

After the battles subsided, a series of coincidences diverted his attention, thus lightening his military misery. The explosions that had pelted the beachfront uprooted a stand of briar trees that previously graced the landscape. A silver lining to Henry's dark cloud appeared when he had recognized the hardwood roots as an ideal material for making pipes. In addition to his providential discovery, he had also found fragments of thick plastic from shattered enemy searchlight lenses for making mouthpiece stems. An avid smoker at the time, Henry found these materials quite suitable for his artistic expression.

With his discovery of materials for carving, Henry's army life changed. Whenever he could, he focused his attention on locating tools and preparing a work area where he sectioned, boiled, drilled, and whittled until his persistent effort resulted in a variety of beautiful pipes. He sold these pipes as quickly as he could make them. Even Field Marshal Alexander, commander of the Italian front, became a proud owner of one. He presented Henry with a commendation and a large framed photograph of himself smoking one of Henry's pipes.

The income from the sale of pipes, combined with the savings Emma had managed to put aside from her employment in a state office as part of the so-called war effort, made it possible for them to buy their first home right after the war. It suited their needs ideally at the time. The house had a basement where Henry set up his shop. Yet the bitter aftertaste of war remained with both of them. Emma had felt deprived of her husband and a normal family life. While she worked, Henry's mother cared for their twin daughters born in Henry's absence. Grateful for Henry's safe return from the war, they nevertheless felt a lingering sense of injustice due to the hardship and separation they endured.

Pressured by his recurring memories, Henry yielded to the

need to talk about the bitterness he carried inside.

"You mentioned my sentiments regarding the military and the government in general. Would you care to say something that might help me let go of these less that divine thoughts?"

Can you escape from it without subjecting yourself to less desirable circumstances? It would appear that you are basking in the blessing of a fruitful tonality in this respect. So, starting from that premise, can we proceed to see what might possibly be the basis of your feeling of bitterness, that less than ultra feeling?

First of all, Henry, you are reaping a bit of karma that stamped into your consciousness during the wicked-eyed Peter existence. You ruled over many, and most militarily. Not that you held a highly superior position, but in your realm, you felt yourself the master. Alone you stood on the pinnacle, tasted the wine of authority, and delighted in applying the whip.

Do you see now how karma demands that you taste the feel of the lash yourself? And Uncle Samuel waved it over you in your service period. Now, in that period, when your resistance lessened, you found a degree of relief in the briarwood incident.

It is somewhat like this, Henry: karma is one of the unimpeachable laws set up by Wisdom, and your understanding of it will afford an opportunity to accept and yield, rather than resist and remain unbelieving. Accepting what comes, in perfect understanding, turns the bitterness in your mouth into sweetness.

Emma took time out to put a new sheet of paper into the typewriter and wondered about accepting in good faith everything that happens. The Friend explained.

The moment-to-moment aspect is ever peaceful and pro-
ceeds in understanding. Just knowing that it couldn't be
otherwise, because of Wisdom's justice, will enable you to
accept many otherwise troublesome happenings. You can
squirm and twist, rebel and gripe, but karma goes on.
Exchanging a bitter attitude for one of immediate good
thought influence will, in one sense, reverse the procedure,
and oh, what a lift! Does that appear understandable,
Henry?

"I think so. It's been hard for me to accept that such things
as wars are workings of Wisdom. Why wars? Can't Wisdom
find another way to teach instead of having people kill each
other? Incidentally, judging from the look in Peter's eyes, I
should have made a first-rate military man!"

Now, let us back up a bit, Henry. First, do not consider
that war comes from Wisdom. Second, it did not have to
be Uncle Sam in that aspect of warring to teach you, or
rather, I should say, for you to fulfill karma—oh, no. There
are other ways in which you would have felt the lash just
as definitely.

Your picture must include a larger concept. There is an
individual karma, a national karma, yes, even world-wide
karma. And when certain forces are set in motion, Henry,
the results ensue, as surely as a bean seed sprouts beans.
And, because your karma called for, in this instance, a thumb
of authority over you, and since these other forces were in
motion (but don't attribute them to Wisdom) and the nation
was plunged into war, therein was the thumb applied on
you. But remember, Henry, it didn't have to be war to com-
plete that particular aspect of karma, as thumbs have been
applied in other manners, too. In one sense of the word, it
is as if you attracted to yourself that thumb of authority.

Henry sensed something fundamentally sound and logical about this karma business, even if he did not understand the whole picture. It made sense to him that his actions and attitudes came back to him to let him know what they felt like on the receiving end. He could see how hurtful acts, reflected back to the individual through the law of karma, would lead to a better understanding of the feelings of another, and maybe even contribute to an attitude of compassion.

The Friend disclaiming Wisdom's responsibility for war felt especially comforting to Henry and Emma. They tossed around the question of how war originated, and concluded that humans blamed God for the wars that they themselves collectively created. Instead of using their free will to avoid war, in their ignorance, humans even invoked higher powers to help them achieve their selfish and hurtful goals. Henry and Emma could see that Wisdom certainly did not approve of killing, or of one group of humans dominating another. The Friend placed into perspective Wisdom's ever-present love for humanity, and indicated a careful apportioning of karma for individual learning.

Henry had no doubt that the Friend provided solid explanations for what he had to submit to in the army, but his privation during the war still perturbed him, and workings of karma still puzzled him.

The Friend sensed Henry's distress and offered him a less complicated example of karma in action.

Let us momentarily consider a much less tangled incident: that packer.

Oh, yes. Henry's thoughts went to the events of the morning. His attempts to have a customer's order professionally packed for shipment had resulted in repeated delays.

For reasons many—and don't feel that the reasons were not justified—you have told others, 'I'm just too busy to do your work,' and you were told 'Too busy' by the man whose help you needed. But it worked out. You remained calm, you did not barge into some complicated set-up, but followed a very normal procedure, and the results are showing that it is working out quite satisfactorily. That is karma. You meet again yourself, your attitudes, your emotions, your reactions reflecting back to you. But fancy your relief when you understand what is happening! And you do not need to continue in confusion!

The analysis of this minor version of a karmic incident helped Henry to better understand the immutable law. The words, "As you sow, so shall you reap," took on for him a less primitive meaning.

Accepting all, yes all—each and every occurrence—as handed down from the kindly hand of Wisdom, changes the picture considerably. And doesn't that sound suspiciously like the moment-to-moment existence? Accepting all is so simple, but yet so profound; so easy, and yet so difficult; so smooth, yet so bumpy; so clear, and yet so muddled—oh, peace, how welcome your protection!

The Friend conveyed the sense of peace that comes from fully trusting what Wisdom has in store. Henry wished he could learn to accept everything with a peaceful attitude, including karma.

✦

Far from exhausted, the subject of karma raised additional questions as they continued the theme the following evening.

"Your comments yesterday were excellent and much appreciated, Friend. I wonder, though, doesn't a person with many negative imprints from childhood, plus the effects of karma, stand in a disadvantaged position, possibly enough to push them to insanity? Or is there a finer filtering of justice or compensation for the traumas that shape our actions?"

It sounds complicated, the way you put it, Henry, but it works out a bit easier. The clue in this case is the influence from our realm. Without the momentary assistance, protection, guidance, and enlightenment provided by our realm, certainly, the world would be a madhouse in nothing flat!

Emma and Henry reacted to the comment with raised eyebrows, reflexively ready to question this sweeping statement, but it took only moments for them to understand that, left to its own devices, humanity would indeed have created a total pandemonium on Earth. Even with protection and guidance from the higher dimensions, humanity often manages to find ways to invent frustration, disregard basic decency, and take actions opposite to those that lead to peace and harmony.

It is our sincere effort to lead mankind into paths of learning and comprehension, but ever and always is reserved to a human being that instrument of choice. You may choose to deny the entrance of truth, turn your back on comprehension, and start that downward spiral. But, the Wisdom's piece of Wisdom within that is temporarily housed in human bodies ever and always seeks to expand, to quantity, to develop.

In the stillness of the night, perhaps, or in the face of immediate danger, or in the presence of a beautiful sunset, or even in the midst of confusion, an individual becomes aware of that something bigger, that something greater, that something better, that something mightier, and responds. And heaven rejoices, for comprehension can commence.

Henry and Emma could not help but thoroughly admire the Friend's consistently optimistic view of humanity, despite the many negative events on Earth.

We long to assist, but we do not force the entrance. An invitation is readily accepted, however, and an anxious, seeking one is never rudely shoved aside. There is much to this subject also. You are bordering on many subjects now, with much content, and isn't it delightful?

Henry agreed, but tried to stay on the subject at hand.

"Is karma a product of Earth experiences exclusively? From what we have read, I got the impression that consciousness manifests itself in us on Earth, but then gathers excess baggage, and has a tremendous difficulty getting away again. In the East they refer to it as the 'wheel of karma,' if I am not mistaken."

Interesting, Henry, how you see this. However, look upon it slightly more like this: Wisdom's piece of Wisdom, consciousness—in the great sweeping picture—is intent on returning to Wisdom, as it were. Like a magnet, in one sense, there is ever the drawing toward final consummation into Wisdom. But alas, something is missing—the picture is not complete, the frame is missing, maybe, or the blankness of a part of canvas calls attention to itself by the very reason of its blankness. To fill in the vacancies, to quantity, to expand consciousness, is imperative.

One of the aspects of Wisdom's sweeping plan is to unite with a human form for the purpose of adding quantity. Recall what we once said: Some learn more, some learn less, but all learn something. An addition is made, but perhaps not sufficient, so once again, an effort it made to complete the necessary experiences. There are hindrances, yes, many of them, but in spite of such obstructions, a measure of leaning develops in an individual. It is all beautifully mapped and arranged, Henry, and the privilege of choice can be utilized to a massive benefit in a lifetime, if openness prevails.

Now, you have read enough this evening, so, until later, so long.

The information they received sounded considerate and logical. The sessions about karma gave Henry and Emma a number of ideas to contemplate. For example, the statement that *it is all beautifully mapped and arranged* seemed to dovetail neatly with the theory of karma playing itself out in the lives of individuals. But the Friend also emphasized freedom of choice. The two ideas seemed contradictory.

"If everything is pre-planned, then where does our choice come in?" Henry wondered.

This is a big subject, and one that demands much clearness of thinking, alertness, attention, and comprehension in a high degree.

First of all, consider the choice as consisting of, shall we say, the manner in which you will choose to quantity, to increase consciousness. For example, look at your war experience. Had you chosen to thwart and waylay the plan and purpose of the magnetic attraction principle which has worked to attract you to the event, should you have chosen to refuse to comply, to refrain from going (by pulling strings, by using influence or 'angles'), it is possible that you might have avoided that one experience, but not the lessons that the experience taught you. In some other variety of manner, you would have attracted a mass of superiors (in their function over you), even if it had been in your own family situation. With Wisdom, there are no accidents. The particular lessons that could be learned only by being subjected to superiors you surely would learn in some fashion.

Take our conversations that you so much enjoy. You choose to hearken, to respond, to cooperate, to listen, and you are learning lessons thereby. There are other manners in which these lessons could likewise be learned. You could get them by another channel, by reading, discussing, etc., for your choice remains ever in your grasp. Actually, we tell you only what Wisdom dictates, and no more.

This is a partial picture. Do not attempt to make it fit every condition, for it is a varied subject, and we may refer to it from another angle at some later time.

As he occupied himself with the material, Henry's mind opened onto a simple but profound truth. The Ten Commandments provide clear ethical guidance, but people choose to ignore them. People break God's laws and then blame God for the consequences.

Just then, Henry wished he could have his Friend, Bernie, hear and understand the principles involved. But Bernie, not ready to hear about such things as karma, would most likely "let go of the guiding hand," as the Friend put it, should Henry mention the source of his information. As disgusted with the war as Henry, Bernie simply concluded that God did not exist. "If there was a God, why would He permit wars and killing?" he usually said, not as a question, but as an unalterable declaration of logic meant to support his idea of God's nonexistence. Any attempt to discuss the subject met doom from the beginning.

Henry learned to recognize this type of attitude—the barriers, conclusions, and locked-down decisions—as difficult, if not impossible, to soften or dislodge. Bernie made his decisions only once. After that, no amount of discussion could impact his philosophy or introduce newness into the framework of his thoughts. Bernie's belief system consisted of a disjointed scaffold of ideas, glued together with superficial observations and convenient rationalizations to create an impression of a cohesive structure.

A year before he died, Bernie began to notice "strange coincidences" in his life, which opened the door for Henry to gently suggest the existence of a higher intelligence. In small increments, he had also seen the logic in Henry's explanation that people make wars, not God, and that God allows humanity to make mistakes for the sake of learning.

It pleased Henry immensely when it made sense to Bernie that death ends only one aspect of our existence and begins another; and that we come to Earth many times, leaving each time a bit wiser. By the time Bernie had found himself in the hospital's intensive care unit with a fatal heart condition, he felt comforted by the knowledge that his spirit, or soul, would survive his physical extinction.

A few days after his passing, Henry received a direct message in Bernie's usual shorthand style: "This is Bernie. All is well. It is the way you described it. You will like it here. I do."

19

Turmoil in the Shop

✳

Motivated by his success, Henry had hired an assistant in anticipation of the future growth of his business. Wayne, an older man whom Henry had known as a friend of the family, worked well for a while, but as his health declined, he began to miss scheduled workdays, and the quality of his work also deteriorated. As Henry's frustration mounted with each of Wayne's mishaps, he would find himself taking a break outside to cool his temper, which irritated him even more because of his loss of productivity.

"I must be badly out of tune with wisdom in my shop. I don't know how to manage the situation with my employee. I get upset with him, and when my emotions flare up, I begin to fall apart. This afternoon, I couldn't even put together a simple letter to a customer. In situations like this, is it better to just push ahead or wait and ask for enlightenment from you?"

It is perfectly possible that, in this case, I can help you out. However, with due respect to the precious possession of openness, next time, it might be different.

Your concern about shop matters entails some faulty lessons that you glued to through the years. Some of them are showing their ugly heads now and demanding that you pay attention to them.

You may recall the time when an evidence of success was measured by the length of fish. Your trout fishing incident was a formative one. It troubles you more than you are aware. Much distrust was instigated by your mom's fondness to make it look like 'Henry is a man.' But you knew differently, and a sense of shame overtook you, erasing any possible pleasure. You now translate this incident to the workings in the shop and can't understand your frustration. Comparing your fish, which now happens to mean the extent of the shop output, is destroying your sense of accomplishment, and frustration overcomes you.

The mention of one of Henry's experiences so long ago surprised him. The Friend stirred Henry's memory of an outing with relatives whom his mother tried to impress, as usual, with her son's accomplishments. He remembered with dread his youthful impressions of fishing—impaling the poor worm on the hook, the writhing and gasping of the caught fish, and his frightful embarrassment.

His mother held his hands on the fishing pole when a big fish succumbed to the lure. She burst out with excitement, announcing Henry's catch, while he squirmed under the gaze of his relatives. He could not understand why outsmarting an unsuspecting fish should bring such a feeling of triumph to the adults. If anything, it pointed out the deviousness of adults and the need to beware of their tricks.

The idea that this past incident impacted his present feelings about performance at the shop sounded rather remote, but he tried to remain open to it. The Friend had warned him that experiences in childhood create deep impressions. Analyzing the fish incident made him wonder how many other early impressions that he could not recall had also shaped his psyche. His apparently insignificant memory of a family outing illustrated to him a pattern of unrecognized workings of the subconscious mind.

"No wonder why confusion takes over so easily, especially when I'm under stress."

A basic hint to you: when you are in the midst of what you term turmoil, your whole world looks different to you, and your feeling translates to all areas of endeavor, it seems. So, writing a letter sounds hard to do. During these difficult times, try to excel in mastery of self, in the tangible force of ideals, and if you find response in others, lead them to the process that will enable them to expand and find accomplishment. Do I make myself clear? Do ask for more details if any perplexity remains.

Henry began to see that he had assumed the role of a mother hen with Wayne. Had he subconsciously imitated his mother's attitude? Did he want to hold his hands on Wayne's to assure a quality product? He saw himself hovering over his helper—like his mother had over him—watching his every move for fear he would mess things up again, trying to catch his mistakes before they happened. He shuddered at the image.

"Do you mean I take too much responsibility and should release responsibility to Wayne?"

Certainly, in some areas. If repeats of work become necessary, remember that cold steel does not weigh as much as your good feelings. And the lesson thus learned by Wayne will remain with him, and you will not have to sacrifice yourself on the altar of expanding the consciousness of others. This does not even remotely imply that the output of your shop should be sloppy. Maintain fine output, but with not so much of yourself in it, Henry. Classify this as another fine example of reaching for the moment-to-moment feeling. Pretty elusive, isn't it?

"I suppose letting go of some of my concerns would make me feel a lot better. But I have to keep tabs on the way things go. Trying to balance all this takes so much finesse, but it all goes out the window when I come unglued."

Understanding, comprehending, completely knowing all aspects of a problem would rule out resentment, that is, of the type we are discussing, and which flares forth in your existence.

"Judging from your statements, there would be no resentment without a misevaluation. That implies that I am living in delusion most of the time! But isn't there any valid reason to get angry?"

Righteous indignation, such as evidenced by Christ in the incident with the moneychangers in the temple, is of a different nature. His 'anger'—although I use that word very guardedly—His emotion was not against the 'do-er,' but the deed itself. Translating the principle into the terms of your shop, it would mean that you are angry at the resulting inferior product, but not the man; your understanding would cover the area of the do-er of that work, the maker of the product. In other words, differentiate between the person's essence and the person's action. It is a fabulously valuable lesson, if you are able to grasp it now, Henry. Your anxiety to know and understand indicates to me that you can grasp its very fine shade of meaning.

"Christ had a good reason for showing emotion toward the deed, but deeds don't do themselves. I've got to do something about Wayne's work."

Yes, Henry, your job downstairs, done wrong, that won't do. Correction includes doing something to the do-er, and this is where your choice comes in. You can fire him on the spot; you can understandingly instruct; you can walk away; you can produce it yourself. You are free to choose.

In the instance of Christ, He in His wisdom knew that only one avenue of action would effect a desired result—casting out of the do-ers from His Father's temple. Not every incident did He handle thus. For example, the storm on the sea while He was asleep brought forth a remark, 'Oh ye of little faith.' He rebuked the storm, but didn't send the disciples swimming.

So, Henry, you face your problems. Mostly you understand, make your choice, and proceed. But, once in a while, some past misevaluation blocks out understanding, brings confusion, won't let you choose, but insists that you choose, and off you go in a whirlwind. That's why we probe deep to find those offenders who want to run the show. Ask more if you wish.

The Friend's statement encapsulated the concept of personal integrity, and what happens when parts of self don't work in harmony with each other. To Henry it meant that he needed to set his own house in order before he could properly address the predicament of another. The principle of respecting other people enough to approach them with dignity while dealing with an irritating problem sounded good, but not so easy to do. However, the matter of distinguishing between the deed and the doer began to come into focus for Henry.

"I think I got the fine shade of meaning you mentioned. One of the problems in Wayne's case is that he is slipping, but the big point is that getting angry at *him* won't solve the problem. I am angry at the situation, not at Wayne. Had I fully seen this, I am quite sure I would have had less turmoil about it than I had today."

Now we are going places, Henry. That is ultra thinking. You understand the problem. Would you care to go one step further and ask yourself, 'Now why did I feel that resentment? Where is that engram that dares to dictate those sensations to me? What impels that type of reaction in me that I recognize as less than ultra?' That is for you to answer, Henry, if you choose.

Henry reflected for a moment.

"I thought of one possibility. When I was small, old folks gave me a bad time. They set themselves up as examples of perfection, which had the effect of challenging me to find proof that they weren't. Does this sound right?"

Mmmmm, yes, that's one aspect of it. Keep going.

"Here is another—the perfection standard gets offended. I feel embarrassed and begin to apologize for my work. I don't like to do that."

Yes, good, Henry. Cancel out the thought that perfection standard and good workmanship are the same. They are not. As to that other aspect of receiving criticism—oh, that's a nasty one. It has troubled you often. Go on, you are doing well.

"The fear of criticism may have impelled the anger, as there must have been hundreds of angry incidents in my early life, all involving criticism."

Shall I hint something? It isn't going to be necessary to live again all those sundry experiences in detail. Lump them together, gather them in a bag, and throw them overboard.

"Well, Friend, you make it sound so simple. Is there an

automatic falling away on some level? Don't I have to at least recognize each incident to make a proper re-evaluation?"

Quite a bulky subject at so late an hour. My hint as to bagging these together applies to this situation, but not to every situation. In some instances, meticulous attention to details brings relief; in others, scanning high points aids in elimination. But in this particular case, the two or three hundred incidents can be treated as a general subject. My main point is to stress that no one method is The Method. Nor will the results always be the same—I mean, in terms of recognition and evaluation. Will you remember?

Before Henry could answer, Emma's fingers typed:

Good morning.

The couple smiled at the indirect suggestion not to extend their sessions late into the night.

✶

Henry muddled through another day of dismay. Disjointed thoughts danced through his mind, ranging from finding a bigger shop so he could keep a distance from Wayne, to a temptation to close his own shop altogether and look for work elsewhere. None of his speculations felt comfortable. Not wanting to hurt Wayne's feelings by firing him, Henry wearied from the strain of holding on to his decision not to show any anger toward him. He could hardly wait to talk to the Friend again in the evening.

"I feel the need again to address my attitude toward Wayne, my shop, and the turmoil I can't escape from."

The Friend began on a humorous note.

The atmosphere is charged with electrical energy particles, and the flow of ideas, new and untried continues. Yes, let us ponder a while on the momentous problem that shoots the emotional temperature up and the feeling-tone scale down.

First of all, your shop. It is yours by virtue of necessity to enlarge certain areas in your background that were left blank. Let there be no question that, as of now, your possession of the shop is necessary.

Now, your Wayne. He came to you fulfilling a definite need. Your head was bowed down under a weight of stupendous tasks, and assistance was desirable. We discussed sending out work, or hiring laborers. As is your privilege, you made a choice, and better so, as evidence has borne out. Wayne's illness interrupted the flow of energy. Now, Henry, something else is interrupting the flow: It is hard for him to admit to himself that he needs to quit. He forces his body to respond, although it rebels. So much of his energy must be used in that direction that not too much is left for the shop work. Now, what to do? Again, Henry, your choice.

With an understanding of the conditions, your strength of patience will bloom. He tells himself that he is vitally needed: 'Work must get out, orders must be filled, and I, Wayne, am needed.' It encourages him to forsake his home.

Surveillance of his work appears mandatory. So, for now, if his worth to you warrants, establish yourself as an observer. This is a garb you might wear for delightful instruction to yourself, too. Or, you can dismiss him.

"Wayne has always earned his keep and has been a gentleman. For one thing, I hesitate to dismiss him, as it might give him a bad emotional setback. For another, maybe somehow

I can overcome my turmoil to the point where I can see the reality of the situation, and then, hopefully, I can make the right decision."

Yes, Henry, Wayne has been paid twice — by check and by your very sentiment. You rightly discern the matter, so far as turning turmoils into triumphs. We have discussed some aspects of it already, but the way is open for you to look at your tendencies that puzzle and perplex you.

Various reasons for Wayne's appearance exist. Kindness of Wisdom permits opportunity for lesson material. Sharpening your tool of good thought influence and keeping it sharp for every incident, great or small, would energize Wayne considerably. He has several burdens which he does not mention. He, too, is in the schoolhouse called life, and the pages of his lesson book are sometimes blurred and hazy, hard for him to decipher. His present situation lends no support for him to like himself, so his resulting doubt makes him try to appear more sure and certain. Thus it often is, Henry, with members of your tribe of Earth people. Underneath the spoken words may lie a contrary reality.

In the light of the Friend's deep empathy for Wayne and his concerns, Henry felt embarrassed about his outbursts of temper. He felt ashamed that he hadn't thought of using his good thought influence on Wayne. A clumsy silence ensued.

I think I sense your concern, Henry. Recognize now that it is these 'hissing snakes in the tank' that are stealing the show. When understanding lightens the sky of perplexity, your actions will contain the seeds of triumph for all. You may boldly escape from this turmoil, Henry; there is no need to dwarf your spiritual growth, to compress into one day so much turbulence, to drown out the voice of Wisdom's ways. The life abundant of the moment-to-moment aspect cannot fit into such a turbulent schedule.

"What should I do when turmoil comes, like the one I had today, that drives me out of my own shop? If I could muster a good attitude, would it crowd out my resentment?"

What to do? Frankly, your physical placement is not the important factor, but rather, the necessity to face in openness each jarring incident. Can bitterness abide with good thought influence? Nay, verily. Good thought influence would drown out, smother, and completely eliminate resentment.

Another thing—it is the bitterness of resentment that drives out the strength of the good thought influence, for your turmoils are of a temporary nature, and you and I both know that you wish the guy well, even if momentarily you feel you could tear him limb from limb! (I enlarge for emphasis.)

Yes, the main idea is to face the problem—not the man, not the outside of the shop, but the problem. Wherever you can do so best, that's the spot for you.

As to controlling resentment, that's the stickler! There would be no resentment if there were no basic misevaluations forcing an erroneous command. So, be thankful for that which hints (oh, more than that—it blares it out) and tells you that a squeak needs oiling, as it were. Your peace comes from a proper solution.

Ask more. I delight to assist as far as I can go, but you are the do-er controlling the wheel of the machinery.

"It's strange—the other night, when you explained it, I could feel sympathy toward Wayne, but tonight I feel like I am on the run."

The other night, momentarily you saw one aspect of the situation. Ponder well that reality changes not, only reactions to reality.

Now, let's look this squarely in the face, Henry. There remain but two, no, three things to do. One is to let things be, torment yourself, and just hope for relief from the predicament. Two says eliminate the cause. That, too, you may do. Number three says change the scenery within your focus until more understanding reigns. Yours in the choice.

Suddenly, Henry understood a basic concept. He heard, and repeated it many times to himself, but never before did the thought hit him with so much power, that one could maintain a peaceful attitude, when childhood misevaluations did not cloud the issue at hand. Deep inside resided the wherewithal—the caring and the knowledge of what to do—while the hidden misevaluations obscured the path of action between himself and the other person or situation. Just as he gained this realization, doubt crept in as to whether he could follow through on his new understanding the next morning.

I'll help you, Henry, and rest assured that your decision will be a right one, not because I help you, but because you will do the right thing, as long as you walk in openness.

The following day, Henry had a friendly talk with Wayne, who took the opportunity to let Henry know that he wanted to retire. He only wanted to make sure that Henry could handle the work in the shop by himself. Genuine and mutual kindness lent an endearing touch to their parting.

20

The Power of Hindrances

✳

Now that he worked alone again, Henry returned to his normally brisk pace of tending to his responsibilities. He enjoyed his solitude and felt satisfied with his productivity. Within a week, however, several problems descended upon him in a single day. Nearing the end of a production run on the drill press, he caught himself drilling holes of too large a diameter, which rendered a large number of his workpieces worthless. Soon after that, he powered his milling machine, forgetting to first adjust the settings. Immediately, the cutting tool snapped off and clattered across the shop floor. Startled, he looked in disbelief at how narrowly the fragment had missed striking his hand. At the end of the day, he discovered that he had neglected to verify an invoice, which had resulted in his having sent a shipment to an incorrect address. He felt that he should have known better than to allow any of these things to happen. His frustration with himself had reached that familiar, awful boiling point once again.

"Friend, can you tell me anything about my turmoil today?"

Which one, Henry? You turmoiled considerably today.

"I thought there was only one, about fourteen hours long."

The Friend ignored his sarcasm.

Perhaps, but consider how its branches spread out to

include so much—your own attitude toward work, your spilling of influence on others who walked into the shop, your disinterest in new experiences proffered to you today, your angry attitude toward family's radio listening, your denial to respond to the glow around you—see, Henry how far-reaching are the effects? Each angry tangent would in itself be a source of wonderment when the basis of misevaluation was reached.

Groping for a way to escape the weight of his negative emotions, Henry blurted out a guess.

"There was probably a fear of consequences somewhere. Can you tell me anything about that?"

Every act you perform, Henry, every step you take, every thought you entertain even, has its consequences. Some of them are apparent and can be readily traced, but others are subtle and unrecognized. Your power of good thought influence is an excellent example of producing direct consequences by indirect means—unseen but very powerful.

If everything he did had consequences, Henry reasoned, then perhaps even his own small acts of mentally sending good thoughts to others could have a positive effect on a troubled situation.

Oftentimes, what you mark as small events perform for you, and through you, masterful results. A good example is your 'chance' acquaintance with Emma. Remember the non-importance of the event as far as your neighbor was concerned? It was a friendly gesture on his part, that was all, a small incident, and look what results it concocted.

So, Henry, can you see that any event ends in some consequence? Obviously, there are some events whose far-reaching implications you can partly foresee. However, until certain dormant senses are aroused, the future remains pretty much of a blank.

The Friend's logical explanation about consequences had a calming effect, but after a few more enjoyable and productive days, Henry inexplicably found himself almost paralyzed by inertia. The number of orders appeared manageable, but he simply could not figure out how to get himself back into the flow of work. Henry wondered if Wayne's absence contributed to the empty feeling in the shop that seemed to suffocate his vigor.

"I wonder if you could help me understand why I got so bogged down today."

Yes, Henry, that's all it takes—understanding. Very few perplexities that confront you contain elements that will not disappear when understanding reaches you. Openness is paramount.

Again, several factors are involved. There is a bit of karma working, for one thing. But recognize early that this should not discourage. The principles of justice are a blessing to those who learn to abide within the framework of understanding. For example, if you think that what is happening is directly traceable to a karma incident, then allow a watch-and-wait attitude to rule, with a sense of 'well, this is it, let me see how it works out.'

Maintain a pliableness to any situation, instead of a rigidity that makes you feel like you will crack. Yes, pliability, a willingness to be molded into the situation, and a comprehension that allows an experience to be completed will start a better vibration in motion. Such an understanding will render for you an inestimable position of peaceful acceptance. That is one factor.

Another is a misevaluation within your present existence,

*not a past life. You learned too well the erroneous idea that
'It's your fault and you'll have to suffer for it.' So suffer you
must, even if it's self-inflicted. Your tendency is to carry over
the load of yesterday. Repeat to yourself the superior viewpoint of kindness to self for relief from those experiences
long ago.*

*Still another factor operating in this instance is a basic
desire that others grant your interests the same importance
that you do. This, too, stems from a learning that granted
great importance to the little boy's position when very small.
Any subsequent efforts by loved ones to tame the tendency
did not successfully help to re-evaluate the earlier lesson.*

An interesting contradiction, Henry thought. On one hand,
he saw himself as unimportant and ignored; on the other, he
fancied that his interests should have great significance for
others. Both conclusions could have resulted from his parents'
handling him with different attitudes at different times. It surprised him however, that the two opposing feelings could coex-
ist in him and not cancel each other out. The Friend confirmed
that opposing stances can and do exist at the same time.

*Recall, for example, that shame instilled in you very early
was not modified by your parents' subsequent attitude which
conveyed how proud they were of you. Thus it works. Do
you desire more assistance?*

"Yes, another interesting aspect of this was my apparent
immobility and inability to think of the next thing to do."

*Oh, yes, I didn't mention that one, did I? Well, this one
traces back to statements similar to 'Why don't you think
about what you're doing?' or 'Oh, no, not that way! Let me
do it,' (and you still wait for someone to do it). And 'Christ,
but you are slow!' or 'Why don't you make up your mind?'*

and 'What kept you so long?'

Therein lies the present, Henry, back in those instances, though the now manifests only a similar situation, not the same one. 'Come along! Not so fast! Straighten up! Sit still! Get out of there!' These commands reached you as generalized messages, as words which, for you, were not tied to definite instances. Is there any wonder that a basis for turmoil was established? Fear not to comprehend, appreciate the power of such commands, and rise above their power over you now. You have much to work on here, Henry, very much.

"Did I interfere with my master plan by getting so upset?"

While asking the question, Henry spotted yet another irrational fear — a fear of interfering with his own life! No wonder he felt paralyzed, he thought. Fears pervaded all his thinking.

"Never mind my question, Friend. I caught myself having an unnecessary fear. Instead, I'd like to ask you about my handling of the new customer today. I took an immediate dislike to him, and my instinct told me to show him the door, but I don't know if I can trust my feeling."

You refer to an incident that is not yet completed. Wait and see. You see the original step in operation, but the climax has not yet been consummated, and you may choose to alter the set-up along the entire event, as ever there is your function of choice. Try to comprehend the significance of this happening as it unfolds, and allow your impulse to terminate in peaceful serenity.

"I'll try. As always, thank you very much, Friend."

✳

A glorious spring day beckoned Henry out of his compara- tively dark work area. Emma encouraged him to follow his urge to get out and enjoy the pleasant weather. Henry used errands as an excuse to briefly leave his shop during his nor- mal business hours. Wishing to understand some details of his adventure, Henry mentioned an incident to the Friend.

"On my trip to town, I had a long list of things to accom- plish. The incident with the locksmith really got my goat. He seemed to deliberately take his sweet time after I told him I was in a hurry. I saw in that a possible karmic implication, but I'm not sure. Would you care to comment?"

Oh, yes, that! Well, that largely stems from your inten- tion to accomplish within a limited period of time a lengthy series of tasks. The perplexities in which you indulged were pretty much based on what might be viewed as karmic, in one sense, but in another sense, they had direct bearing on your attitude of the moment, as events seem frustrating when you are in the midst of the rough handling by so-called engrams. Or I may say it this way: When you are indulg- ing, rather than understanding one of these hindrances, it is apparent that no matter what may occur, you will see the new event through the dust kicked up by the engram mate- rial. As a result, the delightful things that come your way are not as delightful. Small rocks in your pathway suddenly loom up as boulders, and irritation scratches the already disturbed inward soil of emotions.

Note that abiding in the moment-to-moment aspect would completely blot out any irritation, and each new experience would be openly welcomed as instruction via relationship, either with persons or circumstances. Is that helpful?

"I don't know if I am on the right track. I can understand

that dwelling in the moment-to-moment condition for even a moment could start a trend away from difficulty, but once these irritations start, they seem to have a quality of building on themselves. I find it difficult to shake them off. And speaking of choice, it is easy for me to see the proper thing to do, but I don't see why I seem to end up 'choosing' aggravation."

Therein lies the power of the hindrances — they claim you. Yes, even to the extent of demanding from you your power of choice. In the midst of the merry-go-round on which you whirl when in the throes of a dandy turmoil, the weapon to wield is named 'understanding.' Not to shut the eyes (that wouldn't stop the mechanism); not to plug up the ears (that wouldn't successfully close out the sounds); not to fight those around you (they are often spinning on a merry-go-round of their own); not to jump off (escape wouldn't solve the spinning event); not to force, or strain, or mold your-self or others into any fixed pattern (for that only changes the outward appearance). No, the only honest solution to resolving the turmoil is an understanding attitude.

Find out what makes the hurdy-gurdy spin, what makes the noise of the contraption, and then no longer can it rule and master you. The risks of investigation are not nearly as great as the risks of maintaining a stern, unyielding, and unresponsive attitude.

Do you like my picture of fact?

"Yes, I am very pleased with your analogy. We are always grateful for your comments. Many times we even get a laugh out of them. They give us a genuine lift."

Good, good, good.

"Another question. The events of my life point out the pattern that I have to constantly work very hard; I have to suffer and do self-demeaning things—in other words, I have to compromise myself in order to have any success at all. I have a big list of these things that dictate my actions."

Even more than you suspect, Henry. This tendency acts almost like a passport, or a ticket to the merry-go-round ride. It is far more universal in Earth people than usually recognized, although it may show itself in many different types of conduct. Some will act important, some will speak in whispers, some will rave and rant, others will take delight in wearing a leash around their necks to be pulled around by others. But under so much of such behavior is that basic tendency to forget to be kind to yourself. A great gift is the understanding of this basic tendency. A release from its subtle and sometimes not so subtle evidences is a big step forward.

"Somewhere I learned that if people have only a little bit of trouble, they can straighten it our before it gets out of hand. Lao Tsu might have said something to the effect that trouble would strengthen you and was not to be looked upon as detrimental, but I think too much trouble does more harm than good."

What better mirror than the one called 'trouble' would an individual require in which to see oneself? Therein is the trouble's contribution. But often trouble is not permitted to accomplish that result. Would your turmoil lead to enlightenment if it did not produce in you an increased understanding of yourself, Henry? That is one aspect.

Then there is another, and that is karma. Trouble, or events that look like trouble by the definitions of Earth people, if recognized as a direct result of Wisdom's unfailing laws of consequence (because of forces set in motion earlier)—yes, if so-called troubles would be thus recognized, they would not crush, they would not defeat, they would not push you down, as it were. Understanding's wings will lift the troubled one, and comprehension's light will answer the 'why' question, if openness permits the rays of light to enter.

For example, the cruel torture of your war years would have been more readily acceptable, if recognition had existed of the need to quantity consciousness to fill in the 'blanks' left as a result of 'wicked-eyed Peter's' previous actions. Clashing, groaning, rebelling, arguing against, and fighting—that type of attitude will not only be burdensome, but will unfortunately suppress the possibility of new enlightenment entering. An active acceptance, and alert understanding, a responsive reception—this type of attitude will increase your possibilities in an ever-expanding existence. You do well to search for explanation of any problem area, Henry. There is no virtue in abiding in darkness when light is available.

"The length of time it takes for an idea to take root and start working in consciousness is a strange thing. It is almost as if the mind is like a blob of clay or putty. If an experience is pressed in too hard, it becomes an engram; if it isn't imprinted strongly enough, it has to be pressed again. The impression seems to require just the proper penetration to be effective. I am guessing that this is the way understanding works. A new fact that invalidates a misevaluation seems to take a while to counteract one's usual reaction. Must one consciously digest the new idea for some considerable time and consciously apply it in many instances to be assured of a proper routing out of the old misevaluation?"

Your putty analogy is 'putty' terrific. It spells out an interpretation that is a masterful picture of fact. As to the task of readjusting misevaluations, do not insist on knowing their intricate patterns. Suffice it to say that this digestive process will assist in the desired accomplishment. But also recognize that an adjustment could happen suddenly as well. Often there are so many more facets involved than the apparent ones, that if a readjustment were to take place immediately, it would 'knock you blind' as it did Paul. A longer period of time works best in your case.

One other remark: The more of these misevaluations that are properly corrected and neatly filed away, the more readily the subsequent ones will yield to the gentle touch of understanding. Already, if you searched, you would recognize that. But I will leave that to you, should you wish to examine it further.

Incidentally, Emma is directly absorbing much of this understanding. All is well.

The acknowledgment that Emma had understood the teachings relieved Henry's concern that many questions he asked had relevance to him only. His preoccupation with himself troubled him despite Emma's constant assurances that she enjoyed her role as a scribe. While the discussion focused on Henry, Emma absorbed the insights, while keeping a record of his and the Friend's conversations. At the same time, she found herself in awe of Henry's persistent effort to improve himself. She even told him that witnessing him confess his vulnerabilities strengthened her feelings of love and admiration for him, which in turn prompted Henry to let her know how much he valued her participation and help. In a renewed sense of togetherness, they admitted to each other that, with their complementary skills and common interests, they made a great team.

21

Bless All Who Cross Your Threshold

✳

Henry's experience of social encounters caused him such discomfort that he learned to dislike having company over, expected or unexpected. He could usually tolerate his customers, if they got right to the point. He expected concise questions and answers from them. Anything else he considered a waste of time.

In deference to Emma, he voiced few complaints about the visits from her extended family, which included relatives of all ages dropping by to share their family news. During these visits Henry usually retired to his shop. On one recent occasion, he had emerged from the shop with company still in the house and occupied himself reading a newspaper. Emma and her visitors viewed this as an improvement in his conduct.

Since the forthcoming wedding festivities involving Emma's relatives would spill over into their home, Henry decided to consult the Friend. He felt the time had come to examine the issue of his reluctant hospitality.

"Is it all right to take up the question of my difficulty with company? I find it hard to envision doing as the Bible says: 'Bless all who cross your threshold.' As I see this one, openness isn't nearly as feasible. It is possible, though, that I might take a step toward accomplishing something in this area."

The blessing can be mutual, Henry. In this instance, your guests can be blessed, or you can be blessed—and yes, it's

possible that you both can be blessed. Can you consider that in some instances those who walk across your threshold require, in earnest need, those influences and atmosphere contained in your establishment?

The crafty, 'gimme-all-I-can-get' attitude facing so many in business ventures these days—don't you think it is a relief for them to breathe the atmosphere of good will, helpfulness, or shall I say, good thought influence that can be felt in your environment? There is some overflow, Henry, and it splashes on those who feel the urge to visit, but know not why. Oh, they won't tell you, as a matter of fact, won't even act the part often, partly because they don't know it themselves, but there is that aspect present.

Also, without the influx of others, you, Henry, and you, Emma, would miss a chapter in the book of lessons. Your need is not known to you, and it isn't entirely what you think it is, Henry. It isn't only to learn to get along, to learn to put up with, to learn to share thoughts, but there are other reasons and needs, too.

Cultivate an attitude of 'Well, I wonder why they came?' and an openness to welcome one, two, three, or more lessons that will make your visitors appear different in your view of them. Don't you think that it is just barely possible that, even in the matter of guests, you can't win until you quit arranging things you way?

Henry had no awareness of arranging things his way beyond arranging his shop layout or the furniture in their house. He tried to understand what the Friend meant and could not imagine the changes he would need to make.

Emma, on the other hand, interpreted the comment as intended, having already experienced Henry's tendency to insist on having things his way. In her desire to please him, she frequently found herself yielding to his wishes, finding that it gave her pleasure to do so. She remained silent while Henry contemplated the meaning of the message. To him, it seemed to say: let go, be open, and accept whatever comes; do not interfere with the flow of things.

As the understanding descended upon him, he felt the tension of anxiety lessen. A sense of gently letting go seemed to wend its way into his thoughts. He reflected on the Friend's mention of the beneficial atmosphere in their home.

"That overflow you mentioned—it seems rather strange to me. I wonder, with all my turmoil and touchy attitude, why people would even want to come around."

For one thing, Henry, your turmoils are not seen by them as they are experienced by you. Your focus narrows to include only the turmoil, but they get an overall picture, a general view. There is quite a secret hidden in this pointed revelation to you, Henry, and a powerful weapon you can use.

I have told you before that one of your strong points is your energy-producing vibrations of good thought influence. Of course, if you choose not to use it, you are permitted to file it away in a drawer and choose to spread some other sort of attitude instead, for whether you please or not, influence emanates from you. It does so with all who walk the Earth. You may sense a temporary irritation with company, but your basic trend is full of good will, well-wishing, honesty, straightforwardness, and kindness. That is your overflow.

Henry fell silent. The Friend outlined Henry's strong points, citing the qualities that Henry himself sometimes viewed as disadvantages or liabilities, while at the same time valuing and cultivating their positive aspects. Henry knew he cared, perhaps too much, but usually assumed a pose of indifference to hide what he considered his vulnerabilities. He found security in trying to shield himself from those who would take advantage of his kindness. But the Friend unveiled Henry's soul and exposed his true character—his genuine and deeply caring nature so familiar to Emma.

Henry tried to understand the implications of revealing his benevolent attitude. Did this mean complete surrender to the whims of the outside world? He did not think he had the energy or desire for that. Yet, feeling urged and supported by the Friend and Emma, he tried to visualize himself emerging from the protective cocoon of his emotional isolation.

"I was wondering about the overflow you mentioned. Does that mean that the way I think affects other people even if they are not around me?"

Oh, definitely.

He almost wished he hadn't asked. A sense of responsibility began to press on him to use the gift, which the Friend said he had, namely his attribute of good thought influence. He could no longer avoid accepting the gracious invitation to contribute consciously to the same cause as his much-admired Friend on the other side—to help people in their spiritual growth.

Sensing some complex possibilities, Henry tried to ward off the full impact of his realization by looking first at the basic requirements. He knew that to provide good thought influence, he needed to feel good inside, to feel good about himself. But how could he accomplish that?

"Would it follow that I could send energy to myself? Can one think good thought influence toward oneself?"

Remember the urgent need for kindness to self? It all ties in. Be kind to yourself, and sense your spiritual muscles growing! Be kind to others and (I shall whisper it softly) to all who cross your threshold, and watch their shapes change!

"I wonder if I underestimate the power of kindness by thinking of it as a liability or weakness. It feels to me like it might require a lot of effort on my part to protect myself from possible backlash."

So much is involved right here, Henry. It's largely about turning the other check, or going the second mile, which are familiar to you, because you understood all that some time ago. 'Do a little more than they expect,' you have said, and 'It'll look better if I put a rim on the instrument.'

You see, Henry, you tend to lose sight of such goodness when turmoil bogs you down, when engrams shout for attention, when locks close tight the door to understanding. These are hindrances and obstructions to the moment-to-moment aspect of existence. But looking at them definitely reduces their power, Henry, and openness permits the exposure of these as usurpers to the throne. They want to lord it over you; they want to command, but together we can relegate them to a place of non-power.

As you get better acquainted with these obstacles, you will discover behind their masks of importance only a non-entity. Acquaintance with them acts as a re-evaluation. We are speaking in general terms tonight. Perhaps our discussion will lessen the hold of all of them. Is it getting clearer?

Henry took a deep breath. He felt an increasing sense of lightness, if not deep elation. He hesitated to call it a happy feeling for fear it would vanish, but quickly recognized this fear as a result of a mistaken assumption from his childhood. He laughed out loud and marveled at how easily he could identify this misevaluation against a background of good feelings.

He shared with Emma the reason for his sudden laughter and told her about the increasing happiness he felt, thanks to her help and to the persistent efforts of the Friend. After some hesitation, he finally gave himself credit as well for his early successes in regaining his precious freedom from the weight of the past. To him it meant the very liberation of his soul. He turned to Emma, his true and faithful friend, his life's companion, and let his profound feeling of caring envelop her.

22

Responsibility

✳

The family festivities, for which Henry tried to brace himself, centered around the wedding of Emma's oldest cousin. Relatives from near and far bustled in and out of the house in preparation for the big event. In the past, so much commotion would have overwhelmed Henry and sent him scurrying to his shop, but he held on to his determination to remain calm, while avoiding idle conversations. Instead, he tried to shed some good thought influence on the mass of Emma's relatives, inwardly chuckling to himself about his silent virtuous activity.

It occurred to Henry that he did not know how much responsibility he needed to take as the host to so many people. Emma seemed to handle the situation very well without his help, taking care of their girls and the visitors at the same time. Soon the entire issue of responsibility surfaced for him as a big question mark.

His recent experience with Wayne, his former assistant in the shop, still left him with confusion as to when to involve himself in other people's activities and when to let go. He wanted to ask the Invisible Friend about it right then and there, but his question had to wait, as two of their visiting relatives had decided to stay as houseguests for several days. When the guests had finally left, Henry felt relieved and eager to resume the evening sessions.

After telling the Friend how much he missed their conversations, Henry presented his question.

"I sometimes take too little or too much responsibility than I should. I wonder if you could comment about it."

There are various classifications of responsibility—to self, to family, to business, to country, to mankind. But in the final analysis, regard it all as responsibility to rightly and adequately treat the Wisdom's piece of Wisdom within you, and thus Wisdom Itself.

Frankly, Henry, don't take this to mean that you must bear a burden of great responsibility. Recall that you retain within you a piece of Wisdom, and when your actions, emotions, thoughts, and deeds are governed or sharpened by the force of that piece of Wisdom within you, then those acts, deeds, and thoughts cannot be other than correct ones, accomplishing your responsibility to the proper degree—not too much, not too little. That is why it is so important to 'get one's own house in order,' as it were. Hindrances stand in the way, obstructing you from properly fulfilling your responsibility to yourself and to others.

"I think I take on more responsibility sometimes to compensate for some sort of inadequacy. Maybe I do that to prop up my sense of importance."

Yes, you think you have found an inadequacy within yourself and you now obey the dictates of the belief you created. It is like a big hammer held over your head. You would do well to recognize that none of your friends, acquaintances, and business associates would point to an inadequacy in you, oh, no. All comments would be about Henry's adequacy. You have created a misconception about this, and when did it start?

Early, as you recall, we mentioned your determination to take responsibility for yourself because others failed you.

Then, in the process of time, a sense of inadequacy developed from the admonition of instructors, and you felt the insufficiency. May I lead you to the general premise, and allow you to search for the details? You manifest many fears: fear to direct, fear to correct, fear to hurt, fear to use the powers you contain, or to reach for others that are yours by right of heritage.

Yes, Henry, I sense a fear that you will offend us if you do other than what you consider we might approve. That is one of those attempts to lean on us—and not so commendable. Yours in the choice! Yours is the action! Yours is the handling, the forming, the fashioning! Elimination of the fear, which you recognize, and substitution of it with confidence, which is your tool, will invite a great deal of happiness to you.

"Since I don't yet have the confidence, I would appreciate any helpful guidelines as to when to be accountable for what."

A helpful clue to use is the very fine formula of 'honesty—motivation—attitude.' For example, should you feel compelled to do something, whether for self or others, and when a question presents itself, it might be well to glance in that mirror, look yourself in the eye and say, 'Hey there, exactly what is your motive, what is the driving urge, and what is your attitude?'

Honestly searching your own heart reveals lip service, 'to be seen of men,' or service demanding recompense. Nothing less than honest responsibility will result in mutual benefit for you and those immediately affected. Ponder this well; it has more truth than at first appears. Quite a working principle, I assure you.

Henry's thoughts wandered to an incident in his child-hood when he felt a conflict between something like a sense of responsibility to his parents and honesty with himself. His parents wanted—essentially forced—him to participate in a Cub Scout jamboree. Their insistence brought on an indis-putably honest response from little Henry—a loud, scream-ing protestation that embarrassed him and his parents. The Friend picked up on his thought.

Consider the jamboree incident as duly important, for it started a lot of rough edges for you that must now be smoothed away. Identify yourself with the little lad who faced a threat of abandonment if unwilling to jamboree. Consider your feelings then. Relax in understanding that the force of intense distaste for the proceedings need not interfere now.

"Your words are very comforting, especially after my hav-ing felt unsure about my social responsibilities these last few days."

Be ye kind to yourself. Aiming toward perfection is delight-ful, if you set your sights properly.

Henry chuckled at the comment. The Friend had made an obvious reference to Henry's earlier struggle with his perfec-tion standard, and now praised him for his more appropriate use of it in his desire to maintain a high level of personal con-duct. Henry could now set his priorities straight and aim at *honesty—motivation—attitude* as the Friend suggested. He could see great value in streamlining his self-examination by asking himself these questions.

Identifying with the image of himself as a kid, Henry came upon another question.

"I wonder if you can give me some clues as to why I am so scared of ridicule."

Your tendency is related to many early instances in which you showed or threatened tears and were ridiculed out of them. There was an incident of boys watching you and laughing when you tossed a ball and missed. Another time you balked at an instruction that the teacher imposed on you and you were laughed into shame. There were many other incidents that you'll be able to recall.

Every explanation brought Henry closer to his goal of freeing himself from his energy-consuming impediments. Now that he allowed himself to have more feelings, he realized how deeply his early conditioning had also affected his sense of accomplishment.

"For a long time, I have been vaguely aware that something must be robbing me of a sense of fulfillment. Time after time, I have worked hard and done worthwhile projects only to find that I missed the sense of achievement that I expected. This sense of missing something took on great proportions in my life, to the point where I took more pleasure in contemplating an undertaking than actually doing it."

It is good that you recognize the existence of this tendency, as this will enable us to reach into some areas that are bothersome to you. You have correctly analyzed that you have missed the thrill of accomplishment.

One reason for it dates to your early experiences with over-enthusiasm. You were taught to expect such expressions of enthusiasm by others to mean your accomplishment. You were not permitted to have a real taste of the fruits of accomplishment by yourself, but, instead, the fruit was picked for you, all sugared up, and then fed to you. Receiving praise from someone else became the measure of your success. You have done well, Henry, very well, in spite of this definite handicap. When the delights of understanding reach this area, you will discover much pleasure that has been missed in the past.

The Friend provided just the kind of reassurance Henry needed, with compassion for his feelings as an adult and for his past experiences as a child.

"These childhood experiences seem to dictate my behavior. The more I look, the more I see how confused I was. I trust that, at some point, all my efforts will have a big payoff."

Certainly, looking for misevaluations is not a happy pastime. As a matter of fact, the very strain of looking may become a barrier. Have you tried lending your thought to the general direction you are pursuing, and then entering into such instances as freely and easily as they present themselves? There are some very important things taking place, and not all of them will you be aware of as they happen. Surely, not all is contained in recalling past incidents, since that is only one link in the chain of progress.

The caution here is not to make this or any other a standard system that must be followed. There are instances when re-experiencing, re-living, re-entering into past events is highly beneficial. You have some that will be addressed this way, and you will know what release truly means, but not all past events must be examined in this manner.

Henry wanted to know how reliving the past and living in the moment fit together.

"Examining formative influences seems to clash with the idea of moment-to-moment living. I take it that delving into the experiences of long ago could be seen as momentary necessities, though."

Moment-to-moment living allows for whatever appears within the focus of one's being. Let us consider momentarily one phase of your trouble with turmoil. *You would call it painful, but moment-to-moment living would rule out all pain and an identical situation would result in pleasure, if only because of the contrast between the former turmoil and the present experience of moment-to-moment peace.*

Think again of that unwanted company issue. Moment-to-moment living does not rule out the possibility that into your focus would come those who you feel could contribute nothing to you, nor you to them. But fancy in that moment your relief and untold joy in realizing an absence of turmoil when faced with such company! Lessons can be learned from this experience, even if no apparent contribution passes between you.

Moment-to-moment living does not rule out painful occurrences, but does rule out painful reactions, and perfect poise and calm results. So, in that respect, there is no pain, no ache, no discomfort, no nervousness, no griping, no wishing it were different, no clamoring for change. Acceptance of all—and I mean each and every experience that comes to you as a gift from a bountiful providence, and assurance that no mistakes are made—will rule out the force of pain as a squelching agent, as it were.

This is one aspect of the moment-to-moment existence that we have sidestepped until now, but I feel you are now ready to understand. There is a world-apart difference between the discomfort resulting from hindrances based on your engrams, and the discomfort resulting from the experience itself. Learn to differentiate, and you will reap surprising relief.

"I see what you mean about reacting in a way that causes discomfort. Can you elaborate on ruling out painful reactions?"

Wherein, Henry, lies the pain of, let us say, your temporary upheaval with respect to Wayne or Donald, for example. Is it physical? No, they haven't slapped you. Is it mental? Not from them, as they are not sowing confusion. The soreness lies in your reaction, which reaction is based on some, several, or many happenings, or teachings from the past that resulted in a wrong conclusion, a misevaluation. The moment-to-moment aspect dwells in the now, not in the past. An alert one recognizes that each experience is a new one, and a past decision will not fit the present experience.

The more Henry understood the principle of living in the moment, the more he realized the difficulties involved in its achievement.

"Do you know of many people on Earth who have mastered living in the moment the way you describe it?"

Well, Henry, few have found this haven in its entirety. But I know two that have tasted its luscious fruit for specific periods of time. Openness has usually preceded many glowing experiences, and you know what I mean! It is not a foreign feeling to you.

May I comment also that the moment-to-moment aspect may be enjoyed in certain specific areas of relationships, such as when a flow of wood carving ideas and energy find you, and yet be absent in other areas of your life. In analogy, it is almost as if a gemstone must catch the light correctly to show its brilliance and its beauty. So, as every aspect of your being is focused light-ward, the brilliance and beauty of your consciousness can shine forth its radiance and brilliance.

These comments sounded good, but Henry knew that he still had much turmoil to conquer and that he needed more understanding.

"There is another question I have been intending to ask: How do engrams, or what you call misevaluations, come about? Is it a karmic payback?"

Let me put it this way, Henry: The misevaluations were made due to intentional or un-intentional teachings and learnings. These teachings and learnings came about as a result of a need for the development of the persons involved.

Let us suppose a few instances designed to illustrate the point:

Mama, by virtue of her position, gives an instruction to do something. The child rebels. If mama refrains from brutal punishment, no engram develops. However, if he does not respond, for whatever reason, and mama does not understand, and in anger administers brutal punishment—an engram is born in the child. The child will, until understanding's bright rays eliminate the misevaluation, continue to feel the urge to rebel, even when his behavior results in punishment. But when understanding reigns supreme, the child understands and has no need to rebel, while mama understands and has no need to punish. An engram is a misevaluation that results from lack of understanding.

Do engrams have their place in karma? Yes, Henry, they are steps in the path that need understanding. See them as events on the way to clarity of mind and the freedom to expand consciousness.

"It's remarkable how a misevaluation can affect one's life so deeply."

Let me hasten to return to the picture of the punishing mother and rebellious child. As the child proceeds through life, he observes that his disobedience results in brutal punishment. Life has taught him that lesson. He retains his basic misevaluation, but it goes underground, and he appears to 'behave' in order to avoid further punishment. He learns to act as if he is obeying, but does not learn to obey as an act of appropriate obedience. Note how deeply underground this may go. To all appearances, he may become a model citizen, but can you conceive such a one living moment-to-moment?

"I can see how these misevaluations can get very complicated. I am sure some of ours are deeply buried, too."

A glaring example was Emma's underground tendency to force upon you her way, in preference to handing you the privilege of choice. She learned it as a child, because of an early overburden of demands forced upon her. Due to this, you, Henry, had been prevented from enlarging certain areas of your consciousness. It was subtle, very subtle, but understanding now rules out this irksome tendency.

Recognize here that no blame is intended for either one of you. Here is an illustration close to home. See how enlightening the tool of relationship can be?

The last statement opened the door for Henry and Emma to a deeper understanding of the value and purpose of human relationships. In everyday interactions, and mostly outside of their awareness, partners display toward each other their learned misevaluations. While remaining blind to one's own mistaken ideas or behaviors, one can nevertheless observe the inappropriate response of the other and offer a helpful perspective on the issue at hand. But instead of accepting such commentary as an opportunity to straighten out possible misconceptions, the one receiving a helpful comment frequently defends his or her long-held position. Thus many arguments ensue, sometimes ending in an unnecessary separation of the individuals. Both partners can learn invaluable lessons from each other, if they choose to remain open and willing to take a fresh look at their erroneous convictions.

Henry and Emma wanted to continue the conversation in spite of feeling tired, but the Friend diverted their intention.

Now retire, as you need rest.

In reviewing the session before falling asleep, Henry and Emma admired the Friend's refreshing orientation toward human affairs. Rather than labeling deviant behaviors as pathological, the Friend simply viewed them as self-defining indications of a need for learning and for a further expansion of consciousness. As everyone has unique intellectual and emotional strengths and weaknesses, the requirements for each person's further development differ accordingly, while each person also serves as a direct or indirect teacher to the other. As a result, interactions between people produce an intricate, dynamic tapestry of intertwining needs and responses. Teachers and learners interchange their roles in a continuous flow of effects they have on each other. Viewed in this way, relationships provide ongoing opportunities for individuals to learn, to exchange knowledge, and to sharpen their awareness.

If people could recognize the great value of this process of mutual assistance, it would strengthen their respect for each other's individual needs for growth. The inappropriate demands people place on each other to think and feel alike would sound absurd. If a person's right to have a different opinion could receive respectful acknowledgment, most heated arguments and disagreements would simply disappear.

One could even see most prisoners and criminally inclined individuals as needing special tutoring, rather than punishment. Punitive measures tend to mask or compound their many problems, typically bringing about social ostracism and further affecting their behavior in undesirable ways.

"Ignorance still weighs heavily on humanity," Henry said with a sigh, "but as the Friend says, 'Some learn more, some learn less, but all learn something.' We are all still learning."

"It all fits together, doesn't it?" Emma asked, ready to end their reflections for the night.

"Yes, it does, dear, in a very wonderful way," Henry answered. His mind tried to encompass the enormity of their insights, as he gradually slipped into a deep and restful sleep.

23

Dealing with Fears

✳

Henry continued his self-observation and gathered his latest findings for his next discussion with the Friend. He found that some of his negative emotions, especially his fears, had long since become habitual and hidden under layers of denial.

"Regarding fears, today a frightening thought shook me up. It seemed to tie in with a sense of insecurity and despair. I had a sudden fear that losing either my health or my business could lead to the downfall of my family. As I see it now, these fears can be very vicious. I fear that even mentioning them might give them more power. Since fear is engrammatic, perhaps I can start dealing with it."

This one you have tended to shy away from. By its very nature, fear of this kind belongs to the dark, and will vanish when brought to the light of understanding. It is of a type that can be handled rather easily because its greatest force lies in its secrecy and shame. Break its shell. You will find within that shell not the dreaded dragon, but a lifeless form that dared to make a big sound. This, of course, is symbolic language, you understand.

"I even have fears that you will be unhappy with me because I haven't completely given up smoking. This is one fear, but I have many others: fear of arguments, a fear that I won't attain anything for my family—although I don't know exactly what it is that I want to attain. I get glimpses of an optimal way of life, such as moment-to-moment living, but I suspect that fear prevents me from having as good a life as I think I could have. I wonder how much I live my life because of fears motivating me rather than the enjoyment of life itself."

Henry, you felt the force of these fears as you mentioned them. Now, just to illustrate the point, recite them once again, and see if they are as powerful. Do they not appear less monstrous?

Dare to face them, and they lose their potency. Such is their nature. But be aware that beneath is something that prompts such fears.

Henry thought about it and suddenly remembered hearing the command "Behave!" shouted at him as a child. He realized that the sound of the word had instilled in him a great fear that something bad, unnamed, and definitely unpleasant would surely happen to him if he didn't yield to the ill-defined demand. He shivered at his vivid recollection of the sound of that dreaded word, and thought that perhaps his overwhelming fear had created a portal for other fears to gain entry.

"I think I am finally starting to understand. I assume other fears later followed in the wake of the first big fear experiences I had. I have a feeling that I may expect to remove some of these associated fears more easily now. A big 'thank you' is in order from me to you."

Your increasing comprehension is a source of extreme pleasure to our realm.

In your early years, the words meant little to you, but the tone of voice did, until the meaning of the words became intelligible in later life.

You like to understand all that happens; that is good. Try to retain an open attitude. It will be a delight to witness your continuance in this healthy pursuit of removing hindrances.

"I will certainly try. Thank you for the encouragement."

✦

Henry continued his search through a variety of books for ideas that might help him to break through his denial mechanisms.

"I read that you can't build character without being uncompromisingly honest with yourself."

Such teaching as you encountered can result in enslavement or liberation, depending on many factors at work.

Your situation is different: You read the words (about being honest), sense the intent behind them, and would like to conform, insofar as possible. But, as authorities speak, in books or otherwise, darkness overtakes you, for here is another one of those danger areas to you and many others. You want to respect authorities who you feel can teach you new, enriching things, and yet you harbor no inner respect of authorities. For this reason confusion results. You are torn between two extremes. You want to understand the new, but the elements of distrust of authorities bar the entrance of enlightenment.

Tonight, that honesty to self, admirable as it is, wants to take over, to the exclusion of kindness to self. Kindness to self is not the same as honesty to self, nor is honesty to self the same as kindness to self. To be truthful need not spell unkindness, although you have heard claims to the contrary. Your parents had not the strength to correct the impression, either then or later, to you personally. This effort at correction is being made now, but the finer details should reach you by the avenue of your mental muscle. Can you now differentiate between the two—honesty and kindness?

Henry could see how, in his otherwise admirable honesty, he could have easily acted ruthlessly enough to override any kindness he might have felt toward himself. Also, the conflict between Henry's desire to learn from authorities that teach worthwhile lessons, and resentment toward authorities that intrude and lack kindness, escaped his notice until the Friend pointed it out to him.

"The more clearly I see, the more I see that this authority business overlaps into so many other issues that I despair in my attempts to sort it all out."

The Friend did not let him slip into helplessness.

Are you aware, Henry, that much material concerning authority has already been exposed? We have looked at it from several angles, but some issues, of course, have not yet been drained of their poison. It is as if a toxin had been introduced into the bloodstream. So many areas of the being may be affected that it would be difficult to drain out the poison in one massive step without draining the entire blood supply.

The work on this is continuing and proper enlightenment will enter, when root sources are tapped and exposed. Even your feeling of despair stems from this source. Remember, you were told that you've got to obey no matter how you feel, and that you wouldn't feel that way if you obeyed. It's a mad circle. But its force is lessening and you will, in time, experience complete relief from its crippling effects.

"Thank you for your efforts."

No trouble at all! Simply a pleasure! You are the one in trouble! And pleasure will catch up with you too!

"That's nice to know."

After some hesitation, Henry decided to address his lingering confusion.

"For all the times we've talked about it, I don't think I know what being kind to oneself really means. Would you explain it to me again, please?"

An absence of condemnation, Henry, a complete absence of blame or regret. You see, what happens with blame is that you form a separate 'you' that judges some other 'you,' and openness is dimmed. To progress, walk into the area, look around, examine, see, and understand. Then all is well. Then there need be no such separation, for reality will be manifest, with no condemnation present.

Unkindness to self slashes off a part of your awareness, as it were, and with that part of awareness, tries to force the rest of your awareness into unwholesome complicity. Combine all awareness, keep it together as one, camouflage it not, deny it not, but simply be. If you think that the small piece of awareness is smart enough to direct the rest of it, is it not to be suspected that a union and agreement of the parts of awareness will accomplish more than the broken-off part doing the dictating?

"Of course, and as difficult as it might be, I'll try to make the adjustment."

What keenness of being results, what energies are loosed, and what actions of worth come about! That is freedom — freedom even from the self, the divided self, for you push aside the false and enter into the land of the real.

Henry thought about his glimpse of insight into how aspects of oneself can antagonize each other.

"This problem of kindness to self! So many times you have

told me to be kind to myself, but, as I read your words, I feel unworthy. Does it mean that I am trying to achieve too high a standard, or that I am reading condemnation into your words? As I think of it, a perfection standard is ridiculous, because even Christ said something like, 'There is only One who is perfect.' Is it something like this that is giving me trouble?"

Yes, Henry, yes. This is a basic tendency that destroys openness. Just as Emma's sleepiness sometimes stops our exchange, so your lack of kindness acts as a barrier, so openness cannot remain. This perfection standard! Do you honestly feel, Henry, that, within your realm, you could reach perfection?

Actually, Wisdom desires that you live by Wisdom's dictates, not that you reach a hypothetical place called perfection. There ain't no such animal. Nor is it expected of you. The most advanced one walking the sod is a pleasure to Wisdom, but is not perfect. Try to make an effort to tear down that idol. Openness is much better, for openness is perfection in the sense of arrival at that place of relaxation, so Wisdom can give comprehension. Find a new definition for perfection, so confusion won't result.

Despite overplaying his deficiencies, Henry resolved to adopt these new attitudes. He knew they would have positive effect on his life.

24

Forgiveness

✳

Income from the manufacture of the new instrument began to flow, allowing Henry and Emma to begin their search for a new home. On the spur of the moment, they decided to visit a real estate office. An enthusiastic young salesman immediately began to offer them suggestions, while disregarding Henry's attempts to explain what he wanted. After a few minutes of disjointed conversation, Henry lost his temper. He told the salesman to listen better next time and abruptly walked out. Stunned, Emma quickly apologized and followed Henry outside, trying to remain calm. Henry's outburst shocked both of them. They remained silent during a tense ride home, after which Henry retreated to his shop to contemplate his behavior.

Anticipating a discussion with the Friend, Henry wanted to get a thorough look at his reflexive action. He did not think he had a big ego, but in his remorse, he wondered what gave him license to vent his feelings at a complete stranger. Pulling together the information he had gathered from various sources, he came up with an interesting composite picture of the ego.

To begin with, Henry knew that one's ego does not represent the true self. The true self, what the Friend called *Wisdom's piece of Wisdom,* exists beyond time, and represents the will of God. The ego, on the other hand, represents the will of the mortal personality. It fancies itself a guardian of the person, while crowding out, competing with, or simply remaining unaware of the divine presence. Henry could see how the clash between the two showed itself in the prayer, "Not mine, but Thy will be done."

He then surmised that the presence of the two differing parts in him could explain the double-mindedness and conflict he so often experienced. At the real estate office, part of him had reacted aggressively to the salesman's primitive tactics, while a deeper part evaluated his outburst as unnecessary and hurtful to the feelings of all involved.

Henry proceeded to search his awareness for manifestations of his ego. He came up with several questions about his attitude that he suspected of having caused his inconsiderate behavior: Could his financial success have triggered a sense of superiority? Did he expect special treatment from the salesman? Did he resist openness to the new?

He also noticed definite similarities between his father's and his own behaviors. Although Henry had less of a hot temper than his father, who often flew into a rage, he could nevertheless see the inevitable effects of his past indoctrination. Henry hoped that understanding the root sources of his impulsive actions would help him mitigate his feelings of irritation.

His gruff reaction to the salesman still bothered him as they began the session.

"Good evening, Friend. I have noticed my attitude changing for the better, but I find myself still carried off by my temper. Inside myself, I just watch, while my personality reacts impulsively as it did toward the salesman. True, he probably needed someone to point out to him his irritating behavior, but as I thought about it later, the wicked-eyed Peter incarnation must have influenced me. Also, I may not have been open enough to comprehend the reality of the situation and may have missed its intended meaning. Could you tell me about this?"

Your comprehension is enlarging, Henry. Note how many possibilities presented themselves to you. No longer is it a case of 'I know exactly what I'm doing.' As to the incident, Henry, many factors were at work, some of which you recognized. The traits of the 'wicked-eyed one,' which have been so successfully hidden under the positive attributes of your current lifetime, will, at times, manifest themselves. Another factor entering the incident was, as you suggested, lack of openness at the time it occurred. However, you were open later, and are open now to seize the lessons for yourself.

We would like to offer you our teaching as it pertains to anger, whether in self or in others. Our recommendation is: Silence in the presence of an angry person. We extend that to include yourself when anger's bonds attempt to enslave you. Silence is a powerful weapon. You have used it in many instances and found it ample. Words un-said are more easily repented of, as it were, than those sent out into the air. But this is not in any sense meant as a chastisement to you. Recognize only that your freedom tastes good to you and you are enjoying it. If you feel that way again, let it out, but understand what you are doing. In understanding there is enlightenment and relief from tension.

Freedom, freedom from the bonds of the past—how joyous it can be! Freedom, freedom from the pangs of guilt—how envious is that place of peace. Freedom, freedom from the chores of unfinished comprehension—how bright is the light of understanding.

You are tasting new-found powers, and like a child with a new toy, scarcely know how to handle it. In a sense, you are feeling the joy of liberation, and are aware of definite and perhaps perplexing personality changes. Just watch them, marvel at them, but also try to understand them. Therein is progress into a mature state of stability, true freedom, and advancement. I like your facing this incident so completely and so unbiased in attitude. Now it can really bring benefit to you, Henry.

The Friend's praise felt good to Henry. His efforts at self-analysis seemed to pay off in valuable insights, but it occurred to Henry that to feel even better, he needed to deal with his lingering anger toward his mother.

"Friend, how does one let go of a grudge? I think I have followed your reasoning quite well. I now realize that, in Wisdom, there is no room for blame, yet, I have many engrams connected with my mother. I still sense resentment akin to blame connected with her. I truly know that she did her best according to her enlightenment at the time, just as everyone does, but when I say I don't blame her, I mean it only at the intellectual level and not at the feeling level. I don't feel quite sincere about this, even though I have reasoned it out. I am saying one thing and feeling another—a good example of a divided self. I have reviewed my position several times and assured myself that I do not actually blame her, yet, when I am in her presence, I feel tense and annoyed, and I can become angry with her quite easily."

This is a rather delicate situation, Henry. Your reasoning about blame is so very correct. This entire matter hinges largely on the big subject of forgiveness. Notice again the strength of your good feeling when approaching this subject from its positive angle.

Forgiveness is one of the attributes of Wisdom. Recognize, momentarily, how much Wisdom overlooks that which is less than ultra in each of us. In patience, in consideration, Wisdom continues to permit even the very blasphemous to continue clenching its measly fist with self-importance. Wisdom tenderly nourishes even the tiniest spark of decency and openness that may flourish there. We depend on the strength of that gracious attribute of Wisdom more than we realize, because we all fall short of His glory. Even our best intentions are apt to be quite clumsy in view of the brightness of Wisdom, but His forgiveness encompasses so much. And, Henry, as you progress, you assume and acquire and develop those very qualities of brightness within yourself.

I would encourage you to immerse yourself more completely into the flow of Wisdom's generosity and, as you absorb the attribute of forgiveness, you will find many such annoyances dropping away.

Even with the Friend's encouraging words of a few nights ago, Henry and Emma found themselves in the midst of an argument. The girls clamored to go out for hamburgers, and Henry supported their idea, thinking that Emma might enjoy a night away from the kitchen. But Emma, not recognizing Henry's consideration, insisted on saving the expense by preparing dinner at home. Their diverging intentions put them at odds with one another. Both insisted on justifying their respective positions, while the complaints they aired against each other stirred their feelings even more. Eating dinner in silence, they avoided looking at the girls, who excused themselves without finishing their meal. In the bitter aftertaste of their mutual accusations, their feelings about each other reached the lowest ebb ever. Discouragement colored his every word, as Henry began the session with statements instead of his usual questions.

"Big turmoil today. It seems I'm not learning how to control this, but learning only how to have bigger differences in our home. There must be something basic that I don't understand."

The Friend responded with immediate reassurance and an explanation of the predicament.

You are concealing successfully from yourself the miles you have covered, Henry. I can see some landmarks behind you marked 'triumph.' For example, no longer ignoring your feelings, no longer avoiding company, the instrument you built—so you think you have made no progress? Shall I turn my other cheek for another slap? No progress! Worse, you say! Think rather on your accomplishments within, Henry.

Let me venture to say that, from my vantage point—and as of the moment it is more inclusive than yours—do hearken to the knowledge that you are gradually dropping the influence of the debilitating commands made to you, and you are stronger now than prior.

"I'm glad you think so, Friend, but tonight's disagreement left me feeling drained of my strength. I would like to believe you, but I feel my irritation even now."

Don't you think I know what I am talking about? I am continuing to perform a careful surveillance of data reaching you, but your calmness would, at this point, act as oil to the squeaking wheel. You tend to permit yourself to get excited too readily. I extend this precaution, lest the turmoils make too deep an impression, as you tend to sink so low.

Now, Emma. To you I have something to say: At times, your bothered, toiling, cheerless attitude is adding a burden, not releasing one. You sometimes grope about, find some thread to hang on to, and won't let go. Now, release yourself. You are hindering yourself, spreading perplexity to the girls, and certainly not helping Henry, as you may think. Pace your step to be with higher aspirations, instead of following that by-path you have chosen this time.

Now, both of you have mopped the floor with yourselves. It is time you rise above that sort of thing. You are to progress with grace, in harmony, with dignity, or you will ruin your chances to improve. Now think that over.

A long silence ensued. Henry finally spoke.

"You say that I'm gradually reducing the strength of the old commands. It seems that, as I uncovered these engrams, I should have done something more about them, but apparently I didn't, perhaps because of my lack of understanding."

Oh, I think I grasp your problem. Would it help if we state that we work together on this? But Henry, your part is essential as, in your realm of choice, you are allowed to obey the old commands, or to search for causes behind your actions and thereby not obey those commands or insufficient, misunderstood, or untimely parental teachings. Your mind-matter, as it exercises unused muscles, will find that clearly defined portions of this work are apparently done by helpers, others than just yourself, but you remain in control throughout the process. The same goes for Emma.

The Friend freely admitted to doing part of the work, but also affirmed the understanding that freedom of choice resided, at all times, with Henry and Emma. The reins of control remained in their own hands.

The couple had no problem making amends with each other after the session. Both felt chastised, but also forgiven. In the past, they would have hung on to their negative feelings for several days, only grudgingly releasing their hold on pride. This time, they felt the relief of not carrying over any murky emotional undertones into their attitudes toward each other.

Emma could see how her well-intentioned insistence on thrift perpetuated some of the oppressive feelings of poverty she had experienced in her childhood. Her parents taught her hard work and frugality. As the oldest of five children, Emma always had chores to do, in addition to taking care of her younger siblings. Her present life contrasted greatly with the life she had known earlier. Relieved by this realization, she turned to Henry and let him cradle her in his arms.

25

Openness

✶

Henry began the evening's session by expressing his curiosity as to the degree to which his life appeared transparent to the Friend. Although he liked the Friend's ability to understand his thoughts and feelings without having to verbalize them, Henry also felt uncomfortable having someone look so deeply into him. What else did the Friend see and not tell him about?

"Since we can communicate without speaking in words, I conclude that you can receive our questions and answers through our thoughts, and thus be in position to see any quirks in our thinking—for example, that we are clinging to ideas from the past, and things like that. I like to think I have an open mind, but I feel some embarrassment about how my problems may appear to you."

Openness is the basis, the very foundation of our avenue for reaching you directly. Witness how impossible our approach would be if openness was prevented by fear, or set ideas that demand only one possible method of learning and comprehension, or a stubborn refusal to acknowledge what exists when evidence indicates otherwise. Yes, openness must prevail, if growth is to occur.

As to our reading your thoughts, your ideas, consider again the vibration picture. When we are in tune with one another, and our vibrations throb together, as it were, true knowledge of thoughts exists. And note that we are aware of the thoughts behind the thoughts, the urges, the driving force, the basic foundation of your thoughts, while you, as yet, are not as well acquainted with yourself.

True, Henry did not know every motivation behind his actions or how much his behavior mirrored influences from his childhood and his karmic background. Henry's eyes opened to the observation that he and most of mankind seemed to unknowingly function on a sort of automatic pilot, a kind of waking sleep, blindly thrusting unrecognized assumptions at one another and the world. But the Friend challenged Henry's convictions and, having access to higher intelligence, endeavored to help him get better acquainted with himself.

"You seem to imply that I will become more aware of my driving urges at a later time, but as yet I do not know what they are."

Consider my 'as yet' statement very flexibly and not in the extreme. The fullness of 'as yet' continues in even greater force after the page is turned and you leave your present existence to start a new chapter in the higher realm. The aspect of time and space presents limitations in your sphere of operation, but you will become even more aware of your driving urges when you come to the other side.

You can acquaint yourself with yourself by observing the motivations which spur you to do those acts that you honestly are aware do not constitute ultra movements. Face your attitude squarely and let the clearness of day drive out the shadows of darkness. Thus you become cognizant of the driving force behind your conduct.

"Powerful stuff, Friend."

Henry realized that the ancient dictum "know thyself," worn to a cliché, hardly discloses the process of consciously delving into the deepest self, our divine origin. He couldn't help but wonder how many people really analyze their values beyond such trivia as the flavor of ice cream they prefer, or what they would do if their nickel got stuck in a vending machine. The call of Wisdom has echoed through millennia, but few have heard or responded.

It became clear to Henry that knowing oneself required a search for the authentic self, which meant hard work. It meant excavating the remembrances of times when you could not call "time out" or yell "foul!" It meant looking for shards of broken promises, removing mental silt from sunken hopes, and searching for remaining pieces of once whole and wholesome dreams. Henry could see that removing accumulated misevaluations and other emotional obstacles would allow a more direct communion with one's innermost self, that fraction of a fraction of Wisdom that resides within us all.

One other factor also enters the picture. As you have been told, Henry, your thought process is improving, and thus I am slightly more aware of the possible trend that you will follow in your thoughts, plans, and ideas. Your thoughts are following a more orderly, systematic pattern and, for you, a more beneficial track. Is this helpful?

Henry looked back at how his thoughts used to dart around in his head, and noticed that his thinking had become less disorganized in the months since he had acquainted himself with the wisdom offered by his otherworldly Friend.

Another real assist in our case, Henry, is that our consciousness mingled in our relationship during our Earth experience together. We readily find a common ground.

"Nice to have friends in high places," Henry said, but the Friend did not respond to his attempted humor.

Henry saw that his learning would stretch far beyond his

present existence on Earth. However, he felt no urgency to leave this realm. He wanted to understand his motivations, conquer the challenges awaiting him, and develop his gift of good thought influence.

"We were wondering if there is some mysterious quality about thoughts that isn't readily discernible to us. In other words, a thought's influence might not be visible, but its effects may be quite real."

Thoughts are a powerful, potent weapon. Yes, thought influence is a good way to term it, Henry. Vibrations go outward. You sometimes sense their force and will sense more as your sensitive response continues. Odor is almost perceptible, if poisonous thoughts are released. Great damage can be done, unless kindness governs the thought realm, too. Much could be said about this vast subject. Enlarge on the thought by yourself. The subject will come up again later.

The following evening, they picked up the theme where they had left off.

"It seems the vibrations you mentioned are one of Wisdom's principles. May we consider the vibration of thought as similar to radio waves? I was wondering if the frequency of thought vibrations could be measured with adequate instruments."

Get a fact-picture of vibrations and compare it to dropping a pebble in water, causing ever-widening circles. Yes, Creator's handiworks send out vibrations. Unleashing proper vibrations by choice releases into time-space ever-widening circles of influence.

Carefully consider the potential force of your inner

growth. All you touch will vibrate to new frequencies. The vibrations will progress outward and onward. Bear in mind that no strenuous effort is required, only calm, unhurried relaxation. Your influence is felt, even when no words are spoken or gestures made.

Measuring thought influence? Interesting. Perhaps someone will do it.

Henry had the notion of building a device with a proper sensor to register vibrations of thought, but in the light of the potential power of direct influence by his own thoughts, the idea of using extraneous equipment lost its appeal. A new sense of accountability now filled his being. He felt like a little boy who, while playing with his toy train, suddenly found himself at the controls of a real and powerful locomotive. He knew he needed to learn more to regain his level of comfort.

"I'd like to ask again about the art of good thought influence. I find it exceedingly difficult to detach myself to the point where I can say, 'Well, they see the problem in their own particular way and, unfortunately, it conflicts with my way of looking at it,' and from there to wish them goodwill."

Before I venture into the field of good thought influence, let me point out to you wherein your openness fails, as revealed in your comment. You say it is 'unfortunate' they do not see things as you do. Openness would say rather, 'Goody, another opinion with which I can compare mine, and learn something I did not know before.' This does not imply that as a result of examining another's point of view you should immediately change yours. Not at all. That's not the point. The point is: Learn to let go of judgment. Learn to say, 'Well, it could be,' and find no reason to defend your viewpoint.

Unless openness is there to hear your viewpoint when

you speak, what happens? You are simply wasting words, driving deeper within the other person his or her notion or idea, as mistaken as you think it might be.

Henry stood corrected. He felt he should have remembered the wise teachings that acceptance of another's point of view does not constitute condoning or agreement, and that propagandizing one's own views does not work either. The Friend often stressed the two points about individuality and choice.

Instead of becoming angry at himself for not having made the connection to the previously presented ideas, Henry decided to think in terms of having strengthened his current learning. Instead of condemning himself, he found himself practicing acceptance of himself without harsh judgment. That constituted remarkable progress for someone habitually demanding perfection from himself. Yet, his progress did not alter his wish to proceed cautiously in order to avoid making mistakes.

"Does good thought influence work in reverse? Can a person's vile thoughts bring harm to someone else? Thinking negatively could be dangerous, couldn't it?"

Well, it could, but there are several basic premises. For one thing, the power of good thought influence is much more powerful than a contrary power. Also, those most apt to exert negative power would seldom care enough about another, as their main focus would be on themselves, since their preoccupation is with self.

Another thing to consider is that the receiver of the contrary force would have to be open to it, or its effect would be lessened. Recognize that dangers exist, Henry, but are not troublesome as long as hatred and fear do not cleave a wedge for their entrance. You have a substantial portion of the power of good thought influence, Henry, and will find it continually increasing with use.

Henry felt reluctant to use his thoughts for influence. In spite of hints and encouragement from the Friend, he simply did not feel ready. He felt something holding him back, but could not identify it.

Transfer your thoughts away from the negative aspect. Emma intuitively understands that entertaining the existence of the power of bad thoughts at once starts their power working. It is well to understand that the negative exists, but there is no need to dwell on it. Again, be aware that good thought influence is more powerful than a contrary notion. Also, the basically profound fact remains that the good outweighs the bad as far as your possibilities of reaping results. Stack good on top of error, and error will get smothered at the bottom of the pile.

You have nicely shied away from depressing subjects, as you are aware, Henry. That's smothering the brute! It is likely that you need to remind yourself that authorities also confuse you by dwelling too strongly on detrimental aspects, rather than on the uplifting, inspiring aspects of thought. Proceed now in your testing of these basic concepts.

Henry felt he could not leave the subject without getting more clarification about the negative side of emotions.

"Judging from your comments, hatred and fear are the two emotions we should guard against the most. I suppose they exist because of lack of comprehension. Can we control these emotions with understanding?"

For the most part, feeling of inadequacy—the largely felt sense of lack—opens the door for entrance of both of these emotions. Their power lies in the intensity with which they force themselves upon you. A little fear, for instance, you can combat, but an intense amount can immobilize you completely.

Witness your fear in early years when loud thunder from heaven waved its fiery skirt of lightning across the sky. Now apply that to hatred. You would not hate or dislike, if there did not exist a feeling of lack or helplessness on your part. This may seem a little odd, but think about it, and you will understand.

Henry pondered the statement. People probably would not hate anything if it did not make them feel small and inadequate in the face of it. Yes, from time to time, everyone perceives deficiencies in themselves.

"When I feel something lacking in myself, don't those feelings result from engrams?"

We should enlarge on the subject of inadequacies, Henry. Perhaps I misled you. I meant to imply that in your youth you had a lack of understanding about lightning and thunder. There is a vast difference between so-called engrams and true felt inadequacies, as I think of them.

For example, take the emotion of fear. In you, fear was triggered in many different ways in the past. The light of comprehension has shed its beams into a few of the dark corners, and you have discovered that they were not as fearsome as you had supposed. Think how fear would vanish if, when perplexing events presented themselves, all, or most of the aspects of the problem were clear to you. Now, apply this to the other emotions you have.

"Could my feelings of lack interfere with my good thought influence?"

As you understand the basic teaching of good thought

influence, there will be no room for anything but goodwill. The same holds true of other emotions.

Where do feelings of lack originate? Only in lack of experience. And may I point out that hindrances, obstructions, engrams prevent experiences from ripening. All of that, capped with a lack of openness. If you will enlarge your thoughts in this field, it will become evident to you how the emotions of hatred and fear generate a poison that prevents the effectiveness of good thought influence.

You do well to ponder these thoughts deeply, Henry. There is much more than meets a casual glance, and we will again return to it at a later time. Suffice it to say now that your bag of experiences is piling high, and your capacity for good thought influence is continually expanding.

Thinking about his reluctance to exercise his God-given abilities, Henry discovered the very obstructions the Friend mentioned—a sense of inadequacy and a fear that he might send out vibrations contaminated by negative emotions. Painfully aware of the need to shake his negative engrams, Henry once again felt the cruelty of his perfection standard.

"You mentioned being kind to yourself as perhaps the most important of the tools in removing the adverse command phrases and misevaluations. I wonder if you can help me understand it better."

Kindness to self, in effect, commences good thought influence that works on you directly. Consider carefully how necessary it is to have assurance, instead of criticism, to consolidate your thoughts and ideas. Criticism creates a barrier that hinders clear thinking. Clever manipulation of the forceful tool of kindness to self is vastly real and serves to enlarge capacities, rather than stupefy and dull. Of course, undue and unwarranted assurance would also be a hindrance, but you do not happen to suffer from this ailment of emotion.

"I appreciate your kindness and your answer to my question. It was important for me to know that, so thank you for making me feel better."

Largely ask and largely receive. We delight in sending you our good thought influence. Knowing its power for good, can you blame us for wanting to show you the ways of it? That you accept and want to test it by your own actions brings us delight. Keep on keeping on, Henry.

"I certainly will. Thank you again."

26

Good Thought Influence

✴

The idea of sending out good thought influence fascinated Henry. Part of him rejoiced at the prospect of serving the greater good of humanity, but another part viewed the matter with caution despite the Friend's continued encouragement. Henry noticed once again that his perfection standard stood in the way of venturing into this new experience. Still, he wanted to build a solid foundation of knowledge before attempting to use his gift.

"I wonder if I understand thought influence as well as I should. The pebble in the pool is a good analogy, but would you care to elaborate?"

Thought influence is a mighty powerful tool. Take care to use thought influences that uplift, encourage, enlighten. It is very beneficial to others and to yourself, too. It bounces back to you in echoes that resound louder than the emitted 'sound.' Think about this matter, Henry, and recognize that a commenced thought influence widens out all around you. It triggers, as a response, a very tangible echo from an unexpected source, then collects and magnifies it. It is good that you dwell on this thought, Henry. Try it out!

"How would I know if and when my good thought influence worked?"

How would you know you are producing an effect? Much of it, Henry, is unconscious. You are mostly unaware of its outflow or effects.

Let's see. How else can we frame this? Did you know that you tuned into the vibration wave band that carried the inspiration for your carving just before the rays of understanding revealed it to you? No, but you did tune in. How do you know? Results—you executed your carvings. Similarly, you are largely unaware when you are handling the tool of good thought influence, but you can, at times, look at the results. They will prove the pudding has solidified into an edible custard.

Now, there is one aspect of good thought influence that we may not have adequately covered in our comments, and it is its force when intentionally directed. This you have not yet recognized, but try it sometimes and marvel at the results.

"A moment ago, Emma and I had a discussion about a friend of ours. Both of us had the urge to send our good thought influence to her. Does the length of time count? Or the intensity?"

Now you ask me for a method. Suppose I said two minutes, would you clock yourself? Can you measure your intensity? No, Henry, time and intensity are definitely immaterial. It is as if someone you know suddenly appears in your thoughts and you shed goodwill on their behalf. Your mind travels in memory through many incidents with that person. It may last a second, or an hour.

I will tell you something tremendous. Let's say someone surfaced in your thoughts due to a definite need on his part. If in your awareness of this individual you live again portions of the experiences that you have shared, you can, in this manner, alleviate the pressure of a past occurrence bearing its unwholesome effect on the individual's present life.

Your friend may suddenly feel a burst of easiness, which he may not even analyze. But you, although miles away, may have been the one to alleviate the condition.

As to the friend of yours, with you in your thoughts this evening, she is wavering on the brink of troublesome ordeals that will task her very sanity. She recognizes that something happened earlier tonight, but knows not what and may never know. But if you really wish to help, send a big dose of goodwill and good thought influence in her direction whenever you think of her.

Henry and Emma concluded that an appearance of any person in their thoughts may indicate that person's need for good thought influence. Henry now wondered if he could help someone in an emotional tailspin to regain equilibrium with his good thought influence.

"Can I help a person not to enter a negative pattern as it is developing?"

There is a way, but it is a different way for every individual, because the cause of the descending spiral is different each time. That is the difficulty with methods, with schemes, with hard and fast rules. One basic premise that I might mention is that no one can be forced out of a pattern against his will. Any 'forcing' sends the individual down the spiral even faster, as there is added to the original burden the need for defending his stand. It is a delicate undertaking to attempt to provide assistance to another, as seldom are we aware of the exact ingredients necessary to accomplish the expansion, the needed quantifying of consciousness within the individual.

Let me say this: One of the hardest things to do is to do nothing, but reserve to another their privilege of bumping, stumbling, bruising, and falling again. There is one unfailing weapon to use with extreme profit, and that is the powerful act of good thought influence: silent, but forceful; unseen, but felt; unobserved, but potent in its power.

A master of the art of good thought influence can accomplish more than the most eloquent elocutionist. But it cannot be learned by faking a sincere attitude, for the rays of understanding must genuinely enlighten your being to fully comprehend the situation and personalities involved. To the extent that unbiased, entire, complete goodwill is wished, to that extent will its results be powerful.

Feeling the Friend's consistent encouragement, Henry solidified his determination to practice his good thought influence. He sent mental messages of strength to people who might need it, thoughts of wisdom to a friend who had asked his advice, and thoughts of peacefulness into the general atmosphere in the event that anyone else could use them. Henry's attempts did not escape the Friend's observation.

Plainly and clearly is the concept of good thought influence forming within you, Henry. Yes, you reap benefits of good thoughts thrust outward. Your part in enlarging your honorable, pure, caring attitude, away from darkness, toward the light, is most certainly productive of enlightenment to all you contact with such thought influences. Here is a tool with which you can reach every corner of the world. Presence in physical form is not required to exert influence by thought. Relish the feeling of confidence that each individual plodding along has the capacity to reach out and influence others. This 'talent' is not limited to a select few. All may share in spreading the ever-widening circles of influence.

The Friend explained that only ignorance or rejection of this principle would prevent the benefits of its use. It so happened that in Henry the attribute of caring had reached a high level of development though several lifetimes. The Friend pointed out that anyone can develop or increase their power of good thought influence in their present lifetime.

There remains much for you to understand about this great subject, but it is imperative that the understanding of the foundational truth be instilled firmly. Continue your thoughts on this line, for amazing results will show themselves. You already sense a good many rebounds.

The comment about there remaining much to understand did not escape Henry, but he felt himself treading the right path.

"Do you mean my positive thoughts have already rebounded back to me?"

Rebounds actually become what one might call evidence of the existence of this principle. Thought influence, as we have discussed it, is one of the unvarying laws, rules, or principles that Wisdom has established.

Love extended is never lost. A loving attitude, sent out as a caring thought toward another, can have a healing, strengthening, and enlightening effect. Who has not felt the refreshing stimulation of meeting a good friend? It is a joyous, elevating feeling. One feels a little freer, a little better than before, in the presence of the friend's benevolent attitude. This principle works far and wide across any and all distances. Good thought influence travels to the intended one and makes him or her feel a bit lighter, a bit stronger, a bit more relaxed, although the person may not know from where the influx of the energy arrived. Good thought influence raises consciousness, as simple as that. To wish well to all you see or think about, to think good of them beyond their shortcomings is to wish them to learn that which is good. A sent out wish, 'May they learn,' contains a potent message.

Since wrong behaviors result primarily from not knowing any better, Henry now understood that wishing someone an increase in learning means sending them extra energy for their faster progress toward Wisdom. Even in the middle of a confrontation, mentally repeating the words "may you learn" can soften the ill feelings of either party involved. Sometimes the results may not appear immediately, but wishing someone well has a cumulative effect and triggers the assistance of ever-present positive energies.

✳

Henry awoke feeling unusually tired. That evening, the Friend explained that Henry had performed a helpful service during his sleep. What the Friend told Henry strained the limits of credibility. On that occasion, according to the Friend, Henry had physically appeared to a toddler abandoned by his parents. He lessened the child's trauma of desertion by providing reassurance, comfort, and a little amusement until other help arrived. According to the Friend, most of the required effort came from the other side, but Henry had depleted some of his physical energy in the process. The Friend assured Henry that his tiredness would soon pass, and it did. Once again, Henry had to make allowance in his understanding, this time a big one.

As time went on, the Friend continued to call on Henry for assistance. Sometimes situations arose when the high-frequency energy, on which the Friend operated, needed an attuned human intermediary to scale it down to a rate that others could more easily assimilate. Several more such incidents took place without Henry's awareness until the Friend told him about them. Emma kept shaking her head in wonderment, as information from the Friend about Henry's escapades flowed through her fingers onto the typed pages. She admitted to herself that her admiration for Henry grew with each new revelation of his activities.

With an unexpected knock on the door, Donald, one the few people whom Henry welcomed at any time, came for a visit. Donald's own source of information, his daughter, told him that three entities worked with Emma and Henry. This did not come as a surprise, since the couple had long suspected that the Friend had helpers. Not only the use of *we,* but also the variety of ways in which information reached Henry and Emma, indicated that the Friend did not operate alone. At the next opportunity, the couple satisfied their curiosity.

"Was the information from Donald substantially correct?" Henry asked.

You are aware now that visitations to you, and to all Earth children, take different forms at different times and stages of receptivity. You can be reached in many ways. You have witnessed visions in sleep, direct comprehension, word pictures, mental pictures, and events formulated or fashioned to depict the exact lessons you needed.

The chief concept you must learn is non-dependence on any one particular method of receiving information. Unbiased, undefined, unbounded openness, just plain openness—that is what must remain with you. Your delight in receiving is commendable, but reliance or dependence will act as a definite barrier between us.

Now, you heard your friend describe our set-up, as it were. This is how it appears to his source looking on into our territory of vibration. She amazes me with her accuracy. Indeed, influences are reaching you through three entities. But do not attempt to define too exactly or pretend to establish any type of control, or whoosh, away it will go! The strength of our communication is as strong as eternity, but hangs on a wire as thin as a spider's web. Relaxation, lack of tension, and your interested participation are essential from your end. From our end, we, in our element, cooperate, intertwine, and gladly contribute to our mutual benefit. Would you like to meet the others?

"Of course we would!" Henry responded with excitement.

As if at a simple social event, the Friend introduced the other participants in the transmissions.

Our engineer, who has so capably conducted the flow of charge, as it were, is a master of fashioning, but prefers to say few words. Our English translator busies himself with studying your language and acquainting himself with your terminology and interests. A great scholar, yours truly, you have met on previous occasions, oh, several delightful times, Henry. We are tuned in on a vibration wire direct to you. We find our source of data in a higher realm, as well as in the knowledge we possess by virtue of our position in relation to you.

Lean not, depend not, and our delightful group effort may, if Wisdom so dictates, continue. Profoundly fun, isn't it? Keep the channel open and in openness receive, but expect nothing exact. Receive only as presented to you. All this is for your interest and assistance.

Time to retire. Good night, you two.

Henry had momentarily raised his hand for a handshake and quickly put it down. Emma could not help but laugh at his reflexive gesture to clutch a nonexistent hand. She wistfully reminded him of his initial reluctance to communicate with their unusual source, but Henry's uncertainty had by now turned into a fond recollection of meeting the Invisible Friend.

The session ended abruptly, but Henry and Emma found themselves feeling energized. Meeting the other members of the team left them with an even greater sensation of close camaraderie. That night they went to bed chuckling about the bewilderment they had to overcome to reach the level of comfort they now felt in communing with the invisible realm.

27

Helping Others

✳

Ever since Henry heard it in his youth, the meaning of the Christian concept of carrying one another's burdens had eluded him. He tended to think of the concept in literal terms. From personal experience, he felt that he carried his own burdens all the time, and often someone else's as well, which struck him as an unbalanced deal. He remembered hearing it said or implied that relying on others to help you carry your load renders you vulnerable and indebted. Henry wanted to know the real meaning behind the words.

"Someone once told me that if I carry another's burden, it strengthens me and weakens the other. It doesn't sound quite right to me. Just thinking about it makes me feel tired, not strengthened. Can you enlighten me?"

Henry's understanding required refinement, which the Friend thoughtfully provided by preparing Henry to directly correlate the concept of helping others to his practice of good thought influence.

You are bordering on a very important phase of your existence. It is as if you sense a need for expansion so as to include other people, as if your consciousness is reaching out to unite with that element in another that links you both to Wisdom.

Seeing the other person as containing a piece of Wisdom, rather than focusing on a possibly distasteful ego or personality, struck Henry as an uplifting distinction.

You will find, in reaching out to others, that their degrees of comprehension will vary greatly. Be aware that many avenues of Wisdom are open to Earth children. Others might be reachable with an approach that would leave you cold and indifferent. You would find their interests dull or unenlightened from your point of view, but Wisdom includes all in His great scope of unity.

Henry felt himself climbing the ladder of understanding. The idea that individuals may have different understandings of the same truths struck him as a revelation. He knew that people sometimes confused truth with their personal opinions, but he had never considered the possibility of seeing the same thing from perspectives other than his own.

You may be fired up with desire to help, but unless you are prepared, you may be deeply grieved because of misunderstandings that may arise. You would do well to remember, Henry, that the subject of openness is of relatively recent acquaintance to you, and completely unfamiliar to many others. They may not be ready to grant you the generosity of openness you desire.

From your position of inner knowing, you greatly desire that your contacts result from the flow of ultra movements, not from sandpaper action rubbing edges off with less than ultra operation. As confidence replaces uncertainty, there is much you can do to assist other pieces of Wisdom to enlarge, to develop, to grow, to expand.

As if to issue a gentle forewarning, the Friend reminded Henry that his experience might include some exposure to incidents of a less than pleasant nature, and that lessons present themselves in this fashion as well.

It is the beginning of a sprouting growth period in you.

You need to see the basic concept correctly, so no injury to self, hurt feelings—or even worse, condemnation of self—could follow, if the pure light of understanding temporarily dims.

Your concept about carrying one another's burden is a proper concept, if applied in certain cases only. Opportunities to help another to help himself will come and are most beneficial. Those with flickering rays of consciousness may sometimes require the kind hand of sympathy to raise in tenderness by carrying another's burden, and doing it over and over, until sufficient enlightenment arrives for the weak one to find strength to help himself.

Henry wondered if he had he ability to discern between appropriately giving assistance and unwittingly encouraging laziness.

Much more will be said about the subject. Impress indelibly on your mind the basic pattern before we proceed into the deeper significance of bearing one another's burdens.

"I've had some qualms about trying to help people because of the possibility I might be hamming it up and taking on responsibility where I shouldn't."

It is well to ever regard Wisdom as interested in the progress of His own as housed in each person on Earth. As such, Wisdom would not direct another to your sphere unless you had to take part in the continuity of that soul's growth. Therefore, Henry, learn to relax in understanding that opportunity presenting itself also includes the capacity to handle the situation. You would not be expected by Wisdom to go beyond your capabilities. Also, pause to consider that you do not know what lessons need to be taught, or the form they need to take. What from your standpoint may appear as an awkward, clumsy gesture may be the necessary spark to inspire another. As you retain an open attitude, you will know what course is yours to take.

Henry soon had an opportunity to put his new lessons to use in his shop. His new helper, Mike, had an annoying habit of constantly seeking attention and praise for his work. Henry had not immediately recognized this situation as proper for an application of carrying another's burden.

"I can't complain about my new helper's outstanding workmanship, but something about him irks me, and I don't quite understand why. Could you give me a clue?"

Henry, he is more friend than foe to you. Like a child, he loves an audience to watch every step he makes. His craving makes him reach, reach for that audience.

As soon as the Friend began to explain Mike's behavior, Henry could see in Mike's adult form the naiveté of a child. He even felt amused by Mike's innocent mannerisms.

You are aware of the external aspects, but not quite so clearly aware of the driving urges behind the results. His attitudes irk you because within, you pretty much classify a showoff with mimickers, apers, and hypocrites. But Mike is not a hypocrite; he really feels that way. If you wish, your influence can benefit him, but not with a lash of name-calling or dismissal.

"How can I benefit him?"

Largely by understanding the driving force that leads your friend into one mix-up after another. If it becomes clear to you, Henry, you will then be in a position to drop a word here, another there, as opportunity presents itself; not with a zeal to conquer, not with a fervor to alter and change the man with your superior enlightenment, but with gentleness, kindness, patience, tenderness, and with the tool of good thought influence.

This particular relationship approaches very nearly an opportunity to assist with another's burden of incomprehension. It is well you decipher for yourself, most emphatically, that carrying his burden implies that you understand him better than he understands himself. Only as you shoulder, as it were, that element of comprehension unknown to him, and are able to gradually shed to him that understanding, in that manner only can your influence be of a generously helpful type.

Is it clear to you that, if your energies are spent in being irked, there would be no possibility of sending forth to him the benefit of your additional enlightenment?

This explanation threw an altogether different light on the situation. The burden of dealing with another person's naiveté, or perhaps ignorance, sounded like one of the main aspects of this helping principle. In contrast to lending strength and wisdom to another, the Friend highlighted the burden of dealing with people whose lack of understanding creates a variety of frictions, difficulties, and inconveniences for the one trying to help. Maintaining a positive attitude, coupled with the inability to share insight with a person who might react in a negative manner, can weigh heavily indeed, Henry reflected.

The same objective of not becoming irritated with another applies to carrying another's burden as well as to good thought influence. In an earlier silent conversation with Henry, the Friend had commented that good thought influence contained the essence of carrying another's burden. Or did it work the other way around? Either way, Henry could see how emotional energy handled improperly would take away from both good thought influence and his own peace of mind.

As to the method of actually presenting the rays of under-standing, consider for example the manner of approach your Invisible Friend has used in an effort to guide your feet though the many briars, poison oak, and nettles that we have together found lining your pathway. 'Go ye and do likewise.' But do not take this as a command, Henry, for it is not intended as such. It is to do only as you feel an urge to benefit, as you and your partner both trudge on your pathway Wisdomward. This is rather deep, Henry. Does the significance reach you?

It did, and it meant that the Friend, with superior knowledge of Henry's needs and misevaluations, had also followed the same principle with Henry, even while instructing Henry in its use. The Friend gently led Henry toward an awareness of his shortcomings, so he could see them clearly and, at his own pace, release them to the past. Henry could not recall or even imagine the Friend getting irked or impatient with him.

The general direction of the teachings clearly took a new turn. The Friend's tutelage, so far, had centered on helping Henry and Emma divest themselves of their negative programming, but now the Friend began to offer advice on how to use what they had learned for the benefit of others. The two eager students felt as if they had reached a certain stage of completion, which elated them, but also made them more keenly aware of the new level of responsibility they carried.

28

Urges and Desires

✳

God will provide. Emma had heard that expression frequently in her youth, although no one seemed to take it seriously. Then she met a woman, Gerry, who shared a modest apartment with their artist friend, John. Gerry actually lived by that belief. Time and again, she found herself miraculously relieved of her financial predicaments. Emma marveled at Gerry's faith and suggested that Henry ask the Friend about it.

"Good evening, Friend. We were just talking about Gerry's actions and attitude. She seems to live very precariously, and just assumes she will be provided for at the last moment. Emma was wondering if there is some conditional principle operating—if you do such and such, then you'll be taken care of."

The conditional principle you speak of operates within the territory of urges, apart and distinct from desires of the ego.

"These urges you mention sound like intuition to me. She must really know how to tune in on them. Would it help us to know how she does it?"

Frankly, no two persons' urges are identical, although there may be some resemblances. That's why your psychologists must write books upon books, volumes upon volumes, and still miss covering the important picture.

Now, Gerry's urge is vastly different from her companion's urges. She is aware that the circumstances of cashing the check from her uncle, for instance, would have been inappropriate for John, but for her, it was the thing to do. Her operating on the edge of financial precariousness is for a different reason than for your artist friend. They wrestle in one particular sphere, but Gerry wanders on the edge of nothingness for a different reason.

In her case, she is heading into a territory of liberating her consciousness from worry, for the worries stifled her last appearance on Earth. She needs to learn release from worries and she is doing it successfully. Of course, her openness and expansion do not include mastery of other problems that beset her, but her progress has been remarkable. She is definitely on her way. John, too, shines as an example of apparent progress, and his influence, or sandpapering of Gerry, is going beautifully. So much for that.

The Friend obviously did not want to intrude into private territory beyond what the couple already knew and what served as an example for the purpose of teaching.

The principle in question highlighted an important issue that had to do with whether one followed desires of the ego or the urges of inward consciousness. As Henry and Emma understood it, the distinction seemed to consist of following the gentle prompting of an inner voice that points the way to expansion of consciousness, as compared to chasing elusive satisfactions by pursuing a never-ending string of desires, usually based on misevaluations. From this vantage point, they realized that they would fare best listening to the fleeting urges of higher consciousness, which subtly guide actions for the greater benefit of one's spiritual progress.

Henry wanted to know more about the nature of desires.

"I can think of one or two reasons to not be in a desirous mode. If I can understand better how desires are not good for me, then maybe I can moderate them. This matter could very well use some of your special brand of enlightenment."

Desires, generally speaking, are based on premises that do not contain the aspect of Wisdom's seal of approval, shall I say. An example would be your desire to stay away from too much company. We both recognize that this whole area was quite badly tampered with in you. As a result, you came early to an erroneous conclusion. So, there is a misevaluation based on early rushes of energy from introducing you to company when you were not ready to make their acquaintance. You were so proudly shown off, but to you this action violated the understanding of your needs and definitely did not lend you strength.

Henry remembered his discomfort as a child, when he had once found himself the center of attention of a large number of adults at a church gathering. He did not understand their remarks about his appearance, nor their expectations of him. He wanted to run away, but knew it would get him in trouble. He turned to bury his face in his mother's dress, but his obvious sensitivity and feelings of discomfort brought only hilarity. Thus, his *desire* to retreat and hide took a firm root and persisted far into adulthood.

So now—with the exception of your select loyalty group and your curiosity about those far away in foreign lands—those in between hold no interest to you. You desire that they keep their distance. Now, for the moment-to-moment aspect to truly expand within your being, that particular area must be leveled and smoothed, and these undue emotions brought into the focus of understanding. All the proper tangents need to be covered. I chose this example of an undesirable desire because we have already worked on it considerably. Build on this premise, on this thought, for ample learning.

The example rang true for Henry. He could see how some of his desires, because of his various experiences, had lodged themselves in his thoughts and feelings.

Now, that is one type of desire—the desire not to want. Then, of course, there is the desire of wanting. The main objection here is that, even should the want be granted, therein would be no settling back into moment-to-moment attitude, but rather a new want would soon replace it. For, strangely enough, the Earth atmosphere does not contain sufficient spiritual oxygen to fill your spiritual lungs. Ever there is the shortness of breath feeling, of 'not quite enough,' the 'unrest beneath'—so then, why cherish such desires?

The Friend dismissed the desires of want in an easy, offhand manner, whereas Henry just then realized that his desires motivated most of his actions, almost as if he lived *for* his desires. He tried to focus his attention into the moment, wishing to minimize the sudden confusion he felt.

The Friend continued.

There are desires of yet another kind, and I am now thinking of desires to receive from other pieces of Wisdom homage, respect, acclaim, renown. This is more general than you think, and is contained not only in the so-called lead horses pulling the wagon. Again, this is largely of no concern to you, Henry, for you do not desire such.

"You know me well, Friend," Henry interjected.

You correctly comprehended my thought about the urges and that they are different from desires. But how to conquer these desires? How to lay them down? How to rise above their command value? One obvious first step is to recognize the futility of claiming them, for, as you can understand and recognize that they form but a mirage, then no longer is there the pull toward them.

Easier said than done, Henry thought. To understand that desires have no greater reality than illusions could present a bewildering challenge to many people. The Friend's teaching aimed at gently puncturing any inflated fantasies of attaining happiness by satisfying desires. Henry realized that living by desires sidestepped listening to the urges of a higher order.

Your consciousness, when allowed to portray its wishes, will draw to you experiences, understandings, towering problems or massive undertakings, elegant conditions, quiet reposes or mingling with the masses, according to need. But these experiences will not be forced, strained, nor stubbornly fixed, but will naturally transpire in the fullness of time. Now, don't get the idea that these experiences imply a ridiculous, frenzied, spinning type of pace, or the opposite, inactive type of living. It is rather a serene, calm, dignified, poised, quiet, refined, positive type of living. Oh, in some cases the events may be anything but serene; they may be full of bluster, but I speak of the inward state of being. Do you wish to ask more specifically, Henry?

"When I look at my motivations, I see a gray area where I can't differentiate between my urges and desires."

With desires, you feel compelled to handle, to adopt, to condition, to manipulate matters in your own manner, according to your own wishes. If you find yourself wanting something to be 'just this way' and no other way is acceptable, no other way is comfortable, no other way is quite right—that, Henry, will be the red light that signals to stop and consider before barging forward. The green light of 'go' from urges of consciousness contains the feeling of peace, of contentment, of 'I am glad it's this way, but if it were otherwise, that's fine, too.' Another hint is that fulfilling an urge grows into more contentment, while a desire adds frustration and confusion to your inward being.

Now, Henry, these clues must be looked for within, not necessarily in the outward condition of things. For instance, I will return to your issue regarding company again. Although it is still causing considerable annoyance in your soul, for the sake of clarification, think of it thus: When your desire for fewer visitors fades away by probing, probing, probing, far, far into the basic root, then your attitude about it will shift toward openness. Then, if your consciousness urges such contacts, you will find yourself most keenly interested, most alertly concerned, most delightfully amused, and most graciously mingling with your company. To all outward appearances, it would look as if a lot of confusion had been added—more noise, more mess, more broken dishes, more spilled beverages. But, it is the inward state of being that is the place to seek clues for the actual condition. Is this any clearer?

"Your comments help to clear up the matter. However, before pursuing these thoughts any further, I feel I should test it for a while."

Let me hasten to congratulate you, Henry, on your quickness to perceive that it is well to action-test these profound teachings, else they will escape from your awareness.

A few days later, Henry returned to the issue of urges and desires. The Friend obliged with additional explanations.

"I have found that I desire good things for myself and other people. Now, is that bad?"

An alert attention, a true listening to the urges of con-
sciousness, will permit, attract, and open up the necessary
field of activity to be traversed. A forcing of interest could
result in a detour, a sideline trip away from the best pos-
sible path to be traveled.

'Straight is the way and narrow the gate, and few there
be that find it.' Do you recognize the importance of that
'timed to interest' formula? Consciousness attracts to itself,
if permitted to do so, those experiences that will best awaken
and those experiences that enlarge.

At the mention of straight and narrow, Henry remembered
to ask a question he had about it, suspecting that religious
institutions might have distorted the meaning in the same
way they did the idea of faith. Henry followed the emerging
sentences intently as the gentle clacking of the typewriter
resumed.

The teachings of Christ were often veiled, and purposely
so. Those who explained them later also stamped their own
interpretation of them. 'Thus said the Lord' became 'Thus
said the interpreters,' and many people, many individual
pieces of Wisdom, went to sleep, for no further individual
activity or seeking was encouraged.

It became stylish too have an answer to every inquiry,
and a standard one, always acceptable, was: 'Here is a
book of rules. Do this and you will be all right.' Thus form,
method, and dead role-playing took the place of the vital-
ized newness of which Christ spoke. Herein is the picture
of the downward trend of the church, but ever there have
been individuals within its confines, within its borders, who

remained open and refused to be lulled into false sleep and
indifference. Yes, the narrow way came to mean a narrow-
minded way.

The narrow way means a universal way, in which the
advancement by individual pieces of consciousness is con-
fined to a relatively narrow field of 'urges' of consciousness
that, properly followed, lead to the fullness of life.

The Friend once again gave an explanation that did away
with dogmatic and authoritarian points of view. Henry and
Emma wondered how many other misconceptions would fall
away with the help of their new understanding.

29

Consciousness

✴

It occurred to Emma and Henry that they did not know what the term "consciousness" actually meant. The dictionary definition, "knowledge of what is happening around one," did not satisfy them. The couple understood the idea of expanding consciousness, frequently referred to by the Friend as the process of "quantitying," as an increasing awareness on the part of individuals, but a better understanding of what constituted consciousness seemed to require deeper explanation.

"For some time now, I have been meaning to ask about the attributes of consciousness. I know a few, but I imagine there are more of which I am not aware."

Consciousness is bigger than the universe you know. The experience of your universe is only a part of the quantitying of consciousness.

All consciousness is one, just as all wind is air, for wind is air in particular manifestation. Or as all ocean is water, but water in a form of manifestation. Or as all clouds are water, but in a form of manifestation separate from the ocean. So is all consciousness, whether it be manifested as the little plant by the side of the road, or the buzzing bee that drinks its nectar, or the giant mountain with its flowing slopes and jagged pinnacles, or the blooming trees—all are consciousness, but in different forms of manifestation. To man has been added the tool of choice, reserved to no other form of creation which you recognize on Earth.

Consciousness, as you are aware, we have also referred to as Wisdom's piece of Wisdom. As such, consciousness has the potential power to display every attribute of Wisdom, for within the human form are embodied the possibilities of expansion into the revelation of great attributes now unknown.

The tendency of the Earth people is not to claim for themselves those attributes to which they are entitled by virtue of being a container of Wisdom's piece of Wisdom. You live below your privileges, below your capabilities, below your capacity. You Earth people recognize not the force of the attributes to which you could lay claim, or, if someone does recognize some such facet, openness stops, a shrine is built, and one enlarges on the new 'find' to the exclusion of further and mightier attributes.

Now, occasionally, someone glimpses the possibilities, 'forgets' the limitation assigned to your sphere of time and space, and would, in great delight, 'show everybody' what force he can produce. There are many pitfalls in the way, but no need to misunderstand the fact that attributes, as you recognize, are many, and using them will bring recognition to you.

"These attributes that we don't lay claim to—I am assuming an attribute is something like the good thought influence that you say I have. Is that also considered an attribute?"

Yes, verily, and so is consideration for others, kindness, generosity (and that implies much more than giving), understanding, comprehension, honesty, uprightness, sympathy, tenderness, manifested love—these are some, and you will think of others. Then there are some not so obvious, not so clearly recognized. A good example of that is your strong attribute of good thought influence. Others might include

an enlargement of the 'carry one another's burdens' prem-
ise, and that is a large field of activity. Others would include
the healing touch, as well as power over nature.

This, however, is a territory which needs much instruc-
tion, and I would prefer that you leave the matter open
and contain the information to yourself for the time being.
To excite some individuals to a knowledge of their powers
without a solid background of experience is like handing
a sharp knife to an unlettered child—it isn't safe to do.
Many such powers are not in evidence because the immedi-
ate need for using them is not in the fore. There is no waste
in the economy of heaven.

You have a great deal of information presented to you
tonight, so best you digest it and make it your own by com-
prehension. Good night.

"Thank you very much for your efforts this evening. At times
I feel it superfluous to thank you, as we feel you know every
thought we have."

Appreciation makes it possible for us to continue.

"In that case, please accept our heartfelt gratitude."

Henry and Emma read a book about the uses of light and
sound for healing purposes. They wondered if they could
learn these healing techniques, but approached the subject
with much hesitation. Having had a taste in her childhood
of people reacting adversely to the unconventional, Emma
reminded Henry that one can become stigmatized by those
who cling to dogmas and prefer to insulate themselves from
unfamiliar ideas. Henry agreed that they needed to carefully

contemplate the social ramifications of such activities. Realizing that they needed much more knowledge should they ever want to "claim" such an attribute, they began their next session with a basic question.

"You presented us with the concepts of a few new attributes in our last session. Do you mean to say that a new idea can grow when we begin to action-test it?"

Observe a seed. Enfolded therein is the secret of the universe, for consciousness expands as, and if, it is fed with experiences from which truth, honesty, love, tender kindness, unselfishness, harmony, peace, and great balance with all its implications are garnered—that is your privilege on Earth—and to be gathered, you will note, by experiencing. These experiences are found along the pathways of life, and are present precisely as the need of consciousness dictates, and in the exact circumstances in which each individual human manifestation finds itself.

"Can you describe the process of how the seeds of new thinking grow?"

Concepts, Henry, are not separate and distinct forms reaching awareness. For the most part, concepts are built on many, many previously understood facts. Without an adequate foundation of functional factors on which to hang new concepts, such new concepts might be largely inoperative as mental muscle builders. Especially when openness is present, there is a continual production of new concepts, and many at the same time. Then, suddenly, often when the final enlightenment or illumination reaches the awareness level, it truly feels new. But, Henry, in the background, on the unaware, unconscious level, much has gone on, much experience, testing, thought, and preparation.

I am going to liken the process to a telephone system. Suppose you desire a word with a gent in New York. Before your dial systems were refined, it was necessary for an operator to connect with another, that another with still a third, and so on, across the map. Finally, in due process, the phone in New York rings, and your party is made aware that you, in California, wish a word with him. Now, insofar as the New York gent is concerned, his activity of receiving the call (contacting new comprehension) starts when the phone rings. But, preliminary work (on the unaware level) has gone on before his phone rang.

Incidentally, here is a good place to incorporate a picture story of your psychological hindrances. These hindrances can make completion of the receipt of new comprehension either hard to hear due to poor connection, or impossible to hear by preventing the connection entirely. The analogy is not to be taken too literally, because in receiving new concepts, a more active part is played by an individual. The seed-thoughts, or basic concepts, are introduced and built upon by you, mainly in the attitude of openness, and may consist of observations, reading, sensations, previous conclusions, and as the new thought-seed finds its fit, its readied place, a new concept reaches your awareness. It is there, if you need it.

"I wonder about consciousness. Does it retain identity after we die? All this seems so strange."

It need not be strange, Henry. Yes, recognizable traits of character are retained in a manner that is difficult to convey. We recognize others by their unique patterns of vibrations.

Identity? Well, in our sphere, it is vastly different; however, we recognize the shell of the human form which housed us when we were in your stratum of operation. This is clearly decipherable to the far advanced, but do not expect complete understanding so long as time and space limit.

Remember this: Consciousness is revealed in manifestation. That is its cloak. You are familiar with the manifestation of consciousness on Earth as male and female. Its counterpart exists in our realm, but not in the same way as you know it, even as a tree exists not in the same manner as you know it, or a stone, or a dog. Individuality remains, as well as the 'remembrance' of the human form in which an appearance was made on the Earth sphere.

It is thus we 'clothe' ourselves in order to reach you. I am Wu Li Tsung because I was embodied in that form of manifestation when we met on Earth. But my form is now different, for the body which I once carried now lies in the dust of the mountainside, long since changed in fashion. However, the impression I made on time's page remains, and I glance thereat to find the clue that enables understanding to pass between us now.

"Some time ago, you mentioned that your consciousness can mingle with ours. I was wondering about how consciousness mingles. Is this how we advance toward absorption into Wisdom?"

Mingling is accomplished in many ways and in different degrees. You have experienced it to an extent, and will probably experience many more delightful visitations. How it is done differs greatly.

"It seems to me I received a direct comprehension today, rather than words. It went something like this: 'Old people are sometimes noticed talking to themselves. Instead, it is rather a conversation with beings from your realm.' Does this sound as if it came through properly?"

This is another manifestation of Wisdom's visitation to you. Thoughts can come through complete, without the hindering element of words. Actually, this is one of the most orderly manners of communication, as it is free and unhampered.

The general premise is that the aged ones are closer to our realm than supposed. Sometimes only a slight change in the volume of breath transfers to our realm. Hence comes the notion that they live entirely in the past. More nearly, one can say that they live in the future state, part of the time, as they are gradually absorbed into this realm. How nicely your definitions of relationship are shaping into a constructive whole, Henry.

"I just had a thought—when Emma and I are in perfect agreement, as we frequently are now, is it possible that our pieces of Wisdom are commingling and thus becoming more powerful to receive?"

You are reaching out for solid food, Henry. That is good. Did you recognize how substantial this thought was? You are growing out of the 'mush' class. This is what I implied when I suggested to you that your thought process is developing. You are beginning to walk, not crawl. In stature, that is, in spiritual stature, you are progressing Wisdomward. Pleasant sensation, isn't it? Oh, there will be setbacks, but don't let that alarm you. The main thrust is Wisdomward, of that you may assure yourself right now.

The growth felt quite real to both Henry and Emma. They had fewer disagreements, and the fact that they had something very special to absorb their interest greatly benefited their relationship. They both felt elevated above their work-day world and looked forward to their evening sessions with insatiable curiosity.

The couple had a rudimentary understanding of various Eastern philosophies. The notion of reimbodiment as a snake or a gnat as punishment for one's misdeeds sounded to them like another authoritarian admonition, but the idea of going backwards on the evolutionary scale captured their interest.

"We know that we can progress upward though the realms, but is it true that we can also devolve downward from where we are presently?"

Correct to a degree, Henry. Keep ever in mind the power-fully massive and inclusive thought of eventual absorption into Wisdom. Consciousness cannot be destroyed. Its form may alter, but consciousness remains.

Let me present a picture of fact to illustrate. It is as if Wisdom hands out a box. You can open the box, utilize its contents, or disregard it and trample it in mud. A mishan-dled box would bear scars that must be removed sooner or later. By your power of choice, you determine in what shape that box—that portion of consciousness—returns for future embodiment. Is it apparent why we yearn to see you carefully nurture, care for, and properly utilize your portion of consciousness?

The Friend emphasized the need to value consciousness and confirmed their understanding that current behavior affects future lifetimes.

"Of course I will take care not to trample my box, but what about the damage it receives unintentionally?"

The understanding is limited at times because of 'black-outs' created by incidents and conditions that make correct evaluation of some situations impossible.

Now, consciousness draws to itself those experiences, those lessons, those particular situations that will enlarge and intensify existing attributes, as well as introduce the missing elements, as it were. Thus, you sense the sum total of past lives, in a way, and call them tendencies.

In the progress of consciousness, if moment-to-moment living is chosen by the Earth person, if openness rules, those very experiences which are required will be attracted by a sort of magnetic compulsion, and consciousness develops. However, if too many misevaluations are 'too well learned' and the urge of consciousness is completely smothered by thunderous and demanding desires, progress is brought to a snail's pace.

The expression "too well learned" seemed to apply very well to misevaluations. It accurately pinpointed the reason for the deeply ingrained patterns of behavior that resisted change. Henry felt his psychological education increasing with every statement from the Friend, as he continued to expand his knowledge.

"There's another thing I want to ask about. I have heard and read that when someone is drowning, falling, or whenever death confronts them suddenly, that their whole life flashes before them in that instant. I was wondering if that is true, and if you could tell us why it happens."

The basic idea is a temporary transfer to the timeless condition. It is as if they already 'stepped over' with part of their being and sensed escape from the binding element of time.

"That's very interesting."

Actually, very elementary, Henry, when viewed from this realm.

Henry thought about it for a while longer. Events must have a very different texture on the other side. He wondered how things looked to the Friend.

"It seems as if eternity limits our ability to experience events that exist in time. Perhaps that it why we reenter time, coming back to Earth to correct our past obligations. Am I coming close?"

Strange how you approach this subject, Henry. Generally, it is regarded that time is the limiting factor, not eternity. But I grasp your point. I will try to explain this difficult to explain condition in our realm: Remorse and regret, as such, do not exist, but the counterpart is an opportunity to influence those on your realm as a method to 'quality' our consciousness. Hence our delight in awareness-awakening in you, for example. Witness the ease of communication. Carefully following Wisdom's dictates graduates consciousness, as it were.

Emma saw the puzzled look on Henry's face and ventured an interpretation.

"I think the Friend means that here, we *add* consciousness, and there, they polish or refine it."

"I think that two consciousnesses have 'quantitied' quite a bit this evening," Henry replied playfully.

Consciousness is ever learning, and a portion of such learning is the very 'harnessing,' the orienting of the individual manifestation into a position of response to the universe. For consciousness, by its presence, also in a way teaches, but ever permits choice to remain in the hands of the individual.

Ours is the plea to accept all that comes, knowing that whatever Wisdom hands out in the process of a lifetime, is intended to be the best opportunity for consciousness to expand.

Impressed with the explanations, Emma voiced her respect for the way the Friend approached the difficult subject of consciousness. Henry concurred, and added that he admired the Friend's ability to state in just a few words such basic principles as acceptance and trust in the plans of Wisdom. They closed the session accepting that the higher function and purpose of the hardships and joys they encountered remained largely beyond their current comprehension, but they knew that the appropriate opportunities for their growth toward spiritual maturity surrounded them daily.

30

All is Good in Process

＊

Before the beginning of a school year, the family usually took a long vacation, visiting national monuments and taking in the sights of natural wonders. Their journeys proved educational for the girls, and allowed everyone to break old patterns while enjoying a change of pace. This particular trip stood out as an exciting time for the whole family. Henry and Emma had little chance to record their conversations with the Friend; however, they received occasional quiet suggestions where to stop, where to eat, or which roadside attractions to visit. Above all, they felt convinced that the Friend surrounded them with special vibrations of happiness.

On their return home, Henry and Emma expressed their appreciation for what they perceived as loving treatment from the Friend.

"We were aware of that unusual energy you sent us during our vacation; it made all of us feel so good! One or two slightly difficult times cleared up quickly and we were able to enjoy our children and our vacation so much more than we ever did. I consider that something very special."

Something special? Did you know, Henry, that the turmoils, the upsets, the twinged, unsettled feelings — they should be the ones that belong in a special class?

Are you aware that your joyousness, your exuberance, your aliveness — that is the feeling of moment-to-moment living? Are you aware that the broken strands of the peaceful existence are the strings pointing to that which prevents its continuation?

You are proceeding fast toward the place of freedom from the effects of the past, Henry. Then life can really begin for you! Then your growth can enlarge into reality, into a vastness, which you only partly fathom. The hindrances are noisy elements: they prevent the silences of comprehension, of understanding, of peaceful existence to shine forth.

Do we give you this special feeling? It is more nearly that you take it, Henry, you accept it, you partake of it, you revel in it. Again, that is part of your heritage, your privilege, your accomplishment. Understanding its importance will enable the continued expansion of consciousness in a fashion that will surprise you.

In the corridors of our realm, we feel the throb of activity, of progress, an urging onward. It is good, it is energizing, it is uplifting. The dewdrops of Wisdom's abundance may be felt directly within your beings, Henry and Emma. The vibrations of the sounds of plucked strings, the echo of the music awakens within you the exuberance of rejoicing. Good you remain open, ever open to Wisdom.

Emphasis on his active part in experiencing good feelings produced a delightful result: Henry more deeply understood the meaning of freedom of choice. He and Emma *chose* to have an enjoyable vacation; they both *chose* to avoid escalation of irritations into problems, and they *chose* to resolve tensions amicably and lovingly. They maintained harmony without even making a special effort to do so. A loving attitude carried them through their potential difficulties.

After their vacation, a new class of communication arrived through Emma's fingers, given as a broadcast to humanity in general, instead of individually tailored tutorials and counsel for the couple. In their efforts to help satisfy mankind's unstated need to advance in wisdom, benevolent entities continuously beam uplifting messages and inspirations into "the ethers." Ever growing numbers of people consciously receive such communications and cooperate with the efforts of those on the other side. Others spontaneously absorb these "ether messages" directly into their subconscious and continue on their way without recognizing or crediting the source.

When openness to spiritual values prevails in one's way of thinking, familiarity may begin to accrue, which allows for recognition and comprehension of higher values at a later time. With conscious cooperation, anyone can better receive these broadcasts by developing sensitivity and trust in impressions that may at times challenge conventions of the rational mind. Few have cultivated the personal transparency necessary to consciously capture this type of telepathic transmission accurately enough for written presentation, yet Wisdom remains available at all times to anyone open and willing to receive the higher inspiration.

The Friend dictated to Emma this next message, which highlights the importance of the conscious use of enlightened choice. It explains that humans do not come to Earth to *judge* anything as good or evil, but to *choose* amongst available options. The importance of the distinction between judging and choosing escapes many, yet the purpose of human life centers on precisely this premise—*the use of the divine gift of choice.*

It is in the realm of negative and positive that humans choose. Their experiences and their learning are then contained in the sphere of their choices.

If humans will only recognize that the entire environment and the entire world are constituted from their own attitudes and their own choices, the result can be an inward change, and the world about them can change as well. No matter what the conditions of the world, a human being, as an individualized part—an individual within the world's confines—can live apart from any of the turmoil and difficulties that others may choose. The individual can still retain inwardly an indefinable and undisturbed peace.

Does this deny the existence of that which is not perfect? Of course not. But one sees all, both that which occurs to the individual and that which happens to others, as the result of choices. The ultimate result of these choices is good; it is the process that is difficult. It is the interim, the interval of unfinished learning that has the pain, and the discomfort, and the confusion, and unrest. Understanding this fully and knowing its full implication as a truth will change the outlook and the inlook of the human.

Learn one will, whether one chooses the negative or the positive. The end result of the choices and of experiences spells progress or lack of progress, the development or lack of development, the slowness or the speed with which one spiritually and inwardly grows. In the final analysis, it is all good. But Earth experiences and Earth choices are the process by which that good is brought about.

One's own life pattern, that for which one came to Earth, may indeed involve contact with that which is called negative in one's own sphere of progress. It may touch the physical form, the mental world, even the emotional existence, for one may have within that which needs to be refined by the very interaction with the negative.

But seek not beyond your own life pattern for the negative. Stay in the positive. Only as it is necessary will the experience come to you that will bring about the progress you need as an individual. It will not and need not in any

*sense disturb the inwardness, that basic peace, the content-
ment that knows that all is good in process.*

While reading the message, Henry and Emma saw clearly
that no matter which lessons one has yet to learn, the great
need for inner peace supersedes all other psychic needs. The
knowledge that *all is good in process* can help us attain this
inner peace, especially if we can keep our minds open to the
designs of Wisdom and assistance from Invisible Friends.

✴

Some Additional Notes

✳

Henry and Emma's conversations with the Invisible Friend continued for nearly fifty years. Much valuable information came their way in almost daily conversations with the Friend and through the "ether messages" mentioned in the last chapter. Henry passed on to the other side in 1999, while Emma remains in contact with the same Source at the time of this writing.

Spiritual wisdom requires considerable time for its absorption. One cannot condense profound spiritual knowledge into a short course, nor can one force this knowledge on someone not ready to partake of higher wisdom. The Friend delivered these teachings in small amounts, usually waiting until the subject appeared "timed to interest" to Henry and Emma, thereby greatly facilitating their process of learning.

Thanks to the remarkable guidance of the Invisible Friend, the couple's lives took on a seldom-encountered quality. They discovered talents they never thought they had and became creative in ways they had never expected or imagined. Over the years, Emma widely shared her ability to communicate with the Friend and transmitted helpful messages to those in need of spiritual advice. Henry produced many carvings and paintings. He also built a harpsichord, several guitars, and devised unique bench-top printing presses. Together, Henry and Emma hand printed several books with manually assembled type. The books, of course, featured messages received from the Invisible Friend. Their home came to resemble an art gallery displaying a wide assortment of Asian antiques and Henry's remarkable handiwork.

Two of Henry's carvings carry a special value. Henry felt an unseen hand guiding his movements as he fashioned them. They represent the Old and the New Testaments in the light of a new understanding possible at this time because of humanity's increasing capacity to comprehend them. The Friend later outlined the meaning of the symbols contained in these two carvings and offered surprising new knowledge about Christ and His mission. We hope to soon publish this divinely revealed material, as it sheds light on the purpose of the two Testaments not previously available. The knowledge offered in *Invisible Friend* can serve as a background against which to view these new revelations.

✳

Once awakened, the hunger for Wisdom grows. Increasing numbers of people commune with invisible entities or feel their presence. As we progress in our evolution, a growing sense of closeness to our divine origin unfolds in our awareness. Our present state of development now enables a greater number of individuals to consciously turn their attention to spiritual matters.

Recent developments in the field of physics have presented us with the concept of *nonlocality,* introducing into mainstream thought the existence of dimensions beyond time and space. Although difficult to understand, these findings open the door to contemplation of subtle superior forces on higher planes of existence. Scientists at the forefront of knowledge have long realized that great intelligence seems to manifest in every aspect of the known universe. They inform us that energies, which we cannot yet properly measure or understand, permeate our entire existence.

Conditioned to the physical plane of life, we naturally tend to seek proof of other dimensions by expecting them to manifest in physical form to our physical senses. Also, most of us have a general tendency to look for answers outside of ourselves. Those captured in the wonderment of UFOs, crop circles, psychokinesis, and the like, would do well to also ask themselves if they may have underestimated the treasures contained within their own inner domain.

Along with our natural eagerness to understand the larger universe, we have an urgent need to get to know ourselves and our fellow human beings. We need to clearly recognize our own level of functioning, and the level of development of others, so we can understand human activities and their consequences in this difficult age of transition. The following brief overview of evolutionary steps may help place the story you just read, as well as ourselves, into perspective.

The development of human potential proceeds largely along the sequential stages of physical, emotional, mental, and spiritual unfolding. These overlapping developmental stages of humanity as a whole follow one another in a manner analogous to the gradual unfolding of capacities in a child—the physical body develops, sensations presage emotions, the mental aspect appears and, together with traces of spirituality, these unfolding capacities enable one to function as an adult.

A great refinement of physical attributes has taken place since the appearance of the human form on Earth. The emotional aspects of our functioning have also undergone a steady upward trend. While raw emotions still tend to predominate, one can see a general increase in people's sensitivity and their ability to handle their emotions responsibly.

The management of emotions comes with the growth of the mental aspect, while the conscious cultivation of spiritual qualities leads to an ethical cohesion of emotions and the intellect.

Our current state of evolution appears to center on the development of mental powers. While we further perfect our physical bodies, refine our emotions, expand our thinking, and plunge into ever more sophisticated technologies, our evolutionary trajectory now extends into the next developmental phase—the spiritual stage of advancement.

At this time, we witness an intensified struggle between the emotion of greed, for example, and the rational view of its destructive effect on society. Many prominent thinkers call for a shift in consciousness. This shift requires the ability to take an ethical-spiritual stance that would enable us to approach our problems with an attitude of love and caring.

Viewing our evolutionary process in terms of the developmental stages—physical, emotional, mental, and spiritual—can explain some of our deficiencies, proclivities, challenges, and accomplishments. From this observation, we may gain an understanding of the cause of our present turmoil, since it represents a developmental stage through which we individually and collectively must pass on the way to the higher levels of existence.

While guiding and assisting humanity in its progress all along, the spiritual realm now actively seeks to increase direct contact with the inhabitants of Earth. People experience this as heightened awareness and greater sensitivity to their surroundings. Openness on our part greatly facilitates such contact. Growing awareness of the assistance freely given from the spiritual realm can help us make better connection with the emerging spirituality in all of us. We can consciously invite invisible help to lead us toward the experience of inner peace.

Evolution takes place regardless of whether we pay attention to it or not. All of our experiences lead to the expansion of consciousness even without our conscious participation; however, it may help us greatly if we choose to consciously cooperate with evolutionary forces. Each one of us contributes to the overall state of human affairs, to the state of the planet, and to the current evolution of consciousness in the world as a whole. At the same time, when confronted with untoward situations that evoke fear, frustration, or a sense of helplessness, we would do well to keep in mind the Invisible Friend's continuing reassurance:

All things work together for good.

✴

About the Authors

Laryssa Nechay has taught and practiced psychotherapy for forty-five years in such settings as Stanford University, Esalen Institute, and the Mental Research Institute of Palo Alto. While practicing in the San Francisco Bay Area and Mount Shasta, her specialties included helping people with emerging psychic abilities to accept and develop their gifts.

Nick Nechay grew up in California amidst the blossoming human potential movement, surrounded by psychics and spiritual teachers. Recently retired from his business as a fine craftsman working with interior designers, he now pursues his literary interests and his inspirations in fine art and electronic music production.

Please use this order form to order additional copies or send a gift of *Invisible Friend*

No. of books ordered
@ $17.95 each: _____

☐ *Please put me on your book catalog mailing list.*

Shipping & handling charges: $3.00 USPS or $6.00 UPS or priority mail, plus $1.00 for each additional book.

Name _____

Address _____

_____

City _____

State _____ Zip _____

☐ Check enclosed

Charge to:

☐ VISA   ☐ MasterCard
☐ AmEX   ☐ Discover

Subtotal: $ _____

California residents add
7.25% sales tax: $ _____

Shipping & handling: $ _____

Total: $ _____

Ship to:

Name _____

Address _____

_____

City _____

State _____ Zip _____

Gift Card Information

To:

From:

Card No. _____ Expiration Date _____

Authorized cardholder signature _____

Daytime phone _____

Send your orders to:
Lost Coast Press • 155 Cypress Street • Fort Bragg, CA 95437
or call 1-800-773-7782 • Fax credit card orders to 707-964-7531
or visit our website at **www.cypresshouse.com**

Thank you!